BOOKS BY FREDERICK BUECHNER

NOVELS

Brendan

Godric

The Book of Bebb

Treasure Hunt

Love Feast

Open Heart

Lion Country

The Entrance to Porlock

The Final Beast

The Return of Ansel Gibbs

The Seasons' Difference

A Long Day's Dying

NONFICTION

Whistling in the Dark

A Room Called Remember

Now and Then

The Sacred Journey

Peculiar Treasures

Telling the Truth

The Faces of Jesus

Wishful Thinking

The Alphabet of Grace

The Hungering Dark

The Magnificent Defeat

BRENDAN

FREDERICK BUECHNER

BRENDAN

A NOVEL

HarperSanFrancisco
A Division of HarperCollinsPublishers

First PERENNIAL LIBRARY edition published in 1988.

Reprinted by arrangement with Atheneum Publishers, an imprint of Macmillan Publishing Company.

Library of Congress Cataloging-in-Publication Data

Buechner, Frederick,
    Brendan.

    1. Brendan, Saint, the Voyager, ca. 483–577—Fiction.
2. America—Discovery and exploration—Irish—Fiction.
3. Ireland—History—To 1172—Fiction. I. Title.
PS3552.U35B7   1988   813'.54   88-45128
ISBN 0-06-061178-2 (pbk.)

94 95 96 97 RRD-H 10 9 8 7 6

FOR

HARVEY & ANITA

In the very shape of things there is more than green growth;
there is the finality of the flower. It is a world of crowns.

G. K. CHESTERTON

CONTENTS

BRENDAN

The Fire in the Woods

E R C said the night the boy was born he saw the woods by the boy's house catch fire. It wasn't any common kind of fire either. It didn't burn bright here and not so bright there. It didn't have the higgledy-piggledy colors of a fire or a foul smoke to choke off your breath and set your eyes weeping. Erc said no. It was in no way like that at all indeed. There was no higgledy-piggledy about it. There was no smoke. The whole woods went up in a single vast flame behind the house, and the color of the flame was such a fiery gold clear through that it turned the house gold and the eyes of Erc gold as he stood in the dark watching and waiting with the tide scudding in among the monstrous hills behind him. For a greater wonder still, Erc said, by the time dawn come and the boy was fully born out into the world and wrapped up snug as a badger against the chill, there wasn't so much as one dry twig blackened or the delicatest feather of a bird's wing singed.

Finnloag was the boy's father and Cara his mother, free born and of the new faith both of them. They say Finnloag had kingly blood in him trickling down from Niall of the

Nine Hostages or one of them, though if you travel upstream far as that, there's not a dung-foot cow-herder
couldn't find a kingly drop or two of his own to crow over
if he felt like it. The name they give the boy was Brendan,
and Brendan is the name he carried with him to the grave
where he's no likelier to need a name any longer if you ask
me than any of the rest of us when our time comes. Save
for life itself and a few small gifts along the way, his name
was about the only thing he had from Finnloag and Cara
nearly. Not that they wasn't ready for all I know to pluck
down the very stars from heaven if he'd ever cried out for
them, but it was a cry he never got a chance to make because
before the cord was tied off and snipped almost, this same
Erc that had been biding his time in the dark come lumber-
ing in and claimed the boy.

Erc was a great cairn of a man. His belly was where the
stones buckled out under their own weight. His feet was
where a pair of them had tumbled to the ground. His head
was a boulder on top that was cracked straight across. He
could open this jagged crack of a mouth wide as a stone
cave and bellow out of it all manner of wild flummeries he'd
learned from the days he was a druid.

"Ah-h-h-h! Yah-h-h-h! God is the wind that blows over
the sea . . . the wave of the deep . . . the bull of the seven
battles . . . the tear in the eye of the sun."

His breath had the musty moulder and damp of caves
to it. The words rushed forth thick as bats but more of them
got left within than ever come out because there's never
been the likes of druids for secrets.

"A bear for courage he is . . . a salmon in the water . . . the
head of the death-dealing spear!"

Erc loved telling how he was weaned from druidry by no
less than the sainted Patrick himself at the mere sound of
whose name the high angels wet their holy breeches, so
they say. Patrick was long since dead by the time Brendan
was born though, and Erc was by then turned into mighty
Bishop Erc. He was high cockalorum over all Brendan's

kindred that lived in squat stone houses like Finnloag's.
They stood ringed round with a ditch and a bank and high
palings to keep out lunatics, gentry, and all such workers
of mischief.

Erc had more cows than all of the kindred together. He
would stand holding a stick to count them as one by one
they shoved through the gate at day's end with their big
bags swollen and leaking as they went and him making such
a clamor out of his big mouth the very leaves on the trees
shook. He was a great one for singing and shouting even
when there was none but the beasts to hear him.

"Three slender things there be that best hold the world
together," cries Bishop Erc. He wears a brown coat that's
long before and short behind. He thumps each bony rump
with his stick as the herd crowds through.

"The slender blade of green corn upon the ground," he
cries. Thump. "The slender thread over the hand of a
clever woman." Thump. "The slender stream of milk from
the cow's dug into the pail." Thump.

One of his baggy ladies starts to moo so deep she could
be fetching it out of the world's deepest well. She raises it
shriller and shriller then, her snout in the air, till it comes
to a squeal so sharp even Erc's shouting can't drown it.

He would never have shouted to Finnloag and Cara that
first still dawn the boy was born that was to be Brendan
though. He whispered more likely. He laid his hand on the
damp small skull and said what he'd come to say. He said
the boy was not to be raised by them. Best they know it from
the start. His words was as hushed as the day just breaking
and not even the waves riled yet. The boy was to be raised
to the glory of the new and true grand God that Patrick
had brought them from over the water.

Erc picked him up and carried him over to the doorway
then. He weighed less than a hare. It was there in the
Bishop's stone arms that he got the first whiff he ever had
of the sea in all her blue guile and haughtiness.

* * *

Cara didn't give suck for more than a week or two before she shriveled up dry as a nut, poor soul, though she'd had plenty and to spare for the two boys and the girl she'd borne before Brendan. Maybe it was the grief of knowing he wasn't to be hers for long that dried her. Maybe she did it to spite the Bishop thinking he could suckle him himself if that's how the wind blew. The child was so shriveled and dry like a nut himself anyhow that they was ready to put him out to nurse someplace else when they say another wonder happened to match the wood's flaming.

One dusk there was a soft clitter-clatter of feet at the door of the house and they went to see whatever it might be. A skittish lovely hind stood there with her fawn at her side. She didn't turn tail at the sight of them and leap back into the trees. Instead she give them such a tender look out of her eye they saw she was asking to enter. So they stood aside and in she went to be sure, her fawn wobbling close behind on the dappled stilts of its legs. Nodding and bowing her stately head the hind picked her way to where the boy lay all but hid in a nest of skins and crouched down low next him. With his famished little mouth he found her teat and drank his full at last. Day after day the hind come like that. Day after day the boy fed. That is the way they tell it.

It seems this hind was from the foot of Sliabh Luacra. I suppose some ninny with nothing better to do on this earth must have trailed her home once and then blabbed it about. Nor was the hound the only one to come from there. It was just where Sliabh Luacra starts her steep climb into the clouds that the Abbess Ita also dwelled. She and her nuns kept their school there.

Even when there wasn't a breath of air stirring, the Abbess Ita looked like she was facing into a gale. Her eyes was squinnied up against the blast of it. Her hair blew every whichway. Her cheeks was stung apple red by it and her teeth bared in a helmsman's fierce grimace. She moved through the world like a gale herself. Pots and cups rattled on the shelf when she passed by. Geese scattered before her.

When she wasn't storming about though, she was often to be found sitting someplace still as sunlight with a lap full of children or up to her elbows in a tub of curds. The smell of her was like the smell of new loaves.

I asked her once about the story of the hind and Brendan. "You'll know it surely" I said. "Many times I've asked myself what you might make of it, being a nun and all with a wide knowledge of wonders."

She was sitting on a stool at the time with a goose across her knees plucking it. My question stopped her fingers in the air.

"There's many such stories abroad," she said, "some false, some true. Why on earth would you be asking me of one with long white whiskers on it like that now?"

"Ah well," I said. "They do say the beast was one that come from Sliabh Luacra the same as yourself. I've always wondered was it maybe you that sent it."

She let the goosedown fly from her fingers like snow instead of stuffing it into her sack. She clapped her hands.

"You're a grand wonderer, Finn," she cried. "What a picture to daub on a wall! A grey nun whispering into a red deer's tall ear to bid it go suckle a child of all things." She laughed.

"I'll go you one better than that though if it's tales you're after," she said. "Have I got your good ear?"

My old dad handed me such a clout on the side of the head one time that from that day on I couldn't hear if Sliabh Luacra fell into the sea should it happened to fall on the wrong side of me.

"That you have," I said.

"Hear this then," Ita said. "I wasn't the one sent the hind. I was the hind myself!"

She clasped the goose to her breast to keep it from falling to the ground as the laughter rocked her back and forth. I don't know to this day if it was truly a joke she told or if the joke she told was the truth. I know this though.

Once in a year of blistering drought when the grass crackled brown under the cows' feet and their tongues swelled black in their heads, the fosterlings in Ita's care went wailing to her with hunger. Now Ita lived and died a virgin. I believe that is true if anything about her at all is true. Had any man ever tried to take his pleasure of her, he'd have been blown clean off his feet by the great wind she was. She had never freshened.

Yet I have heard it from some of those very fosterlings themselves grown to manhood that Ita took and suckled them then and there. They say when she saw her two paps wasn't enough to feed so many, she give them her fingers to suck on as well and the milk out of them was every bit as sweet as the other. When still more children come yammering, she pulled the brogues off her feet to uncover her ten toes. Not a single child of them was lost that dark time though all about them strong men was falling like leaves.

If Abbess Ita truly suckled them like the great blue-eyed double-dugged sow of the world, then maybe for all I know it was she indeed went leaping through the trees with her tail in the air and her dappled wild fawn at her heels to suckle Brendan as well.

Before the boy was a full year old anyhow, Bishop Erc come again one fine day and carried him off to this same Ita to raise in her school.

[II]

H E was a bony bit of a thing when I first knew him at Ita's later. He had skin pale as cheese and a crop of hair the color of sunset and too many teeth in his head even then so when he got overheated speaking, the spit flew. He had a big rump on him but a narrow chest, steep shoulders and a smallish pointed head so his overall shape was then and ever after large at the bottom and slight at the top like a stack of hay. He had a habit of twitching his arms and shoulders about if anything fussed him. When he got telling his tales, you could hear him over the wind. It was the same all his life. He made every villain he ever met more villainous and every grey wave that ever heaved him wilder. If he stumbled into a ditch on his way to make water at night, you'd have thought he'd been beset by fiends to hear him tell it.

"Such a one for asking questions he was," Ita told me once. "He asked about the gentry most of all, the good people it's as well not to speak of at all if you know what I mean. May God in his mercy preserve us both, Finn." She drew the shape of the cross in the air.

" 'What be the gentry at all day long?' he would ask," Ita said. " 'Why, feasting and love-making,' I'd tell him. 'The same as mortal men mostly. Sometimes they play such lovely tunes as well that many a poor girl that's heard them has pined away and died with longing to hear them again.' 'What do they do for working then?' he'd ask, and when I told him it was most of it stitching up brogues to wear on their feet he'd come back with wanting to know why they needed so many brogues. I told him, 'Why the whole world knows that, child. It will be all the dancing they do. They can wear out two pair in a week the best of them.' "

Ita said, "I can hear his voice to this day. It was like a mouse fallen in a pail. 'Why do men doff their caps every time there's a whirlabout of leaves and straw in the air? Who do the sisters set out pannikins of milk at night on the sill? Can gentry give cows the crippen and calves the white scour if you slight them any way at all? Have you ever seen one with your own eyes, Mother?' "

She raised her voice to a squeak like his to show me the sound of him in those days.

"By the blood of the true Christ, Finn," she said, "I saw one down by the river once batting at the water with his hands. And so I told him."

Strip the red beard off Brendan and the bramble of hair

off his chest. Take away the wreckage the sea has left in his face, the rutted ox-hide cheeks and cracked lips and eyes salted an everlasting blear. Cure him of the rolling deck-hugging way he has of walking and scour his skull of all the sights he's seen. Then you'd have the boy again that Ita taught the gentry to.

She taught how the Dagda was chief over the old gods. A bloated tum he had and a herdsman's hood and a club it needed eight men to heft. That was one less than the nine he could fell with a single clout of it. Plucking the harp he carried on his back he'd call into life the four seasons of the year. She taught Manannan Mac Lir the Sea King and King of the Land of Promise as well. She taught Lug of the Long Arm.

Nor did she stop at such learning as that. She saw to it they was all shown by the nuns how to milk, how to plow with an oaken share and coulter, how to grind corn in a quern, how to truss a long-legged pig topsy-turvy for sticking, how to ward off a blight with spells and lay up a stone wall to last. Ita herself taught them battling with her skirts hiked up and her hair in a net. She'd hop and skitter side-ways like a crab to show the use of the dagger, the thrusting spear, the iron-bound shield. There wasn't a boy quick on his feet as her. Howling like a storm through a chink she could hurl a throwing spear farther than the best of them. With one eye cocked shut and a lopside flash of teeth she could spin her sling around her head and let fly to knock an egg off a rock at fifty paces.

She taught them holy matters as well. Her wood church was long as it was broad. It had a thatch on it and daubed with the gaudy doings of saints inside. It had a hewn stone for an altar and seven fine lamps on it lit day and night and a cross worked with faces and leaves twined together. Ita's voice when she sang was like a sheep caught under a gate nor could she keep a tune to save her soul from the fire but she had her little ones chirping mass to and fro so sweet as to wring tears from a limpet. All scrubbed up they was too in their snowy gowns like angels.

"May the shadow of Christ fall on thee. May the garment of Christ cover thee. May the breath of Christ breathe in thee," she told them each morning at sun-up. Winters they'd sit there with blue noses and frozen fingers and the way their breath come out of them in white puffs you could almost believe it was Christ's indeed.

True faith. A simple life. A helping hand. She said those was the three things prized most in Heaven. On earth it was a fair wife, a stout ox, a swift hound.

Beg not, refuse not, she said. One step forward each day was the way to the Land of the Blessed. Don't eat till your stomach cries out. Don't sleep till you can't stay awake. Don't open your mouth till it's the truth opens it.

She wasn't above lending a hand when it come to stuffing their faces as well as their ears either. Oat cakes and cheese and curds she fed them. There was milk and butter to make their bones grow. From time to time they got a bit of broiled beef and berries when it was berrying time.

Now and then Abbess Ita would catch them a salmon herself. Up to her knees she'd stand in a bright stretch of stream where it come tumbling steep over the rocks. There's nothing fairer in this world at all than a glittering crooked-jawed salmon all over red spots when he leaps upside down into the air. To see Ita net him with a grin on her face you'd have thought there was nothing this side of God himself in his gold crown she loved so much.

I think what Brendan learned most from Ita was Ita herself. She was the only mother he knew up to then thanks to Erc running off with him so early and he fed on her sure as if he'd been one of the ones she give her fingers and toes to the time of the black drought. Life sent him sprawling many a time with a thwack over the head and each time it was Ita's strength in him got him back on his feet again and sailing off on God only knows what new tack. You couldn't

BRENDAN

rightly say it was only the truth opened his mouth like she taught but when he got to spinning his tales out through all those crooked teeth of his he had a way of keeping his eyes shut that showed he didn't have it in his heart to look at his own taradiddle but beneath his closed lids was looking instead at the plain truth of things straight and clear as if it was Ita's eyes he was looking through.

His lids was mostly closed when he told me how it was his years of schooling with Ita and her mouse-color nuns ended.

"Such a day for cold you never did see, Finn," he said. "I came on a boy with warts standing in the snow. He was frozen to death nearly by the looks of him. His lips were so stiff he couldn't get a word out when I asked him why he didn't come in by the fire with the rest of us. Then I saw the reason plain as day. The cold had had him weeping and his tears had frozen hard clear to the ground. He was tethered there by his two eyes and would have perished surely if I hadn't broken the silver icy streams of his grief with a stick and freed him.

"Do you know of anyone else in the world at all, Finn, can say he saved a mortal life when he wasn't much higher than your knee? Anyhow I threw some husks on the fire when I got him in the hut where the others were. You'd expect it would smoke a little in the regular course of things, but this was like no smoke you ever saw in the world. Thick as cream it was, all curling and swirling around till the tears ran out of our eyes and we were coughing ourselves into a fit. That smoke, it gathered together into one great cloud right there in front of us, and that cloud, it towered up into a creature so high it had to stoop over in half nearly to keep from hitting the roof. You never saw the likes of it, Finn. It was the mighty figure of a man. He wore a gold chain around his neck and heavy brogues on his feet. He had a shaggy cloak on him longer in front than in back. His eyes were rolling around in his

12

head. The voice out of his mouth was like the breaking of waves against the rocks.

" 'Let the boy Brendan come forward!' he cried. 'I wouldn't give better than a pair of hens for the rest of you, though you may be all very well in your way, but for that one boy Brendan I'd give a meadow of red-eared cows and their calves running onto them.'

"Such was the clamor he made that Mother Ita and the sisters came rushing in to see. Covered all over with snow they were with their noses running. I was cradled there high over their heads in those shaggy arms. They had their eyes turned up to me like I was a sign out of Heaven.

" 'The luck of God to you, your worship,' Mother Ita called up at him through her cupped hands.

" 'Health and long life to you, Mother,' he called down, 'and an easy death when the time comes. I'd best be on my way with this boy while there's yet light.'

"Then the boy with warts that owed me his life and the other boys as well as the sisters and the Abbess herself all got down on their knees to do reverence, and he carried me out of that hut high on his shoulders. I was wrapped up against the cold like the Holy Lamb of God himself."

The long and the short of it was Erc come and fetched him off from Ita's school just like he'd brought him there in the first place. It wasn't till he finished the telling of it that Brendan opened his eyes again.

[III]

T H E sail is swollen stiff with wind. It's painted with the ringed cross of Christ in crimson. There's bundles of dried fish and dried mutton hung from the rigging. They're covered with a green fuzz by now and stink. Bunches of sea-holly tossy there too to keep off scurvy. Whenever the ship gives a sharp list you can hear the pigs squeal for mercy in their pen. There's scarce an hour day or night you won't find a monk or two puking over the side. The sea is an endless tumble of foam-capped blue wicked hills and glittering dales. It stretches far as the eye can see on all sides. Brendan has set somebody at the tiller and him and me have crept off to escape the wind. It's the hellish howling you need escape from. It never pauses for breath. It tugs at your hair and beard till they come out by the roots nearly. It lashes your cheeks with salt. It dries up your eyes.

We're crouched belowdecks with the water casks. There's a cage with three ravens as well. One of them has a ragged wing he can't fold shut and a wen where one eye ought to be. From the baleful sound of his croaking, I'll eat my leggings if he's got so much as one croak left in him when it comes time to send him out scouting for land. There's coils of spare rope down there together with pegs, iron, sail-cloth and such-all else for patching us back together whenever the sea takes it into her head to pound us to pieces. The one that does most of the patching is me. I'm one of the few of them that isn't some kind of monk or other. It's why Brendan collars me when he's feeling least monkish I think.

"The Devil damn you to the well of ashes seven miles below Hell for letting me sail a second time," he says, and I, "A red nail on the tongue that said it," and he again, "A red stone in your throat."

He groans like a man passing a red stone.

"I'll tell you what first set me voyaging, fool that I am," says Brendan. He grasps his throat in both hands and squeezes till his face darkens and his eyes bulge. He's punishing himself for his folly. He gasps when he lets go.

He says, "It was after the Bishop took me away from Ita and put me to school with the monks. I found me a perch high up in the cliffs. Hours on end I'd sit there sometimes watching the water. I was only a boy. I'd watch and watch till I became water myself nearly. Some waves would come in gentle as white lambs. Others hurled so hard at the rocks they soaked me with spray. The time I'm remembering it was a blue soft summer's sea though. Flat as a blue meadow it was that day. Way off I saw a lone wave suddenly. Oh, high-crested and proud it was, Finn. Sure as I'm here to tell you, there came a white steed at the gallop behind it. The water could have been solid earth the way he rode it." He paused for breath.

"A man was astride him," he says. "He had a snowy plume in his hat and a blue pale scarf flying behind. The wave was curling over and racing along swifter than wind. Foaming high as the horse's neck it was. I could see the beast's fiery nostrils snorting over the top of it. Just as the wave was about to dash to pieces on the shingle, the horse sprang free and leapt. It was the sky itself he leapt into with his rider on his back. I saw it with my own eyes, Finn." He looked like he was seeing it again.

"It was Tir-na-n-Og they leapt to, Finn. It was the Land of the Ever Young. There's no death there at all, you see. I glimpsed it for a moment only. It was floating over the water like a cloud. The beauty of it broke my heart, I think. I've scoured the seven seas for it ever since. I'm scouring them now. It's why we're tumbled together down here like two crabs in a net. The curse of the crows upon me for a footloose fool and sinner, Finn, if I never find it."

"Six eggs to you then and a half dozen of them rotten," I say hoping to cheer him.

He groans and breaks wind. The sick raven staggers against the bars of his cage as a wave heaves under us. Brendan has his head in his hands. His mumble is lost nearly in the ship's creaking. It's other memories he's mumbling to help him forget. He speaks of his sister Briga, his elder by a year or so. She went to school at the monks with us. Like a toadstool she was with her big head and short legs. Her smile hung crooked. Her hair flew out to either side. You could hardly see her mouth for the shadow of her great nose.

"I wish she was here with us now, Finn," he says. "She was always a comfort."

The monks kept us starved half to death with not a bite of anything at all till past noon. Brig and Bren and me would go foraging. There was eggs to be found here and there among the rocks and in shallow scooped places in the sand. We'd gather dulce along the shore and hang it to dry till it was fit to eat. The stone huts we lived in was the shape of hives. They was fitter for bees than men the way they held in the cold. The wind keened about them like lost souls. It spattered us with brine when the tide was at the flow.

"Once it was so foggy I couldn't see my feet on the path or the path either," Brendan says. "I was that lost I couldn't find my own hut. All at once I stumbled into my ugly darling little Brig. 'O Brig!' I cried and 'O Bren!' she. We held to each other for dear life. Each was all the other had in the whole world save holy faith."

He raises his head out of his hands. His cheeks are wet. I marvel how he can weep over such a long ago moment when any moment now may be our last the way the sea rages. A bundle of laths has come loose and rolls about between us. He clamps it fast with one foot.

Old Jarlath was abbot in those days. He had a willow whistle. He'd come up behind you and blast it in your ears now and then or steal into your hut with it in the black of night roaring some pslam so loud you'd wake up wetting yourself. It's how he taught us. He said God comes like that. Like a thief in the night. Jarlath was like a bird. He had skinny long legs and a stiff way of walking. He carried his shoulders hunched. He had the staring round eyes of a bird.

"I was the best scholar he ever had," Brendan says. "I took to Roman speech like a pig to slops. All those horums and harums, those quibuses and habebiminis and filioques. They were like berries and honey to me, Finn. Jarlath dropped his jaws to hear me roll them over my tongue. He'd own it himself if he was here now, God forbid. I wouldn't wish such luck on any man. There are whiskery cruel beasts below us at this very moment waiting to swallow us whole."

He draws up his knees and rests his chin on them.

"I knew Scripture better than any," he says. "It was meat and drink to me then. The yellow thick cream of the psalms. The prophets' bitter broth. The fresh lovely bread of the Gospel. 'Ah Brendan, my darling,' Jarlath said to me one time. 'If wit and worthiness were inches, you'd stand tall as a tree.' "

He opens his eyes and fixes me with a stark look.

"I was tall as a dung fork. They gibed at my big rump. They stuffed nettles down my shirt. Brig and you were my only friends, the luck of Heaven to you both. Thanks be to God I had Erc as well."

Jarlath taught him Heaven. Erc taught him Earth. Erc never tired working his jaws like the upper and nether millstones to grind out how it was Saint Patrick himself won him to Christ's faith, but not even Patrick routed the druid out of him entirely if you ask me.

To the end of his days Erc understood the rustling speech of trees, the rowan and blackhorn and quicken most of all. They told him things a man's better off not knowing like how to draw a thick mist out of the ground. They told him the way of driving a man mad by throwing straw in his face. Erc knew about clouds as well. They swell out and unravel into queer shapes that show the shape of things to come if you've the knack of reading them. He knew about stars. He knew the tales of how they come to be stars in the first place and who their grandmothers was. Every once and so often they step down out of the sky and rub shoulders with common folk. You may happen on them at a greyhound coursing or a feast though there's nothing more to mark them for stars maybe than a silvery ring to their voices and their way of leaving no marks when they walk on the cobwebby dew at sun-up.

All the years Brendan was with the monks, Erc would

17

come every now and again to fill his head with such matters while Jarlath was busy filling it with monkish learning and leaping out at him with his whistle to teach him the ways of God. It's a wonder the boy didn't grow up more muddled than he did.

The feet of the monks clatter over the deck over our heads. The sea roars mad to mount us like a bull.

"Erc used to take me out in weather like this," Brendan says. "Just a wisp of a boy and a tun-belly bishop in a currant we were, and all the wild water in the world against us. But Erc knew seafaring. He showed me how to drag ropes to slow down with and the use of an oil-bag to flatten the waves. He showed me the way of rigging a backstay to hold the mast steady in a gale. It's from him I learned how to lace bonnets to the foot of the sail if it's speed you're after."

We poke our heads out of the hatch. There's a mountain of a wave coming at us. Grey wrinkles run down its flanks. We climb it toward the sky higher and higher till half our hull juts out over the top. I'm queasy in my groin with terror waiting for us to snap in two. Then all of a rush it crests and tumbles. We plunge down with the foam-white boiling rage of it. Tons more of water threaten our stern. If just for a wink we slew sideways we're goners. Brendan draws a cross in the spray.

"Erc would sing when the sea was like this," he says. He goes red remembering it. He sings it anyhow.

"Praise God for the pizzle of the whale! Praise God for the watery womb of the world!"

He lays his hand on my shoulder and places his lips to my ear so I can hear.

"Finn," he says, "I felt safer in danger of drowning with Erc than asleep by the fire."

The Cry in the Cave

[IV]

T H E R E was a girl name of Maeve at school among the
monks when we was all of us children in our stone hives.
She had thick straw-color hair she wore down her back in
three braids. She had a mouth like a crushed berry. The
way she stared out of her blue eyes made it look like the
whole world was a never-ending surprise to her. She had
stout legs and arms and a pair of fat small breasts on her
when all the other girls her age could as well have been
boys for anything they had from the belly up to tell you
different. Everything she did she worked hard at whether
it was watering the monks' bony cows or learning her hic,
haec, hoc or kneeling hours at a time with her arms
stretched out for penance or playing at who could spit farthest. Her face was always flushed. She was always damp
with sweat on her upper lip and under her eyes. Jarlath said
she would make a grand nun someday because she was a
generous sunny-hearted girl that never told anybody no if
she could help it. She didn't mind them poking fun at her

either like the time she was making water out in the open one day when one of the monks come on her by accident. Still in a squat with her three braids flying she made a wild scuttle out of there that nobody who saw it ever forgot or let her ever forget either. She laughed right along with the rest of them.

Being a nun was the last thing Maeve herself wanted. She wanted to be a warrior. She wanted to master the sling and the spear like Ita that was great-aunt to her. She practised running through the woods without getting her hair tangled in the branches or cracking twigs under her feet. She learned fending off whacks with only a small shield and a hazel branch. Ita give her a wood sword and one of the children she thrusted and parried with because he had a wood sword as well and also a buckler plaited of straw was Brendan.

They was huffing and puffing away at it one afternoon howling war cries at each other. Brendan's voice was shrill as a titlark's still, Maeve's husky and more like a crow's caw. Hopping up and down they went flailing at each other against the tall sky. Brendan was showing his teeth gasping for air. Maeve's face had gone red and her new breasts bouncing about that she'd hardly had time to get used to yet. They was on a sweet-smelling hairy green slope scattered all over with cloudberries and wild garlic. After a time they sat themselves down to rest. There was a spring boiling up nearby. You could see the gravel crushed small and white at the bottom of it. Dark cresses grew about. They splashed water on their faces and soaked their feet till the cold made them ache. It seems Brendan was telling her there wasn't a cleverer swordsman in the land than himself and Maeve listening with her blank astonished eyes. Midges swarmed in the sun. Then it come Brendan's turn to be astonished. Right while he was blathering away, Maeve pulled her drawers down and showed him her parts.

I don't believe it was out of lewdness she did it at all. I

believe Brendan was so busy crowing about what a fine
fellow he was she just wanted him to know there was this
one little tuck in her flesh she had that he hadn't. I doubt
she'd even guessed the full use of it by then. She could just
as soon have showed him anything else she had that she
thought might make him sit up and take notice. It might
have been a stone with a ring about it, say, or a goose feather
from her pocket or a shell strung around her neck. Be that
as it may, Brendan was onto his feet in a trice and off out
of there like the fiends of the air was upon him. Maeve was
left sitting by the spring with her drawers about her knees
and her round eyes empty and blue as the sky.

"You'd have thought she'd given him a peek at the mouth
of Hell at Lough Derg and him in danger of falling into it
head over heels," Briga said years after. She was a nun by
then with a shawl over her head and her nose jutting out
of it like an elbow and her sour small mouth. "He was pale
as a peeled stick when he come running to me. He prayed
straight through the rest of that day and clear through the
night. He wouldn't come out and tell just what it was Maeve
showed him, but I guessed right enough. Those days I
might have showed my own if I thought it would catch
anybody's eye. I've long since willed it to Heaven with the
rest of me you'll be glad to know. You'd think it was one of
the holy prophets scowling at you in a grey beard if you
was to see it." Briga had a face to curdle milk with but
merry as morning when she smiled.

Brendan told Jarlath what Maeve had done together
with the wicked thoughts it planted in his head. Jarlath
flapped his wings and opened and shut his beak a few
times. Finally he croaked out a penance. He said Brendan
must spend a whole night through in one of the caves thereabouts and call on the mercy of God. More than likely Jarlath had another thought or two about the kind of nun
Maeve was going to make someday but far as I know he
said nothing of it to her. Perhaps he knew she'd meant no

21

harm and he'd only be harming her innocent heart if he come after her over it.

"Father, will I be struck blind now surely?" Brendan asked.

"That you won't because the sight wasn't of your own choosing," Jarlath said.

"It wasn't a mortal sin then?" Brendan whispered.

Jarlath was roosting on his stone chair. His bare feet was yellow as a goose's. He head was shaved bald as an egg save for the stringy locks down in back and the half circle of fuzz from one ear to the other across his brow in the manner of monks. Brendan knelt at his feet like Jarlath had just hatched him there.

"It was a mortal danger," Jarlath said. "If you see something before your time to see it, the devil only knows what may come of it. A child that saw the sea before he knew it was the sea might lap up a bellyful and go staring mad."

Brendan remembered how he'd lapped up the sight of Maeve's bareness and was afraid he could feel the madness rising in him already. He lost no time getting to the cave like Jarlath told him. It was a low-ceilinged cave with a toadstooly smell to it and winged flimsy things that bumped into your face in the dark. There was bats swooping in and out on their nasty errands. It was all he could do to keep from screaming.

He knew it was the one and only true God he was supposed to call on for mercy but he thought it would do no harm to call on the Dagda as well. He only whispered his name in his heart instead of speaking it out loud though. The last thing in the world he wanted was for the Dagda to turn up there in the cave lugging his terrible great club and his brass cauldron. All the boy was after from him was a bit of luck. Likewise for luck he whispered in his heart the name of the Dagda's son Mac Oc. He remembered from Ita's telling it how Mac Oc had been changed into a swan once for lusting after a golden limbed girl. Maybe he would take pity on a mortal that had sinned after the same fashion.

In case any of the gentry was around waiting for the moon to rise so they could start up their dancing, he stretched out his hands and scattered some crumbs of oatcake he had with him. That way they'd have something to munch on and wouldn't take it into their heads to come funning and tricking with him. Only then did he turn to his prayers it seems.

A scrawny hollow-chested wreck of a boy he was at the time, half wore out with growing too fast and dragging his dirty big feet about with him wherever he went. The sky outside was black as death and the cave blacker yet. Jarlath said he wasn't in a state of mortal sin but Jarlath didn't know all of it. He didn't know how in his heart the boy wallowed in sinfulness like a sow in muck, how he thirsted for it like the mixed wine in the navel of the Shulamite woman King Solomon sung of in his holy song or the honey and milk the song said was under her tongue.

Brendan's teeth was chattering so hard his words come out all stuttery like a half-wit's gobble. He prayed as many prayers as he knew of and said as many psalms as he'd ever learned. He stirred in as many Laus-laus-laus tibis and De Profun-fun-fundises and Pater no-no-nosters as he had breath for. There was such a fearsome buzzing in his ears he was afraid it might be the gentry coming for him with their tongues in their cheeks and pulling their eyes into slits with their thumbs. It wasn't like praying for some special thing like his enemies' herds to get blacktongue or the sore on Briga's lip to heal because there wasn't some one simple thing like that he wanted just then. The one thing he knew he ought to want was what he didn't want at all. It was the quenching of the fires of sin inside him. Only he didn't want them quenched. Instead he hungered for them all the more.

No matter how high the boy aimed his holy gobbling skyward though he didn't reach an ear to hear him far as he could tell anyhow. There wasn't so much as a whisker of starlight or moonlight in the sky or anything else you might have cared to call a sign of the mercy of God or anything else of God. There was only emptiness and darkness like God had gone off altogether carrying his mercy with him on his shoulder like the Dagda carrying his six-string harp.

Nobody ever tried harder at making God hear surely. He called on him till the veins on his neck swelled and his face went black. He kept at it till one eye got sucked deep into the socket and the other bulged out like a berry on a stem. He gaped his jaws at Heaven till his lips peeled back from his teeth and you could see down to where his lungs and liver was flapping like fish in a basket. Up out of the point of his head a jet of his heart's blood spurted black and smoking. That's how he told it.

"There came angels at last, Finn," he said. "They were spread out against the sky like a great wreath. The closest were close enough to touch nearly. The farthest were farther than the stars. I never saw so many stars. I could hear the stillness of them they were that still."

I see his pinched face go silvery watching. There's silver in the hollows of his cheeks. He has silver eyes. His shoulderblades cast shadows dark as wings on his bony boy's back.

"Lofty and fair beyond telling was the angels' music," he said. "They heard me cry and they answered me. They weren't singing to me of the mercy of God, Finn. Their singing was itself the mercy of God. Do you think I could ever forget it even if I tried?"

Two things followed from that night in the cave.

One of them was he shunned the company of women from that time forth.

The other was that ever afterwards he wore a string about his neck with a ball of beeswax at each of its two ends. Whenever there was music or singing of any kind at all he'd work the balls into his ears saying he wanted nothing on this earth to make him ever forget the music of Heaven next to which the sweetest trill of birds even was like the yammering of cats and made his head ache like somebody was pounding on it with a stone.

[V]

BRENDAN was a few years short of twenty with the hair on his chin more like an armpit than a beard when Bishop Erc come one day to pay him one of his visits. It was the first time he didn't come alone. Brendan was in the refectory eating his bit of porridge and salt butter toward the end of the day and all the other students and monks there with him. The only sound was the sound of them chomping or the shuffle of their feet on the flags or the scrape of their bowls when they tipped them on end to swipe them clean with the flat of their thumbs.

Abbot Jarlath sat at his raised table with the inky-fingered copying monks. He made a show of pecking at his food some but not a crumb of it passed his lips. He did on little but water and cresses for weeks on end in penance for the sins of the world. He wanted no glory for it in the eyes of men, but for all his trying to hide it there wasn't one of them there couldn't have told you he was on a black fast. Under his shirt he wore a girdle of iron they say cut to the bone but you'd never have known it for the shy smile he had with his eyes lowered and the lids fluttering like a girl. The eyes of a girl he had but the fierce beak of an eagle.

The rule was no talking at meals at all. If you wanted salt you scratched the table with your nails till somebody pushed it your way. When the meal was done Jarlath give three raps in honor of the Holy Trinity. Brendan was mooning over his empty bowl when he saw three figures coming over the brow of the hill where the monks' sheep nibbled such thin greenness as there was poking up.

From the height of him and the way his coat was hiked

over the swell of his rump he knew straight off the one with
the staff was Erc but the other two he couldn't tell. They
was having a hard time keeping up with the Bishop and
was a few strides lag of him. It was past harvest and they
was so bundled up against the chill he couldn't be sure was
they men or women even. Only when they was all but upon
him did he see they was one of each. When they got closer
still he found he knew them by name.

The long-jawed one with the shock of grizzled hair in
his eyes was Finnloag. The plump one without a tooth in
her head was Cara. They was the boy's own mother and
father Erc had brought with him though it's a wonder the
boy spotted them as such seeing he scarce knew them. He'd
seen them when they come to leave Briga to study alongside
him and again the time they brought him a sword Finnloag
whittled him of wood for his birthday, the same one he
battled Maeve with, and maybe there was a time or two
more. But that was about the length of it. The tramp took
days because not being scholars or bards or having a bishop
aboard they had no proper right to travel open roads across
borders but had to slog through fens and woods lest they
be turned back for their pains by the bullies of some small
king or another along the way.

Brendan knew of his parents from Briga mostly. He'd
pestered her half to death with questions. He knew Finnloag was handy at spearing salmon and fashioning churn-
staffs, coffins, barrel hoops and all such as a family might
have need of as the years rolled by. He knew Cara had so
tuneful a way of singing it didn't matter a whit you couldn't
understand a thing she sang hardly for the windy shapeless
way the words come out of her bare gums.

The three of them stood in the drafty door till Jarlath
give his raps and the monks went filing out one by one
with the ropes at their middles aswing and their crumby
beards wagging as they chanted psalms. Finnloag and Cara
stood back to let Erc be first to greet their son. Erc smothered him in his arms nearly. They give the boy the gifts

they had brought him—Finnloag a wood cross for hanging round his neck and Cara a saffron shirt of wool.

Jarlath was last to come out. Erc crumbled down on his knees to ask his blessing, for abbots stand higher than bishops in holiness and already there was talk Jarlath was a saint. They said you could tell it from the way he had of never blinking his round eyes.

"We've need of a place out of the weather to speak a bit amongst us, Father," Erc said. He held his hands clasped under his chin and his eyes lowered to honor Jarlath. "I'm wondering might we have the use of the scriptorium an hour at most if it suits your worship?"

When Erc had trouble rising to his feet again Jarlath caught him under the elbow but he was so feeble from fasting he might as well have tried to hoist a lintel stone into place single-handed.

"Use it and welcome," Jarlath said. "Brendan here will make you a fire as well to keep the chill off."

They all of them knew this was a special honor to Erc because the use of fire except to cook on was as forbidden among them as the use of women or beer. Brendan lugged in an armful of sticks from the kitchen and as the dusk swarmed thick as bees among the stone hives and the wind buzzed ever bitterer he got them a fine blaze going.

Finnloag and Cara sat on a bench with Brendan between them at the long table. Erc stood facing them with his shoulders humped against the wall. There was a cow horn of black ink on the table and the quills of crows and geese. A heap of dried skins lay nearby for copying on. Finished books cased in leather hung from pegs save for a few so holy they lay on a shelf between covers of silver and gold. Some covers was set with gems deep-watered as the eyes of hounds. Shadows wavered, nose shadows, peg shadows.

Erc's mouth chomped slowly open, slowly shut, to chew up the shadows inside himself into words. He started putting Brendan through his monkish paces.

"Who is the Prince of Light then?" Erc asked.

"Him as is son to the King of the Stars, your honor," said Brendan.

"Which is the mightiest work of the Spirit of God?" Erc said.

"The begetting of the Prince of Light on the Queen of Glory," said Brendan.

Erc said, "Where might you find a house with fifty and a hundred windows and all of them looking out onto Heaven?"

"King David's book of psalms," Brendan said. His face was feverish pale. His lips was parted over his teeth.

Erc said, "There are three devils forever leading us into sin, boy. Would you be knowing their three names?"

"The tongue in our mouths is such a devil," Brendan said. "The eye in our heads another. The thoughts of our black hearts the third."

Cara's buttery cheeks glowed red in the warmth. Her nose come close to resting on her chin for she had no teeth between to hold them apart. A gust of wind belched smoke back down through the roof-hole and Finnloag fetched a deep cough. Not a sound did they make otherwise. Erc went on with his testing.

Had Brendan learned to speak the hundred and fifty psalms? He had. Did he know the use of numbers and how to write the Romans' tongue in the abc's of Rome? He did. Could he list all the High Kings from Conchobar on together with the deeds and kindred of each? He could. And tell how the bag-carrying Firbolgs was overcome by the shining people of Dana? And tell then how they in turn was overcome when the bard Amergin split the whole land in two giving the surface of the earth to his own brothers, the sons of Mil, and to the people of Dana the places under the earth and under the sea? Brendan could tell all that as well and so he did.

"The people of Dana dwell there invisible as air to this day," he told Erc. "We call them the gentry." He lowered his voice when he spoke the name. Cara signed herself with the cross. "Some of them dwell in Tir-na-n-Og where there is no death at all," the boy said.

Erc folded his hands and rested them on his belly a little time.

"You'll have heard of Celestine as well, I shouldn't wonder," he said at last. "Him that was once Holy Father and Bishop of Rome herself?"

Brendan nodded solemn as rain.

"Perhaps you can tell me this then," Erc said. "Who it would be that Celestine sent to this land to be Archbishop, First Primate, and chief Apostle?"

"He sent us the son of Calphronn, the son of Potaide, the son of Odissus," Brendan said.

He spoke all the names out in a hushed voice but not the name of the Archbishop and chief Apostle and all that. Erc was angling for it like it was the gold-speckled scarlet-mouthed king of all trouts. Brendan was taking his time saying it. They was both of them stretching things out for the joy of it. It was like a dance they did.

"Coaxing of tongue he was," Erc said. He let his mouth fill up with shadows before speaking again. "Manly and hard-striking. Sweet was the sound of his shoe."

"He warred against flint-hearted wizards, that's what he did!" Brendan said. His voice was half way between a man's and a boy's. It rang out shrill as a stylus on a slate when he was in a dither. "He baptized the heathens," he said. "He thrust down the proud from their seats with the help of high Heaven. He preached the Gospel of Hope, that's what, and delivered us from the spite of devils."

Erc said, "You'd best out with his name then."

"Patrick!" Brendan said. His voice cracked when he said it. He said it again. "Patrick."

They all four drew crosses in the air. The Bishop heaved a great sigh and lowered himself down onto the bench. He turned his eyes from Brendan's now to the boy's parents. The wind had the room blue with smoke. Their eyes was all watery.

Erc spoke to Finnloag first. Besides being cousins Finnloag and Erc fished the same white-haired stream together. They worked their oats and barley, their leeks and onions, side by side. They pastured their sheep and cows in the same highlands. But there in the scriptorium Erc was above all else bishop. Among the jeweled books and all the tools of monkish learning everything other than that was forgot. Finnloag had trouble meeting Erc's eye even.

"Cousin," Erc said. "I've lifted the top of the boy's head off like the lid off a pot. You see for yourself all he's got at the simmer inside. There's more besides if I was to spoon down deeper. You'll be that proud of him both of you surely. You've got good cause."

Finnloag give a thin smile. Cara's head bobbed up and down like an apple on a windy branch.

"If I was to lift the lid off your head, Finnloag," Erc said, "would I be like to find as much again do you think?"

Finnloag had a rutted narrow face and the same great nose as his daughter Briga. His grey hair was forever dropping into his eyes.

"Not so much as the tenth part," Finnloag said. His legs was bowed and his hands hung far as his knees when he stood. His hands was piled one on the other on the table now though and his eyes fixed on them.

"I've no wish at all to shame you as Christ is my witness," Erc said. "A tenth part is more than a plenty for any need you're ever like to have. You're a good man, Finnloag. You've fathered a fine son. You gave him his strong back and his honest heart just as Cara here must have given him his backside. A grand one it is too as may save him being toppled in a high wind some day if it should ever come to that."

Erc reached across the table and clapped Finnloag on the shoulder at the jest but Finnloag only fetched another cough. He and Cara sat there silent with their thin boy between them.

"Oh the pain in that room was terrible, Finn!" Brendan

cried out when he told me the tale later. "My father knew what Erc was leading to. That was his pain. My mother's pain was for my father as well as herself. Erc saw their pain too and the pain of it half killed him for his heart was tender as a girl's though few ever guessed it for the great size of him. My pain came later only. It came with thinking how easy I cast adrift the two people in the world I had most cause to honor." I could see his pain still there in the blue shipwreck of his eyes as he went on with his tale.

"Finnloag my darling," Erc cried. "You gave him the holy gift of life itself. He'll reverence you for it the rest of his days.

"Tell him it's so, boy!" he wailed though he paused no longer for the boy to tell it than the incoming tide pauses.

"But what he's got in here," Erc said, tapping the boy's head between his two proud eyes, "and in his soul," he said patting the boy's flushed cheek, "that's straight from the King of Heaven, Finnloag. It's God himself planted those seeds and it's God must have the harvest."

Erc had a druid way of saying God that had the rustling of oak leaves in it and the sound of shallow waves against the rocks and the feel of mist drifting knee-deep over the blue folds and hollows of the hills. They said he could bring on a snowfall with the right words if he felt like it.

"The King of Heaven wants him for a priest, Finnloag," Erc said.

A stillness like snow come settling down on them all when he said it. "He's not to go home to you when the monks are done with him here."

A man's true wealth is counted better in sons than cows and with those words Erc made off with a third of Finnloag's. Finnloag could have been up over his lips in snow for all he found to say. He was looking down still at his hands piled on top of each other.

Brendan's eyes was bulging like eggs with the honor of the thing. Cara was biting down on as much of her fist as she could fit between her bare gums.

Erc rose up from his bench and come around to them. He set one hand on Cara's head. Her brow went dimpled trying to look up at him. His other hand he laid on Brendan's head like a great stone cap.

The Winning of Kings

[VI]

ITA said surely Brendan should see something of the world first if he was going to get priested. That way he'd know what he was giving up when the time come and know something as well of the world's need for priests.

She had tucked her skirts up into her girdle and tramped all the way from Sliabh Luacra with three of her nuns to deliver Jarlath a child or two more for teaching. Many a steep mile she'd brought them, and I remember them whimpering on a plank bed in one of the hives. They had their little fists in their eye-sockets, and Ita was singing them a lullaby they say she made up one day when she come on baby Jesus sucking his finger in a pool of sun on her stone floor.

> Jesukin
> Lives my little cell within.
> Fat monks chide me to deny thee.
> All is lie but Jesukin.

That was how it went only she didn't have a sweet voice like Cara, and it didn't seem to comfort the children much on their plank.

They say under her shirt she had a great horned stag beetle fed on her flesh so she was in holy martyrdom every hour of the day though I can't help thinking she give him some time off when she went out fishing or chasing after conies with her sling. Apart from the beetle she was as sensible for an abbess as any I ever saw though. It was sensible to look the world over a bit before they priested him because once you're a priest it's like a cleft lip you can never get rid of at all so you'd best make sure it's what you're after before you let them do it to you. It was sensible as well to tell him he should take a friend with him on his journey for any nasty thing come into his head to do out there in the world he might stop short of if somebody else's eye was upon him. It's why they always send them off two by two of course though if I was the devil I'd fix it so every once and so often they'd send out a pair had a knack for the same kind of nastiness and that way they'd only egg each other on. I was myself the one she picked to go with him that time. Who's to know if it was sensible or not? She could have done better but she could doubtless have done worse as well.

It happened one day when we was coming on to some holy feast or other. I was in the kitchen yard helping cut up a pig they'd slaughtered for it the day before. I'd been there for the slaughtering as well, catching the blood in a pail for black pudding when they shoved a knife in its throat and helping drag it over to the pile of straw where they got twists for singeing off the bristle. We poured water on the carcase and scraped it and singed it again and finally with a gambrel between the hind legs hoisted it up to a crossbeam. Then a monk with yellow braids sliced open its belly and groping around up to his elbows delivered it of a steaming tubful of pink slippery insides I carted off to the kitchen in my two arms. They left it hanging overnight to cool with a sack wrapped round its long snout to keep the cats from it and the next day after matins the yellow-braid monk and I set to cutting it up, Ita being at her quern across the yard from us. Hams, trotters, eye-pieces, ears for making brawn with, brains, chops—we was laying it all out in the straw when Ita come over and drew me aside to where we kept a black stone on the wall for whetting. She told me with Jarlath's leave she wanted me to go with Brendan though she didn't so much as know my name then.

"It's a smirchy sort of business you're at with that pig, some would say," she said. "There's many a monkish boy either he'd beg out of it or turn green as a toad doing it. But it's neither of those with you, I see. You could be laying the holy table for mass the way you set those cuttings out. That's the deep truth of things too no matter or not if you know it."

Ita's eyes disappeared entirely when she smiled.

"Smirchy and holy is all one, my dear," she said. "I doubt Jarlath has taught you that. Monks think holiness is monk-ishness only. But somewheres you've learned the truth any-how. You can squeeze into Heaven reeking of pig blood as well as clad in the whitest fair linen in the land."

She said that was why she picked me for the one to go with Brendan and maybe she knew it would be for the best. What she didn't know though was I wasn't a monkish boy like she thought. I was put out to fosterage with the monks for no reason better, as far as I ever knew, than my father was a ham-fisted, beer-swilling fright of a man as didn't want to be pestered raising me. Holiness was the last thing in the world I had my mind on whether it was Jarlath's kind or the pig's. Indeed at the very moment Ita found me I was having unholy thoughts.

There in the straw was all the pig parts laid out for salting, and I remember thinking when you say a pig has lips, has ears, has trotters and so on what you mean is he has them the same as a tree has leaves. So when you take all his parts away there's still the pig himself left over somehow just like when you take all the leaves away there's still the tree left over. But when you take away all the parts of a pig there's no pig left over at all save some mess and stink to draw flies. A pig *is* his parts. That's all he is. And I thought as I squatted there peeling the lips off him it's the same with a man surely. Hack him apart for thieving say or leave him to fall apart all by himself in his lonesome grave, there's nothing beyond that left of him to go to Heaven or anywheres else far as I can see. And if there's no man or no woman either in Heaven, is there a Heaven then at all indeed? And if there should be no Heaven, Heaven help us, what kind of a king is the King of Heaven himself then or is there any such king at all for the matter of that? It was to such a dark pass my thoughts took me that I made the blessed sign on myself with my greasy hand to keep the Devil off and maybe that was the very thing caught Ita's eye and made her say I was peeling off pig lips like I was laying the holy table for mass.

We both did Ita's bidding in any case, Brendan and me— Brendan to see his bit of the world and me to see it alongside him should he need me. When she set her mind to pair the two of us there was none could stop her. Even Erc minded her though she could have passed under his hairy arm and never grazed her head. Him and Jarlath both give their blessing, and Erc give Brendan as well the Bishop ring off his own thumb so he'd have it to show if there was any tried stopping us along the way. Erc said there was a new king to be made at Cashel. We was to say we'd been sent to bless him in the Bishop's name.

So we set off in our worn brogues that spring when Brendan was just a step or two past twenty and me just a step or two lag of him. Brendan wore the saffron wool shirt Cara made for him who knows how many washings and mendings before and me a cloak you could read the holy Gospel through if you half tried. Uphill of the monks' graves a bit was a stretch of flat rocks rippled with water-marks and pocked with sea-smooth holes from ancient times when the sea come roaring and foaming up over them. Wild thyme and yellow pansies poked through the cracks and you could see down over the graves and beyond to the higgledy-piggledy walls around the monks' fields. Jarlath and Erc and Ita climbed up there to watch us go. Ita was in the middle with her eyes gone entirely. The three of them was dark against the clouds. They had their hands in the air.

Me and Brendan wasn't what you might call friends at first. We circled and snuffed each other like hounds not sure whether to start baring our fangs or go off together at a trot. Brendan was the one picked out for no reason I could fathom to be the darling of the world. He was queer looking in his way. He was full of brags when he talked and full of sourness when for miles he'd trudge along mute as a cabbage and always six or so paces ahead of me no matter how I quickened my step. There was times he got to throwing his shoulders about in such a twitch at some thought he was having I was afraid he'd be mistook for a lunatic and the two of us clubbed about the ears and shoved into a pit.

As to what he thought of me, he made it plain as if he spelt it out with a quill. I could tell him the sun had just cracked in two like an egg and he wouldn't so much as raise his head to see. Often, I think, he didn't so much as hear me even. Sometimes he'd fix me so hard with his pale eyes I'd think he marked me but once I put him to the test. I stuck my finges in my eye corners and my thumbs in my mouth corners and pinched me up a face to knock a squirrel off a tree and he never so much as blinked. It was only the backsides of his eyes he had on me for they was turned around the other way to peer in at his own secrets. Whole days went by with so few words between us we might each have been no more than the shadows stitched to the other's sore feet.

They was glad days for me even so being free on the road in the fresh summer of the year and proud to be bound for the making of a king with a bishop's blessing in our pocket. As we left the sea behind us heading east there was brown-backed dappled deer under the trees and round-faced otters fishing the pools and birds everywhere you cast your eye, the linnet in brier and brushwood, the soaring lark, the thrush piping out of the deep heart of the wood. We'd stop in the shade or by a stream to eat of what the monks had loaded us down with in the way of flat loaves and onions or gather dark sloes off the blackthorn or scarlet rowanberries or new strawberries when they wasn't too sour on the tongue. Once we come on a girl drawing water at a well. She offered us to drink holding her cup out to us in her own hands, nor will I ever forget the cool of it in my throat nor how Brendan wouldn't speak a word to her or raise his eyes off the ground so he saw no more of her than her white feet if even them. She might as well have been some snag-tooth hag the gentry sent to devil us for all he knew different. The bees carried honey on their legs and there was cow lilies in the loughs. Curlews fled us into the air skreeking like we was ourselves devils.

Nights we'd sleep under the stars if it was fine or burrowed deep in the brush with our clothes over our heads if it was showery. One night such a storm come up we'd have drowned either way though if we hadn't run into a bit of luck. The rain was whipping about our ears and bending the trees flat. There was no light to see by at all save the lightning that almost blinded us, and we was stumbling along with our chins tucked in and our arms crooked to keep off branches when we tumbled into a ditch dug round a ring of houses. We was wallowing around in the water and muck and how I ever got out I'll never know. I give Brendan a hand up and for a wonder he took it. I think it was the first time he truly owned I was there at all.

The first doorway we come to they let us in. All over muck with our red eyes swiveling, I guess they was scareder to let us in than to try shoving us out. Inside you could scarcely stand the floor was that slippery with cow dung and stalings save where there was holly twigs laying about with the ends chewed off. There was dry places set into the walls along the two long sides. In one of them an old woman was scattering a lapful of husks over the fire smoking the place up something wicked. In another a man was asleep on the yellow hide of a steer. There was a partly bald man making a fire of his own at the far end of the room and a woman feeding him twigs out of a bundle under her arm. The man only grunted at us to keep our distance but the woman give us a little milk and barley bread and showed us we was welcome.

Others was slumped about in the shadows with only the fire in the wet of their eyes to show they wasn't sacks. In one corner there was a rustling and thumping in the straw I first took for dogs till there come a whimpering deep-drawn sigh made me know it was a man with a woman. Brendan knew it too. I once saw a man trussed in a wicker cage for burning. Brendan's face was like that. Sweat run out of his muddy hair. His eyes was pinched like somebody'd hurled dirt in them. There was a tuck of his lip caught on one tooth. You'd have thought Ita's beetle was at his innards.

We went to sleep that night on a pile of straw smelled of piss. The sharp ends stuck us and there was fleas. The storm puddered over us. Brendan whispered he was putting Erc's ring in his mouth for safekeeping. I warned him against choking on it and he tucked it in the pouch of one cheek laying with that side down.

"A good dream to you then, Finn," he breathed in my ear as best he could with the ring in his cheek. It's the first time I remember him calling me by my name since we left Jarlath's. Once in a while I woke in the dark with the hot of his snores on the back of my neck. He was curled up behind me with one arm tucked about my chest.

The only time he had to show his ring come a few days later. There was a mist so thick you couldn't see your hand on the end of your arm hardly or the path under your feet. There was a birch wood on one side and a marsh on the other. The air was still as a cave and we crept along feeling our way without a word between us. It was all we could do just to keep from slamming into a tree. The mist turned to droplets in Brendan's red hair. It smelled of the marsh and the green foggy breath of frogs.

All at once a band of five or six men sprung up in front of us sudden as wizardry. They had skins hanging off their shoulders and leather bands crisscrossed about their legs. They was carrying spears. The leader was a spare clean-shaven man no higher than my heart. He had a nose sharp as a peg and drooped eyes.

"A gentle evening to your honors," he said. You couldn't tell if he was poking fun or polite as you please. "You've lost your way, it seems. Likely it's the fog. Us and our kindred owns this place, you see. We own all the deer and long-legged pigs as well should you be wondering. You'd best come with us to the king then. He's ever one for keeping a sharp eye on strangers."

Brendan's hands flipped at the wrists like hooked fish when he twitched his shoulders but for a mercy he kept a cool head. I stood grave and tall as I could next to him. We had no weapons about us save our thin staffs. We had leather bottles slung at our waists for water.

"I'm wearing a bishop's ring on my hand, your worship," Brendan said. He held his fist out at full length with his thumb in the air. You could see the ragged places where he gnawed on it. "It's mighty Bishop Erc himself that's bid us to Cashel. They're picking them a high king there as you doubtless know."

The spare man hardly more than glanced at the ring with his dooped eyes.

"We're of the old ways," he said. "I wouldn't know a bishop from a weasel. But I've seen grander rings than that in my time though. You'd best come along now."

"So please you then," Brendan said. "But there's one trick for telling a bishop from a weasel should you ever stumble on one. A bishop's curse can wither an acre of corn overnight and leave a whole meadow of cows with their bags shriveled."

"That may well be," said the spare man. "Just fall in with me and my men will follow close behind should you chance to drop anything."

He led us into the birch wood where it was all so sodden there was no cracking or snapping under our feet at all. There wasn't a twitter out of the birds either. I suppose they was off someplace drying their wings. The small man was near enough to touch. At the ends of his braided hair he had silver balls that bounced with his trudging. You could hear the sound the spears behind us made breathing through their teeth.

After a time we started climbing a hill. The trees thinned out some as we went. There was brambles snagging at our cloaks. Brendan was puffing along at my side and I had a stitch in my ribs but the leader never so much as broke his stride till we got to the top at last. It was a bald high knob you could see all the other hills from. We was well above the mist there. It was drifting in the deep glens all about us like the sea. There was a ring of tall standing stones hard by. In the center was another stone. It was stouter and squatter than the others and around the base of it all manner of twining leaves and stems that must have been carved in it in ancient times by the look of them. The top of it was rounded off sleek and there was a kind of collar about it like a man's part.

An old fat man with a gold torque about his neck sat on a slab alongside it. He had gold earrings looped over his ears and a garnet brooch for holding his cloak together. On his head was a greasy soft cap. There was a meager fire of twigs at his feet to keep off the damp. The spears scattered themselves about each picking a tall stone to stand by still as stones. The spare man nodded to Brendan and me to step into the ring.

The man on the slab looked us up and down with only his small eyes traveling. He was clean-shaved like the one that brought us and there was a look to him made me wonder was they father and son though the old one was fat as the other was spare and had a great tumbled sad face on him. He took a pull from a pot of beer on the sod next him and let the trickle run off his chin.

"I'm king," he said at last.

"I'm Brendan, son of Finnloag," Brendan said. "This here is my friend Finn. We're men of peace the two of us. We're bound for the making of the High King of Cashel."

"Let them make what they can," he said. "I can't even make water any more. Not more than a drop at a time anyhow. Besides that it seems like my knees bend the wrong way when I walk. I need two sticks to manage."

He waved at a pair of forked ashplants leaning against the lewd stone. He held his two hands out in front of him then so we could see them better. They was covered in rings.

"Each of those rings is for a king I killed in battle," he said. He lowered his hands and give a belch. "Nowadays I need a man under each arm to set me on my feet. Then I have to wait till my head stops spinning or soon as I start walking I tumble in a heap."

"I'm grieved to hear it," Brendan said. "The great Bishop Erc that's my shield and lord always holds there's nothing for stiffness of the joints like seawater."

"I tried it," the king said. "I've eat all manner of foul herbs. I've soaked in comfrey. I've had my druids switch me from head to toe with yew wands and daub me with muck like I was wattles. I've slit throats galore to him of the Silver Arm." He winced like something was sticking him. "Nor was all the throats I slit beasts' throats either."

The grey clouds scudded low over our heads. The king shifted from one ham to the other and groaned. The bullies leapt out with their spears at the ready and would have spitted us on the spot if the king hadn't waved them back.

Brendan stood steady as a tree with his damp beard hanging in wisps.

"Perhaps I can tell you something new to try, Bauheen," he said.

The king's eyes widened.

"How come you know my name?" he said.

"It's no matter," Brendan said.

The king kept his eyes on him a long time before lowering them. He set his cap beside him on the slab and kneaded his brow with his hand. It made his eyebrows tilt and muddle.

"Time was there wasn't the likes of Bauheen to be found in the whole land," the king said like a man talking in a dream. "We'd stand on the hilltop and rouse the beasts in the glens hurling clods down and hollering. We'd blow ourselves black in the face on our horns. There was the red deer and the wild swine and the fawns all running mad in the bracken. We'd run down on them madder still, Bauheen in front with his blue spear. Each had a leash of hounds and such was their fury the earth was red when we was done. Not a boar was left puffing slobber through his snout. It might be upwards of ten hundred deer fallen and the great stags belling after their dead does. Neither the hinds nor the badgers could be counted there was such heaps of them, nor the clubbed conies. Light on my feet as a lovely girl I was then though strong as a red ox."

He took another pull on his beer looking at us over the edge of the pot.

"And Fiona," Brendan said. "You'll not be leaving out Fiona surely."

The king choked. Beer shot from his mouth and run down out of his nose. He threw his two arms in the air and bent over coughing and spewing. His eyes started out of his head like berries on stems. I would have thumped him between the shoulders only I was scared the spears would be upon me. He stopped finally. His face was blotched. There was tears running down.

"You must be a wizard," he said. His voice was scarce more than a whisper.

"It's little enough," Brendan said.

"Bright as a star Fiona was," Bauheen said. "She had shaggy grey legs and a white belly on her soft as pinfeathers. She could course swift as the wind and fetch down a stag without a mark on him."

He mopped his face with his cap.

"I had them slay me a king when Fiona died," he said. "I had her laid in her grave with a slayed king at her four great feet for honor."

It was more of a drizzling than a misting now. The squat stone glistened.

Bauheen had forgot we was there it seemed. His eyes was closed to where you could see little but the whites of them under the lids.

"Who would you be then?" he asked at last opening his eyes again.

"I'm Christ's man," Brendan said.

"Whoever that might be," Bauheen said. "How come you make so free gadding through my lands like a harper? I'd take you for a bog man from the looks of you."

"I make old things good as new," Brendan said.

"You're a tinker then?" Bauheen said.

"I'm no tinker, no," Brendan said. "I've a higher trade than that. What would you say if I was to make you good as new yourself, King Bauheen?"

There was a pitter-patter of true rain now but it was soft and small. You could smell summer in it. The smoky twig fire spluttered.

The king whistled through his teeth and leaned one of his cheeks against the flat of his hand. He looked at Brendan a while tilted like that.

"I'd give you this," he said. He pointed to the garnet brooch that was wide across as a man's hand. "Should you only be making sport of me though I'll give you and your friend here both something of another sort entirely if you catch my meaning." He spat on his forefinger and touched the stone pizzle with it. "As the Old One's my witness," he said.

"You'll have to stand up then," Brendan said.

I was half sick with fright at what his madness might cost us but his blue eyes and the crammed teeth of his smile was blithe as a juggler's. He moved toward Bauheen with both hands stretched out and I thought please God Jarlath taught him to do it right whatever he's fixing to do. The spears was moving out from their stones. The spare man signed them to wait and see.

Bauheen placed his two hands in Brendan's two hands, and Brendan circled Bauheen's wrists with his fingers as he took hold of him. It was no small matter to hoist a man of the king's heft to his feet that way when otherwise it took a man under each arm but Brendan managed it.

Bauheen stood teetering. His bunchy knees shook under him. His face was twisted in a knot. When Brendan took his hands away and backed off a few paces, I thought the old man would fall for sure.

"In the name of the true Christ walk, my dear" Brendan said in a strong voice. He made the holy sign in the air between them.

It wasn't like a swallow cutting capers before a rain-shower but the king moved forward. He had no forked ashplants to prop him either. The wet seeped up between the toes of his bare feet as he set one before the other. The gold ear-loops swung back and forth to his tread. His cap slipped crooked over one eye. His mouth was agape.

Brendan waited for him in his saffron shirt. The rain was coming in big drops now. Bauheen took the last few steps with his arms stretched out sideways far as they'd reach. When he got to Brendan at last he almost lifted him off his feet throwing them round him and clasping him to his belly.

"You're the great wizard of the world!" the king cried. "I've seen no cunning to match yours save the bees' at honey time."

"The great wizard of the world is him that washes you clean of all your nastiness," Brendan said. "It's our lovely wizard Christ himself."

"Whatever you say is enough for me," the king said.

"Kiss his holy cross in fealty then, Bauheen," Brendan said.

He handed him the whittled wood cross he wore strung on his neck together with the wax balls. Bauheen kissed it.

The rain was coming off Bauheen's cap like a thatch. He was fumbling to take off his brooch.

"You'll have bound over your whole kindred with that kiss then?" Brendan said.

"Every last one of them from this day forth and forever," Bauheen said. He kissed the cross a second time to show he meant it.

To get it to his lips he give it such a tug on its string it come close to jerking Brendan off his feet. You'd have thought it was the grandest joke in the world the way they both of them cackled.

They stood there dripping in each other's arms like a pair of sailormen that's just missed drowning.

[VII]

THE spare man with silver balls on his braids might have told the name Bauheen when he first took us by the marsh. Brendan himself owned as much.

"He might have told it for all of me, Finn," he said. "All I remember is the water ran hot down my leg when I saw those spears."

"I never knew," I said.

"Now you know," he said.

So it may well be he knew Bauheen was Bauheen because the spare man said it and we both forgot in the heat of things. I didn't myself have anything running down my leg but my scalp went cold as death.

The name Fiona was another matter entirely though. There wasn't a soul named the king's dead bitch surely till Brendan named her in the rain. How did he know?

"I believe Christ himself whispered it in my ear to save my life," he said. "Maybe even your life, Finn. How could I know it else?" How indeed?

As for me I believe what we love best in this world shows in our eyes, that's all. There's the blue sea in Brendan's for one. There was a time he loved it anyhow. There's the brown earth in mine for I never had a heart like Brendan's for sailoring but would have spent my days close by the hearth if I'd kept the run of my own life. I always thought in Ita's eyes you could see babies and it was to keep the weather out she kept them squinnied. I believe Brendan knew of Fiona because Fiona was the nut of Bauheen's heart and he wore the garnet because it was the hue of Fiona's eyes, and in his own eyes was the dark shadow still of Fiona coursing and the soft sad shape of her name.

Be that as it may it was good luck however he come by it. The moment the king heard that name on Brendan's tongue he believed Brendan could do anything. If Brendan had said fly in place of walk he'd have flown. He was so beholden to Brendan afterwards there's nothing he wouldn't have given him together with the brooch if he'd asked for it.

He kept to his bargain anyhow. First he let Brendan baptize him all by himself in the deep bed of a stream with his whole kindred gawking from the banks. Then they all come wading in after him. They stood to their chests in the dark water. The children that was too small they took up in their arms. Me and Brendan sloshed among them soaking their heads one by one for an hour or more till at last the entire pack was done.

Then Brendan stood up in a grove of small-nutted branching green hazels and made them a grand speech. He

47

told them how Christ was Prince of Light and King of the Stars and all such as that. He told them every nasty thing they ever did was washed clean away now so they wasn't to foul themselves ever doing the likes again. He told them the Holy Ghost was a gold-eyed milk-white dove would help them stay sweet as milk and true as gold. It was only Brendan with his big bottom and pointed red head talking. He was the selfsame one as Maeve showed her parts to, brother to bandy-legged little Briga. Yet I had to own he cut a fine figure there by the river. Nor did any have a luckier tongue for holy things.

They heard him out like a bard singing victories. When he was done Bauheen got up with only the spare man to steady him and told them it was all just like Brendan said. He told them they better do like Brendan bade them or they'd have Bauheen himself to answer to.

The next day Brendan gathered them at the ring of stones, Brendan in the middle and the rest all about. There was no need for a speech again. We waited in the dark for daybreak. The kindred shuffled their feet some and mumbled but they was orderly enough.

Little by little it got where you could make out faces. You could hear the birds waking. A breeze come up out of the glens and bent the grass.

Just when the edge of the sun first showed, Brendan took up a stout club studded with iron. The veins of his neck swelled as he raised it in both hands. He got it swinging around and around him like Ita taught till it was rather the club that was swinging him. You could hear it whooshing through the air.

The stone pizzle was gold in the sun now. Closer and closer he swung his way toward it, his feet jigging circles in the dew. When the moment was just right he took one step closer. That was it. You never heard such a thwack as it made. It must have shivered his arms to the shoulder. He was all but knocked off his feet.

It didn't leave much of a scar even so, maybe a flake or two smashed off. But there wasn't a one of them there didn't know what had happened.

From that day forward it wasn't the spewing lewd part of a man was lord over Bauheen and his kindred. It was the same lowly Christ as Brendan told them of among the hazels by the river's edge with their twisted boles and the nuts dropping into the water.

Bauheen would have had Brendan stay with him the rest of his days but Brendan wouldn't hear of it. He said he'd see they was sent a priest or two for giving mass and for teaching and hearing their sins. But he himself must get to Cashel, he said. He had Bishop Erc's blessing to bring. Bauheen tried to give him one of his war cars with spoked wood wheels and a fat-hammed horse to draw it but Brendan told him no again. So Bauheen made do with loading us up with as much in the way of loaves and salt fish and bacon as we could stuff in our sacks and only then give the spare man leave to show us down through the woods to where he first come on us in the mist.

Brendan baptized no others on that journey but there was more than a few he softened up against the day another of the new faith should come by. They was poor folk mostly. They'd be gathering white-stalked wild garlic or nuts as might be or grazing their bony cows on some common pasturage. He'd give them a bit to eat out of our plump sacks and tell them news of Christ like it was no older than a day. Nor did he tell it with gull eyes like Jarlath nor grinding it down to a fine dust like Erc. He'd make them laugh instead at how Christ gulled the elders out of stoning to death the woman caught in the act of darkness. He'd drop their jaws telling them how he hailed Lazarus out of his green grave and walked on water without making holes. He'd bring a mist to their eyes spinning out the holy words

Christ said on the hill and telling them the way he shared his last loaf with his friends the night the bullies come for him in the garden.

It was like flirting or courting the way Brendan did it. He'd tease them along till they was hot for more and then skitter off saying he'd be back one day soon or another like him to tell them another tale or two if they'd mend their ways in the meantime. Once in a while he'd get me to join him singing psalms back and forth though it sounded more like cows calling to be milked than monks. And so it was we made our way to Cashel at last.

If I was myself God I'd use Cashel for my chair. If I was Prince of darkness I'd use it as well. I'd fly on my leathery wings to the topmost crags of it for a roost where all the swill of the world would see me and come creeping like beetles to my cruel service. Cashel is a rock rising sheer to a great height. All about it are fields flat as your hand. It rears against the sky sudden and stark. High-flying birds slam into it on dark nights. It's the envy of clouds. If ever you saw it you'd never forget it if you lived to a hundred. There's a massy stone wall crowning it with a deep ditch the full way round and tall towers and timber raths and nailed cross-timbers thick as a man. There's no fierce band of spears and swords and iron-bossed shields could take it even if they had a full year to work at it together with the Dagda himself to lend his club for the battering.

There's many great halls inside for feasting and judging and the like. Full of smoke they are with pads of woven wattle to keep out wild weather and the walls hung with all manner of arms and bright painted cloths that tell of the yellow-haired kings and their high doings. There's huts for guards and foot servants and dry kennels strewed with rushes for the hounds. There's the Hall of Warriors that's got fourteen doors to it. There's the Hall of Fair Women meaning such women as paint their eyes with berry juice and string gems in their hair. You never saw such a mess of kitchens and butteries and bake houses either with brew houses as well where they store their beer in casks of red yew. They've got chambers dug in the earth for holding men prisoner for years at a go some of them and never so much as a peep at the sun for comfort. The chariot chiefs have their bunks about the king's chamber and their horses stabled prouder than themselves among bulged nets of hay and their troughs kept brimming with sweet clear water.

The horses nicker and neigh on the cobbles. The hounds bell. The fowl cackle. There's shield-makers and smiths, cobblers and tinkers for keeping the king's strength strong. There's leeches should he need mending. There's pipers and jugglers and dwarfs to see he stays merry. There's haughty druids for keeping the king's eyes open to the in-between things of the world they say magic comes from such as twilight that's in between dark and day and dreams that's in between wake and sleep. Dew is what they use for their spells because it's neither mist nor rain, and mistletoe that's not just a plant nor yet just a tree. They meet in their moon-color cloaks at in-between places like river fords and pick times when there's fog because fog is betwixt sea-water and air. If ever there's some poor soul lies groaning his way out of life into death you can be sure there'll be a druid creeping up on him to catch a peek at the two worlds at once and the place between them.

As to opening the king's ears to the glory of things there's bards. Bards move through the land like honeybees to settle wherever they deign with the seven times fifty stories they must get by heart before they're properly barded. Twenty-one cows is a bard's honor price if he's taken in battle, the same as a king's. And why not? They've got the knowledge of all past kings and chief kindreds back to Adam in their heads. Besides, if you cross them they've the knack of making songs so spiteful they leave you a laughing-stock down to your grandchildren's grandchildren and raise red, green and white blisters on the skin of your face besides.

Lastly at Cashel there's heads. At least when me and Brendan first wheedled our way past the gatekeeper there was. First off I thought they was some manner of round great nuts set out for drying. Nut color and shriveled they was, leaning against each other on the tops of walls or hung by the hair from beams or stuck on poles. They was men's heads mostly though here and there was a woman's. The oldest ones was gone black. The eye sockets was empty long since and no lips to cover the teeth. Most beards had wore off in the weather or gone to make swallows' nests but once in a while you come across a shaggy one. There was fresher ones as well. They was wizened and tawny but you still might have known who they used to be by the looks of them if you was their mother though I doubt even a mother would have lingered there long the way their mouths was twisted and their eyes rolled up.

Brendan and me was gawking at them when somebody come up from behind and thumped me on the head. It was a pig bladder with dry garlics in it to make it rattle. The man that done it was a frailish lean man that had his cheeks streaked with blue clay. The hair on top of his head was done in a knot. He had a withery grave face on him not so much like an old man's face as the face of a boy grown old before his time.

"You'll want to be watching out for the cat," he said. "She's a sly devil with chewed ears and breath like carrion. I saw her but yesterday. She was playing at dice with a combmaker."

I had no wish to rile a lunatic and answered him fair as I could. "Thanks for the warning, my dear," I said.

"She's the one that got their tongues, more's the pity," he said, nodding up at the heads. "You'll be getting no news out of them if it's news you're after." He caught Brendan with his bladder then. "You've got a lovely mouthful of teeth," he told him.

Brendan let on he didn't even notice he'd been thumped. "Perhaps you'll have news of the king-making yourself then," he said. "It's that that's brought us."

"I'll show you what I have," the man said.

52

He pulled his shirt open and on his bare flesh was painted a face. He had rings painted around his nipples for eyes and two red dots in the pit of his chest for a snout. The crease he got with sucking in his gut was a bitterish smile of a mouth. By squirming about he could make like it was talking.

"Push your belly closer to mine and waggle your bum!" the mouth sung out in a clownish squawk. The man's own lips scarce moved at all. He looked like he'd just come from burying his wife.

"Mother of Heaven!" Brendan said going red and starting to go.

"Mother of Heaven is it then?" the man said but out of his own mouth this time. It stopped Brendan in his tracks the way he said it.

"It is," Brendan said.

"Would you be like to know what's the greatest work of Heaven, I wonder?" the man said. He give us a long look as he pulled his shirt back over his belly.

"Perhaps you could tell us yourself," Brendan said.

I remember still the look of the man standing there by the grisly wall with his blue face and his topknot. He reached his hands out to us like something precious and frail was in them. His wrists was touching and the fingers curved back like petals. His voice was little more than a whisper.

"The begetting of the Prince of Light on the Queen of Glory," he said.

Brendan made to throw his arms about him in a great hug but the man held him off with his bladder. He laid his finger to his lips and signed us to follow. One of the heads had such a evil smirk on its face as we went it give me the shudders.

There was dogs every place—not the hounds in the kennels for hunting, the ones tall as a man's waist with thick silvery coats on them like fog and gleeful shy eyes but lank ones snuffling slops and hoisting their legs on everything in sight though they'd long since gone dry. Tangle-haired children run about naked as birth most of them and brown as nuts. A pair of smiths was pounding iron at their fire and women filling a wood tub at the well. A row of leather-belted men was stretched out in the shade of a wall on their backs. I took them for corpses waiting to have their heads lopped till I saw they was only sleeping.

Nobody paid us any special mind as we went. The blue face man led us to the Hall of Fair Women though it could as well have been the Hall of Ugly Men for all we knew better at the time. At a spot where a pair of walls come together to make a corner a hide roof jutted out from it on poles with timber stumps and other rubble heaped up to close the place off. Wattles was hung for a door and the man pushed through it with Brendan and me at his heels.

It was dim inside. Bundles of herbs dangled from the stones. A cap hung there as well made like a goose head stitched with feathers on it and a flapping yellow bill in front.

"The luck of God be with you," Brendan said giving him his hand.

"The woman of your choice with yourself," the man said. Brendan lowered his eyes.

"If you don't mind my asking," I said, "could you tell us who you are, I wonder, us being strangers to Cashel and not knowing one thing from the other?"

"Who's my granny on the shelf talking, talking to herself?" the man said. He looked at us in silence out of his withery face waiting on the answer.

"A pot on the hob perhaps?" I said, it being such an old one I had no trouble.

The man didn't blink an eye but come out with another quick as a twitch. "Who is it goes off and the priest's dinner with her then if you're so clever?"

It was another with whiskers on it so I come right back at him. "A hen with an egg if I'm not mistaken," I said.

I tried one of my own on him then thinking to humor him.

"There was eight parts of speech when the world began," I said. "Can you say who run off with seven of them?"

"Wasn't I myself the one that caught them at it?" he said. "It was the women."

Brendan saw it was his go then and you could tell he thought he had a grand one from the way he spluttered it.

"What's heavy as a horse that climbs the hill?" he said, "and pinches like a new shoe in a place none knows but him that wears it?"

The man placed his fingers to his temples. He puckered his mouth into a whistle and gazed up at the hide roof pondering. The hide had worn places in it ruddy with the sun showing through.

"My dear, I carry one of those about with me myself," he said at last. "Surely it's a sorrowing heart." The way he slipped his hand under his shirt and laid it on his painted breast he looked like he meant it truly if he meant anything truly at all.

After a bit he said, "Riddle me this one right and I'll tell you who I am if there's nothing in the way of it bigger than a thumb."

We was all sitting with our knees bent up under our chins to make room it was that close. Brendan leaned forward with his teeth showing.

"Tell me who is the monk's mistress then?" the man said.

Brendan flushed dark as the weatheredest head. He closed his eyes for the shame of it, his mouth agape and spittle on his nether lip.

"I've no answer to that at all," he said so you could barely hear him.

"You're a monk yourself then," the man said. "No other would go such a color."

Brendan answered him neither a yes nor a no. Nor was there need to the way he gazed in wonderment.

"As for me I'm the King's clown, Crosan," the man said, "though whose clown I'll be next is a riddle as yet uncracked."

Then at last he come round to telling us what we wanted to know. It seems there was two cousins vying for king, both as it chanced with the name of Hugh. One of them was called Hugh the Black for the color of his hair though the blackest thing about him, Crosan said, was he was of the old faith if you could call him of any faith at all the haughty feckless way he had of carrying on. The other was called Hugh the Handsome, and the handsomest thing about him was he was of the new. Crosan said the way things looked there wasn't a doubt in the world Hugh the Black would be the one they picked. The cowlords favored him to a man being of the old faith themselves and he'd won the hearts of most of the rest for having about him more the proud manner of a king than the other. The women especially was fluttered just by the sight of him.

"There'll need be someone sent straight from Heaven itself to change their minds if we're to get a christly king over us," Crosan said, and the words was scarcely out when Brendan stopped him.

"Heaven sent me," he said.

I knew he was thinking of how the woods flamed up the night of his birth and how the hind out of Sliabh Luacra suckled him. He was remembering the way Ita and her nuns got down on their knees to honor him when Erc come to bear him off to Jarlath's that winter day. Every tall tale ever told of him up to then was passing through his head together with all the ones he'd told of himself. You could see it in how his face glowed.

"Heaven's power to you then," Crosan said. "Without it Hugh the Handsome is good as gone."

We all three of us sat in silence then for a time thinking over what lay ahead. It was me finally broke it.

"Who *is* the monk's mistress then if I may ask?" I said. I felt like a ninny but I couldn't help myself. They both of them gave me a look. The clown had hung his bladder over his head. He flicked it with his fingers to rattle the garlics inside.

"It's the sweet little bell that's rung on a windy night," he said out of his blue solemn face. "Wouldn't a monk rather go to meet that than the wantonest woman in the world?"

[VIII]

NEAR the foot of Cashel on the plain was a school for training warriors. There was oaks growing around the edges and the earth packed so hard and dry from years of leaping about on it you couldn't stub a toe without raising dust. Soon after we come there was a day set aside for showing off all the skull-cracking, liver-skewering, head-lopping stunts they'd learned. All the chief warriors and cowlords was there for the judging and chiefest amongst them the two Hughs. Crosan said we'd get no better chance to see them side by side if we waited weeks.

We'd never have managed without Crosan. By tilting the poles to pitch his hide roof flatter and pushing out the walls a bit where he could without tumbling them he made his hut big enough for the three of us. If we'd slept under the stars we'd like as not have ended up with a hoof in our face or pissed in the ear by some bony dog or taken by some soaked clod for wenches and who knows how used.

Crosan told us the fuss they'd had paring down to just the two Hughs all the ones sprung from the same great-grandfather that was clamoring to be picked high king in their own right. Many come a cropper because of some blemish they had, Crosan said. You couldn't be king if any part of you was wanting nor even if there was anything about you that was bent or kinked or stove in whether from birth or some other ill luck later. They was always hacking and smashing at each other so it's no wonder such a flock of them was passed over on that score.

Crosan played some of them for us. He was one-legged,

squint-eyed, crook-backed, spavined and silly in the head
from bludgeoning, doing each one in turn till he had me
and Brendan holding our sides though Brendan was not
one for such foolery as a rule. Crosan said the ones that was
whole as to their flesh was flawed other ways and he played
those for us as well, the thieves and buggers and wife-
stabbers and so on. He said the nub of it is the king must
be whole if the people's to be whole just like he must be
fruitful if the women and the beasts are to be fruitful. So
that's how come the two Hughs was all there was left to
pick from.

They come down off the rock with all the rest of Cashel
to see the war stunts. Plenty of others come too from many
a green mile all around. There was jugglers and pipers.
There was bandy-legged children just able to walk and old
women and men bent double over their sticks. Dust was
everywhere and the smell of horse dung and sweating and
hay. They had a place roped off for the warriors and planks
laid up for a platform at one end. Two stools was set on it
and two men sitting on them when we got there. Crosan
told us the one on the left was Hugh the Black and the one
on the right Hugh the Handsome. The third man with them,
Crosan said, was the bard MacLennin. He had a purple
face and popped eyes.

Hugh the Black was about as young as Brendan and me.
He had one leg stretched out with his hand on the knee of
it and his head thrown back in a careless proud way. Broad-
shouldered he was with milk-white skin and a haughty
mouth. He had thick black hair you could see the track of
his comb in. His cheeks was painted rose color and his eyelids lavender. He was looking about him in a lazy way with
a sprig of strawberries up to his nose for breathing through.
The way he was dressed you'd have thought he was king
already. His linen cloak was dyed the purple, yellow and
black of a king. It was fastened with a gold serpent. He
wore finely wove slippers on his feet and a gold fillet around

his brow. There was a topaz the size of an egg fixed to it.

The crowds was shouting and throwing muck about and almost knocking us off our feet to see better. They had a row of bullies in holes up to their middles with others hurling spears and rocks at them from some paces off. The bullies had nothing for parrying with save hazel sticks the length of your forearm and shields of hide and wattles. All that showed of them was naked and their hair in braids down their backs. You never saw such a darting and twisting as they fended off what was hurled at them.

Suddenly one of them give out with a howl so sharp Crosan shoved his thumbs in his ears. A spear had struck him square on his hairy nipple and sunk in slantwise to the depth of a span. He was arched backwards half out of his hole. Blood was seeping from him. A few of the spears stopped throwing but most was still at it and the others in the holes still bobbing and ducking. A fat woman started crawling out toward them on her belly like she was fixing to drag off the skewered one. The crowds was hooting at her. It was then Hugh the Handsome stood up. He had his back to us.

He raised one arm for the men to leave off throwing but they paid him no mind. He raised the other in case they hadn't noticed. He waved both arms over his head and called out to them. The spears and rocks kept coming. One spear shivered into the earth right next the woman. She drew her knees up tight to her and laid there squealing like it had gone clear through her.

Hugh the Black took hold of Hugh the Handsome's cloak and with one strong tug had him back on his stool again. Daintily laying his strawberries down on the planks, he made a horn with his hand and set it to his lips. One cry through it was all it took. The spears left off to a man. Hugh the Handsome turned in wonder. It was the first time we saw him plain.

His ears stood out from his head so you could see the

ruddy glow of the sun through them. He had a long nose and a long jaw. The only way he could close his lips over his hare teeth was pursing them. He was Hugh the Black's age give or take but there was grey in his hair already. It strung out from under his slouch cap that was cut too big for him so it come down over his eyebrows. He wore a feather pinned to it with a carbuncle. Hot as it was that day, he wore a blue wool shirt to his ankles and a fringe shawl. He had horsehair brogues. He was shading his eyes to watch the woman trying to tug the man out of the hole.

Brendan tugged at me to lend him a hand helping her. Between the two of us and the woman we dragged him to safety finally if you can call it safety when you're bleeding to death with a spear in your nipple.

We found a shady place for him under a holly bush. We kept his lips moist with a bit of Brendan's shirt soaked in a spring. The woman was of little use. She knelt by the man bobbing up and down from the waist with her face in her hands moaning. The man was the color of ash and shaking so bad I covered him with my cloak. The shaking had the spear's shaft wagging like a mast and the blood seeping out thicker where it was in him. I didn't dare pull it out for fear his life would come with it. There was blood at his mouth as well.

Brendan was kneeling by him. He had his wood cross to his lips mumbling prayers into it. It was slippery with his spittle. He had his eyes screwed tight, his brow knotted. Crosan and me stood watching. The bullies was back at their games from the sound of it. The woman had left off moaning. A bird was perched in the holly flirting her tail.

When Brendan was done praying he took the spear shaft between his two hands and give it a sharp spin pulling up on it. The spear come free. The man's eyes rolled back in his head. Blood welled out of the hole. Crosan went white, and I could feel my legs starting to go under me. Brendan clapped his red hairy cheek down flat on the man's nipple. He pressed down so hard you could see his whole head trembling. His eyes was still screwed tight. The man's blood trickled out under his chin.

"Go," he said like a man strangling. Me and Crosan went.

They was doing leaps now. There was a cross-pole high as a man and they was lined up to clear it one after the next from a running start. The war school chief was standing by to watch if they ticked it. All you could see of him through his helmet was a pair of blue eyes and some straw color hair. Some of the leapers was women and I thought it was as well Brendan wasn't there to see their dimpled hams go bounding through the air pale as cheese.

Hugh the Black had dozed off in the sun. He was slumped forward with his chin in his hand. Hugh the Handsome has taken off his feathered cap and his hair was damp and spiked. The bard MacLennin had come down off the planks and was sprawled in the dust aiming a goatskin at the back of his throat. His great face was that fiery you could all but hear it sizzle when the beer hit it.

In the ring there was a cross-pole set up no higher than your knee then. The trick was to scramble under it as best you could without losing your speed or knocking the pole off. Next was the jabbers as they called it. The chief jabbed thorns in the feet of each runner while they was waiting to go and their task was to draw them out somehow as they hopped along at top speed on one foot only. It was somewhere in the thick of that one that MacLennin lurched back up onto the platform and started hollering out his song. He looked like he'd been holding his breath for a week and was letting it out all at once. He cupped his mouth with his two hands and howled till the crowd quieted and the jabbers come to a standstill.

"MacLennin the Bard I am! Oft have my songs of praise dripped from my lips like honey. My scorn-songs have given strong men the cramp!" He could have been a red bull courting cows from the sound of him.

"Two men there be striving for High King of Cashel,"

he cried. "One of them's sweet-breathed. The other you'd
think was a mossy-toothed whiskery hag breaking wind
when he opens his mouth."

There was some crow caws and moos out of the crowd
but they was mostly as close to still as you can get with
children and dogs running about.

"Set them side by each and see for yourselves. Lo, a
proud hawk-prince, keen as a blade in battle, and next him
a bulge-bottomed boor, wretched of countenance and
feeble," MacLennin went on. He widened his stance on
the planks to steady himself. His bard's green gown was
black with sweat at the armpits.

"Hugh the Black is a choice man of slender fingers. A
bright-cheeked youth, a lover of bards and barding he is,
manly and giving by nature." He give himself another
squirt from the goatskin.

"The Hugh they call Handsome in bitter jest wouldn't
pay you so much as a spavined calf for the grandest song
in the world. He straddles the mangey hump of a sway-
belly limping nag and hunts she weasels only. Red of nostril
and lovely-eyed is the slender colt that carries Black Hugh
like the wind of the west in battle."

Black Hugh had come awake, his eyes glittering through
his thick lashes. Handsome Hugh was making a stab at
keeping his lips shut over his teeth.

"I rejoice to make glorious songs for him whose brow
is the white of the white wild rose, for Hugh of the black
furrowed locks. Lusty and quick to mount as a bull he is
for the breeding of sons," sang MacLennin making lewd
gestures.

"If you pick for your king the limp one instead, O ye
elders and chiefs, then the flow of the milk from the bags
of the cows of Cashel will be scant as the trickle of piss
down a rock."

I missed the rest of the song because Crosan said we'd
best go back to see if Brendan had need of us.

The wounded man's cheeks had gone from ash back

to ruddy. The red bubbles was gone from his mouth. His eye-whites had the eyes back in them. They had him propped on a stone with the fat woman's cloak wadded under his head. They'd mushed up yellow grass and herbs over his torn breast. He showed us a thin smile.

Brendan was the one with blood on him. His straggled beard and cheek and neck was caked with it. He was hunkered near the wounded man with his crossed arms on his knees and his chin on his arms. He wrinkled his brow looking up at us without raising his head.

"I worked it," he said. His face was pale with pride under the caked blood.

The fat woman had her fingers combing through the man's hair. Crosan and me was dumbstruck. We might have been gawking at the wonder of it there by the holly bush still if the chief of the war school hadn't picked that moment to come find out was the man dead. Brendan raised his head to see who it was and the chief seeing him fell over backwards nearly.

"Mother of Christ. It's Bren!" the chief said.

A tumble of straw-color braids come out when he pulled off his great helmet and it was only then I saw he wasn't a he at all.

For the first time since we was all children together at the monks, I found myself staring into the blue astonished eyes of Maeve.

"Bren boy! And Finn!" Maeve cried. She wrapped us both in her arms. She took us each in turn by the ears like a horse trader and tipped our faces first this way then that.

"Ah your lovely brown eyes, Finn," she said, "and a fine new beard on your chin, Bren. I thought at first it was only a bit of fuzz where the red cow's tail slapped you milking. What a time it's been since I gave you your first eyeful, my darling."

Poor Bren. It wasn't easy lowering his eyes the way she had him by the ears. He did it no less, flushing dark as a shoe, but that only meant he was looking instead at the swell of her breasts over the top of her battle belt. The belt was of stiff tanned leather that covered her from her hips to her armpits. Under it she must have had on as many as four or five tunics of waxed skins pressed together and fastened with cords.

"How's Brig?" she said. "And Jarlath? Is Erc alive still? Do the monks still drink in little sips to make sure they won't enjoy it?"

You could tell Brendan was tore in two by the horror and delight both of seeing her again. Mumbling and slabbering he give her the news she was after.

As for herself, Maeve said, she'd gone first to Ita from Jarlath's.

"I'd never have made a nun," she said. "I don't have flat knees for praying. Ita taught me warring instead. She showed me how to make a thick-shafted, solid-socketed spear. She showed me the art of putting your finger in the thong and poising it just right for the surest throw. There was no need to show me swords, thanks to you, Bren. The way we used to go it with our wood ones!" She clattered the one hung at her belt and gave him another bang on the shoulder. "Wasn't we at it the very day I gave you your peek back then?"

She said it as easy as if it was a toad in her pocket she'd given him a peek of but all Brendan could come up with for answering was a strangling sound at the back of his throat like a man being throttled. When she saw how he was rattled she went on to other matters.

"Have a look at this then, Bren. It's a stunt Ita taught me," she said.

She picked a flattish stone off the ground and set it on the stone the wounded man was leaning on. She had her fists on her hips studying it, her three braids down her back. She had that same look in her eyes like the world had just jumped out at her from behind a tree.

Then she pursed her lips up. She screwed them so tight it put dimples in her cheeks and set her eyes fluttering.

Then she did it. She let fly with a bead of spit that caught
the stone square in the middle so hard it split it clear in two.
I'd never have believed it without I saw it with my own
eyes. Even Brendan's feat bringing the man back from
death looked puny next to it. Maybe that's why he made so
little of it. He only shook his head and smiled like she was
a child had just turned a somersault.

She said she had to get back to the racing and leaping
then but would look for us on the rock later. She run off
with her braids stuffed back in her helmet.

After a bit the wounded man said he thought he could
make it home now. Brendan and the woman heaved him up
on his feet. He wobbled there holding the wad of herbs in
place with his hand. Brendan kissed him on the brow. The
woman took one of his arms about her neck and started
walking him off.

The sun was low on Cashel rock by then. There wasn't
much sound out of the crowd over the way. It was quiet
mostly save for a cow somewhere bellowing to be milked.
I thought for a moment it was MacLennin still at his song
but it was only a cow calling for help with her swollen
great bag.

[IX]

MAEVE come to us in Crosan's hut that night. She was
in her war clothes yet. It was a mercy she left her sword
behind because even without it we had to squeeze to make
her room. Brendan had half of her in his lap nearly and
Crosan hunched sideways with his shoulder in my eye. We
could have been gentry the way the rush lamp from beneath
danced in the wet of our eyes and give us freakish gentry
faces.

Crosan laid matters out for us. Hugh the Handsome
wasn't the prettiest man ever got a crown set on his head,

he said, but he was an even-handed man and he was of the true faith. Hugh the Black, on the other hand, was a wench-ing lazy man that didn't have faith in anything save his own looks. Handsome Hugh must be picked over Black Hugh then if King Christ was to be served. That was our work in a nutshell, Crosan said.

"It's the looks of a man men go for, never the good in him if he has any," Crosan said. "The women go daft dreaming he's bedding them and the men go daft dreaming they're in his place. Beside, he's got MacLennin dangling from his belt like a charm, and there's none like a bard for swaying men's hearts especially when he's been known to crack a man's leg over his knee for just breaking wind in his presence."

"There's ways of taking care of a fat rascal like that," Maeve said. She caught me in the ribs with her elbow as she made like she was stabbing one in the belly.

"You could knock out his eye just spitting in it, my dear," I said. Brendan give me a sorrowful look and doubtless would have Maeve as well had he let himself look at her.

"Black Hugh's is the eye to knock out if it comes to that," Crosan said. "There'd be no crowning for him then."

"Surely the want of an eye wouldn't do it alone," Maeve said.

"As surely as thunder sours milk," Crosan said. "If you cut off the plucking finger of a harper, by brehon law you're fined two cows. If a king's finger's cut off, by brehon law he's no longer fit for king."

"Ah well then," Maeve said. You could see she was thinking things out full length before speaking. She must have scrubbed her cheeks since the games the way they glowed. She glanced sidewise at Brendan under her lashes.

"They do some of them say Black Hugh is himself wanting something," she said in a small voice.

"He's wanting a Christly heart in his breast," Brendan said. "There's no doubt as to that."

"Something other than that as well," she said. "Something that don't show."

From the color Brendan went I think he guessed her meaning before she spoke it even.

"They do say he wants one of his two stones," she said.

Brendan sucked a mouthful of air through his teeth. Crosan seized his bladder from the hook and thumped Maeve across the head with it for sheer glee.

"Then Hugh Handsome is king!" he cried. He drew his upper lip back and thrust his teeth out over the nether one like he was Hugh Handsome saying it. "Mind the charge be true though, my dear," he said, wagging his finger. "They'll roast us in cages else."

"After Mac Lennin has first cracked our legs over his knee," I said.

"I've heard them as have laid with him say it for sure," she said. "Just the one stone only."

"It's women's lewd gossip," Brendan said in an awful voice. It was Maeve's lewdness had him shaking.

"We'll have to make sure for ourselves," Crosan said.

"I'll make sure," Maeve said. Her blue eyes sparked bold in the rush light.

She would herself somehow slip into Black Hugh's couch to uncover by starlight the naked truth of him. It killed Brendan nearly to think of it. Yet he knew it was a deed for Christ she was doing and at great peril to herself as well. He couldn't chide her. He couldn't wish her luck either.

The sweat run out of his red hair, and he went on sucking air as we laid our plans. Maeve would do what she must. Brendan, Crosan and me would go to Hugh Handsome while she was at it. We'd warn him what was afoot. Soon as Maeve come back bearing whatever news she might we'd all five of us take counsel together.

*   *   *

Hugh Black had already taken the king's chamber for himself. None in Cashel would have dreamed of telling their heart's darling no. There was cloths on the walls painted with the high doings of the cow lords of Cashel. Hung from the roof tree was a gong of silver he could strike with a stick should he need somebody to pull off his shirt for him or run a comb through his hair. There was a ewer of honey-mixed whortleberry wine for if he thirsted in the night. He had a lidded pot for making water in. His couch was off the floor on legs. There was pillows stuffed with wool for his head to lay on and wove coverlets to keep off drafts.

The chariot chiefs had their bunks around the outside of the chamber. There was guards there too that kept their blue swords drawn through the night in case of a fuss. The guards was the danger though Maeve made light of it. She said she could take on the lot of them with one arm tied. She said they was used to Black Hugh's wenches padding in and out all hours. The chance was they wouldn't so much as raise their eyes to her if their eyes was open at all, they being soakers most of them. For all her bold words though we knew we might never see her alive again. We wished her God's luck as she crawled backwards out of the hut. There's no knowing what Brendan wished in his heart as the dark gobbled her up heels foremost. He said nothing.

Straight to Hugh Handsome we went then. He had a rough chamber scarce bigger than Crosan's off by the kennels and none to guard him save a row of black heads lined up on the roof. A hound lolled on his side at the threshold with a baggy paw covering his top eye. He didn't even stir as we stepped over him. Hugh Handsome lay on his back in a puddle of moonlight. He had a thin pallet only between him and the floor and a deer skin drawn so tight to his chin his feet was left naked. He wore a wool bonnet down over his ears. He was dead asleep with his mouth open. There was no painted cloths on the walls for finery but only his slouch cap with the feather in it. It was hung from a peg. Crosan jumbled him.

His eyes filled slow as cow prints in the rain with the sight of us. The hound slouched up to lick his bare toes but he paid no heed. Crosan told him how Brendan and me had traveled from the western shore with Bishop Erc's blessing. Brendan held out his thumb with the Bishop's ring on it. Only then did he raise himself up on one elbow. He held out this hand to us and we touched our lips to the knuckles.

Crosan saved the part about Black Hugh's blemish till last. Then Hugh Handsome spoke for the first time. His voice was prim as an old nun's.

"A monstrous dark day it would be for Cashel surely," he said. "The kine wouldn't freshen at all under a one-stoned king. The cow lords could never hold up their heads again if it was known through the whole land he was maimed. The corn would wither sure as sin. Better a druid should curse us from a high hill with the north wind behind him and a thorn in his hand."

For a wonder it was Cashel's fate got him clucking. I'd have thought he'd be tossing his bonnet in the air to find he'd be king after all.

"I've never seen my cousin bare," he said. "Nor for all I know could you tell by just seeing anyhow. I doubt you could even tell was there one onion in a sack or two if seeing was all you had to go on." He marked the one and two of it in the air with his finger. "He treats me like a noodle but I bear him no grudge. Indeed I swear by my honor I'll make no use of such idle tales though it costs me the crown."

Crosan told him then what Maeve was about at that very moment. By sun-up, he said, we'd know once and for all if the tales was true.

Hugh Handsome's face darkened. He threw off the deer skin and got down on his knees on the stone floor. He had on the same shirt he wore to the war school. It was hiked up now with his shanks sticking out of it and his pale feet. He placed the flat of his hands together and held them to his face so tight the fingertips pushed up the end of his nose.

Crosan and I stood gawking, the shadow of Crosan's topknot sharp on the moonlit wall. Brendan alone had the wit to bow his head.

"Heaven take charge over this young woman so the bullies and soakers won't do her a mischief," Hugh Handsome prayed. "Let it not be counted for a sin against her that she gives herself unwed to this swaggering man. Thou knowest she does it not in lust but for the sake of thy people of Cashel. Preserve them from the curse of a blemished king if that be the truth of it." He paused to draw a fresh breath.

"Father of Mercies," he said, "have mercy as well on my kinsman Hugh. It is not his fault thou gavest him beauty that makes him haughty and proud. In charity let it fall out that he have both his stones together to the glory of God and his true prince Christ. Amen."

The three of us said our amens with him. Brendan had tears in his beard.

We waited a long time for Maeve to come. Hugh Handsome crawled back under his skin. I sat with my shoulders to the wall and Crosan nodded off at my side. The hound laid his whiskered face in my lap. Brendan stood in the doorway looking out at the stars.

It was to see a little something of the world first that Ita sent him off on his travels. She wanted him to know what he was giving up when the time come and to know as well the world's need of priests. Who could have guessed he'd end up with a clown and a near king waiting in the moonlight on the word of a girl? I wondered did Brendan there in the door think he'd miss the world when he gave it up or would he be as glad to wade clear of it as a cow stuck in a bog.

And who was more in need of a priest than Brendan himself, I thought, his beard still wet with anguish. Did he look at the stars asking himself if among them there was a world where nobody ever yet had his head set up on a roof or had a spear in his nipple or got his heart broke thinking of a young lewd man having his way with Maeve?

I must have nodded off myself after a while. Hugh Handsome's voice woke me. He was up on his feet in his long shirt. Maeve was before him. Through the doorway I saw the first sign of dawn at the sky's edge.

"Was it two then?" he said.

Maeve held her fist out towards him at arm's length. There was a cut place under one startled blue eye and a fat lip on her. Her braids had come loose. She didn't answer him a word but out of her fist raised one finger only.

[X]

WE got into the king's chamber easy as air. All the bullies but one had gone foraging and that one slouched snoring against the wall though the sun was already on its way up. The whole sky was red and feathery.

Black Hugh was sitting at a table with wine at his elbow gnawing the haunch of a stag. He hadn't run a comb through his hair yet and it was all of a tangle. He hadn't painted his cheeks yet either nor was there any need to for they was ruddy enough with the dawn on them. He wore a linen kilt belted over the flat of his belly but was otherwise bare as birth save for a gold chain bright against his skin. We was quite a parade with Hugh Handsome at the head of us and Maeve at the tail but Hugh Black didn't even stop gnawing as we come in on him. You could see his green eyes taking our measure well enough though.

I watched to see how his eyes took in Maeve especially. Having so lately lain with her, would he have some glint of tenderness in them for her, I wondered, or would there instead be some hot glow of the goatishness had cut her cheeks and left her braids wrecked? Did he know she had betrayed his secret to his foes and if so did he hate her more or fear her more? The truth is I've read more meaning in the eyes of a hound gnawing a bone. He looked at us like we could have been leaves blown in over the sill. He let us cool our heels there till he'd torn a gobbet or two more of flesh with his white teeth. He set the haunch down at last and wiped the char off his mouth with a cloth.

"I'll tell you this, Hughie Handsome," he said. "There's more of a man in the one I've got than in the both of yours and ten pair like them."

"Be that as it may," Hugh Handsome said. "You can't be king unless you're entire. That's brehon law."

"The cow lords would sooner pick them a blue-cheeked clown if they knew," said Crosan.

"You'd do well to duck out of the race before they get wind of it if you ask me," I said.

"Should Mac Lennin get wind of it," Maeve said with her fat lip bouncing, "he'll make a song of it will have the whole land sniggering in their beer as long as there's a rock at Cashel."

We each said our piece but Brendan. A breeze riffled the painted cloths on the walls. You could hear a linnet outside clearing her throat for the day's caroling. The sun was higher now and Black Hugh's couch in the corner gone gold where he'd taken his pleasure with Maeve amongst all that tumble of pillows and coverlets. I felt a sadness I couldn't name. It wasn't only sadness for Maeve but sadness for Brendan as well. Pondering that gold couch I felt sad for Black Hugh even. He seemed so fair and young to be maimed, haughty though he was and ripe for a come-uppance. Dawn's a sad time at best anyhow. No matter how fresh-faced and lovely the start of a day you can be sure there'll be some nastiness by the end to mar it.

I feared Black Hugh might be the one to turn nasty. He had a smile I didn't fancy twisting his mouth. His chest was hairless and hard as a shield and he had round strong arms.

There was a dirk at his hand he'd whittled the haunch with, and I knew if he leapt at our throats we'd be lost what with Brendan and me raised monkish and Hugh Handsome with blue milk in his veins not to say Crosan as withered from the night's work as Maeve was wore out and cut from it. Black Hugh's cheeks was flushed and his nostrils wide as a stallion's. His legs was tensed to spring.

"For shame then!" Brendan cried out suddenly with a spray of spittle. "The curse of the crows upon you for using her for a whore!"

He had his neck stretched out stiff as a swan cob harrying and his red beard bristled.

"He did no such thing indeed!" cried Maeve. Her voice was wilder still. "He never laid a hand on me he didn't. I wrestled him to the floor. I got my knee on his chest and his two arms doubled behind him. With this very same hand," she said, shaking it fierce under Brendan's nose, "I could have tore off the only one he's got easy as an apple off a branch. Strike me dead if it's not the God's own truth, Bren!"

It was the God's own truth. Brendan saw it. We all of us saw it. You could see the fight go clear out of Black Hugh. It was wretched enough to be known blemished. He might have brazened that out someway, maybe gotten the elders and chiefs to pick him king anyhow even. He could have said the missing one was up in his belly somewhere like sometimes with beasts so he didn't properly lack it at all. But to be known for a man that let a woman wrestle him to the ground like that was past all brazening.

Hugh Handsome went over to him and laid his hand on his head.

"There's nobody need ever be the wiser," he said. "Don't let them make you king, my dear, and may the tongue rot in my mouth if any here ever breathes a word of this night."

"What will I tell them though, Hughie?" he said in a cracked boy's voice.

"Tell them you're doing it for Cashel," Hugh Handsome

said. "Tell them you think it's an older king Cashel needs. I've a year or two more on my head than you."

Black Hugh's mouth was gone crooked and his eyes teary.

"Tell them as well," said Hugh Handsome, "you're to be Chief of the Counsel and Lord of the King's Herds."

Black Hugh wiped his eyes with the back of his wrist. He drew his mouth straight again. "I'll do it for the good of Cashel then," he said.

The words was no sooner out of him than there come a great burst of sobbing and groaning from behind us. I thought at first it must be Brendan and Crosan and Maeve all grieving at once but it wasn't them.

"For the good of Cashel my darling has done it!" bellowed out the voice like somebody at a burying. What I saw when I turned was the bard MacLennin.

He was slumped against the wall just inside the door with his goat skin bottle dangling from his fist like a wrung goose. He had a lopside wreath of wilted gilly flowers on his head but not so much as a stitch to cover his shame otherwise though he was so matted all over with hair you'd have hardly noticed. He lumbered forward knocking us to the side, and wrapped his arms about Black Hugh like a bear at a honey tree.

"Oh but it's a grand thing you've done!" he cried. "May the skulls on the walls of Cashel grow back tongues in their teeth to tell it! May red-fingered harpers pluck it out on their strings how the ivory-thighed raven prince went and handed his crown to another for the good of the people!"

There's no telling how long the song might have gone on with Black Hugh trapped in those furry arms and bardish slobber wet on his neck and cheeks, but MacLennin started to gobble and stagger so in the midst of it that Brendan and I had to help him to the couch. He had been out all night roistering it seems and was only now ready to lay himself down. He didn't shut his eyes though. He sprawled there among the pillows with the sobs still shaking his shaggy paunch.

"Blemished or no, my sweetling," he called to Black Hugh reaching out his arms to him, "your lovely deed will be told at the hearths of Cashel till its rock turns to dust."

He'd heard much of what had passed between us there in the king's chamber but he'd heard it through soaked ears. He knew Black Hugh was blemished but not the how and the where of it. He knew there had been a scuffle but seeing as Maeve had a fat lip and Black Hugh's was pretty as a strawberry he took Black Hugh for the winner. What set him to groaning and wailing was Black Hugh's saying he'd give up vying for king for the good of the people. The glory of it was too much for him to bear nearly. Save for Hugh Handsome there wasn't one of us he didn't ache to take in his arms and hug to death. His heart was full as an udder at milking time.

"And who might these two strangers be?" he asked with a look at Brendan and me.

"Friends," Black Hugh answered him. He give the word a nasty twist eyeing us. We'd vowed not to tell his shame was his meaning but just "friends" was all MacLennin heard.

"They've counseled me out of the goodness of their hearts," he said with a bitter curl to his lip. He knew where our hearts lay well enough but MacLennin took him at his word. In a great burst of warmth at the thought of how dear we was to his own dearest he grabbed Brendan and pulled him down onto the couch with him.

"Tell MacLennin what makes your heart so good then, my honey, my thrush," he said with his arms about Brendan's neck, half strangling him against his hairy bosom. Brendan's eyes was popping out of his head nearly. His face went black.

"Holy King Christ!" he choked out.

It was a cry for help but the bard heard it as an answer

to his question and from that fine thread Brendan spun as fine a web to catch MacLennin in for the new faith as ever he did for Bauheen before him. MacLennin wouldn't let him off the couch without first hearing the manner of king this Christ was that made Brendan's heart so good, and I doubt Brendan ever preached the Gospel in just such a pickle again.

The fuzzy naked bard with his gilly flowers over one eye took Brendan on one of his knees, his arms clasped about him, and it was there Brendan did it, perched like a bot fly on a bull's hump. It's a wonder he could keep a grave face. Crosan had his cheeks puffed out and his eyes crossed miming MacLennin behind his back. Black Hugh was bent double holding his hoots back. Only Hugh Handsome was sour-mouthed as a carp.

Christ was the king of all kings, Brendan said from Mac Lennin's knee. He was the wizard of all wizards. He turned water to beer easy as breathing. When he commanded the foaming waves to lay flat, they laid flat. He straightened the bent legs of cripples out and peeled the blue milky scales off the eyes of the blind. When he called out of darkness the first light as ever was, the morning stars sang together at the sweet ring of it and all the sons of heaven shouted for joy.

"Ah well, he was a bard then," MacLennin said. It was the part about Christ's voice that struck him hardest.

"MacLennin, he was so mighty a bard his songs have ravished the hearts of men from that day on," Brendan said. "He was a song himself you might say. King Christ is a song on the lips of the true God."

It sent a new batch of tears flowing down MacLennin's cheeks.

"I'll be Christ's bard myself then," he said. "My golden lily-prince here won't have need of my songs any more now he's given way to a ninny." He'd barely got the words out before he sank into a sleep so deep Brendan was able to unwrap himself from his arms at last.

* * *

For a wonder he remembered his vow the next day even and Brendan explained to him how the first thing he must do was get baptized. That way he would wash all his nastiness off at once and take Christ's song into his heart at the same time. MacLennin said that was fine by him.

MacLennin didn't want to be baptized down off the rock in some stream where only a handful or two might come to see. He wanted it done right in the heart of Cashel itself. So he had them lug the great wood trough out of the stables and set it up on planks in the cobbled court outside the Hall of Fair Women. After they scoured it, he had them fill it to the lip with sweet well water. He had bullies go through the streets telling of it and bells rung from the towers when the time for it come round. Everybody was there of course. It was more of a romp for them than a skewering even or a fresh lot of heads to set up on the wall. Brendan wore Bauheen's garnet at his throat. MacLennin wore a fair linen shirt down to his wooly knees and a wreath of white rowan flowers on his head.

The two of them was standing in the trough up to their knees getting ready to start when a queer thing happened. There was doves used to settle down on the cobbles to pick at the horse droppings and just as Brendan was scooping up a potful of water to soak the bard with, a flock of them come swooping down over the wall. The sight of the crowd give them an awful fright. They made a great ruckus clattering their wings over the people's heads and Mac Lennin, who stood taller up there on his planks than any of them, laid about with his arms to fend them off. He must have struck one such a clap he broke its neck. It fell into the water and lay floating there like a cow lily at his knees after all the rest of them had flown off. MacLennin picked it up and laid his cheek to its breast. He looked like his heart was broke.

"It's a sign out of Heaven, my dear," Brendan said.

Mac Lennin couldn't answer he was that shook. He just stood there with his lips to the white feathers.

"From this day forward thou shalt be no longer Mac Lennin," Brendan said. "Thou shalt have a new name to fit thy new life. I baptize thee Colman to the glory of Almighty God."

Colman means a little dove in Roman and from that day on it was the name that great bull of a man was called by.

Hugh Handsome's crowning wasn't for some time afterwards because though he was of the new faith surely he followed the druids' way when it come to luck. It was bad luck, for one, if a king of Cashel went in a cloak of many colors on a grey dappled horse or was still in his bed at sunrise or broke a journey on the fourth day of the week. The call of the cuckoo was lucky. So was the eating of fish out of the river Slaney. Luckiest of all for a crowning was the day of the new moon because that way the king and the moon would wax together in glory. So he had them wait till then.

The Hall of Warriors was where he was crowned in any case. Brendan was there with Erc's ring on his thumb for the blessing. Maeve come in her helmet and waxed skins. Her lip was back to its proper shape but you could still see where she'd got cut under the eye wrestling Black Hugh. Crosan had on his goosehead feathered cap with the yellow bill and it wasn't just his cheeks was blue but his arms as well and his bare shins.

I wondered if Black Hugh would be there in his bitterness. He was. If he was bitter it didn't show though in the proud face he wore under the great hat of the Lord of the King's Herds with the two cow's horns on it. He sat as Chief of the Counsel on a stool next the king's chair. He didn't have his strawberries with him to breathe through though he could have used them, the hall being crammed with as many as it could hold and still leave the square about the king clear for the crowning. There was not a one among them, I thought, would have believed he was anyways blemished if somebody told it. As far as I ever learned nobody has told it to this day.

The old goddess was brought into the middle of the square. A flock of beardless boys lugged her in on wheels. They was stripped to the middle with skirts on them and bronze torques about their necks. It was all they could do to set her up in place. She was heavy and squat and big around as an oak stump. There was blue lichens on the shelf of her nether lip. Her mossy nose was gone mostly. She was hung all over with teats and the opening of her parts was daubed red and fringed. They got a fire of cow dung started in a pan beside her though it was a warm summer's day and the foul smoke wandered through the air to find the hole in the roof.

The king's guard stood ringed about her in their fur-hooded three-corner mantles and skin brogues on their feet. Hugh Handsome sat in the king's chair watching. He looked like the smoke was making him sick the way he worked his nose. He had a lewd round-headed painted stick in his hand and on his lap a pan of milk strained through straw. Crosan was behind him. He stood grave-faced and straight as a tree with his shoulders thrown back so hard it set the feathers on his cap to trembling.

Crosan had told me that morning the seven days of a king's work. On the first day, he said, it's making special laws how to save a harvest or drive off a cow raid or some such as that if there's no overall brehon law covering it. The second day it's playing chess. The third day it's coursing hounds. The fourth day is given to the getting of children though Crosan said Hugh Handsome hadn't ever learned the knack of that and would probably spend the day trying to fit his great toe into his wife's ear. Horse racing was on the fifth day and judging on the sixth if there was tiffs among the kindred. On the last day it was feasting and swilling and passing beer out to any at the gate as hadn't some of their own.

I was looking at Hugh Handsome wondering how he'd take to such tasks when there rose up a great banging of sticks on pots and howling of voices and screeching of horns and groaning. It was like the ruckus women make to drive the foe out of their wits while the men are in the field thumping them to pieces, their hair washed in lime to make it stick up in spikes and muck daubed all over their nakedness. In the midst of it Crosan come out from behind the king's chair. He made cartwheels down to the cleared square and thrice around it, his bladder hung from his belt and jouncing on his rump. When he come to a stop finally before the goddess he made a low reverence from the waist to Hugh Handsome. Then he swept back his arm for a sign Hugh should begin.

All the banging and tooting and howling got even louder when Hugh Handsome rose from his chair. Finicky as a mare on ice so as not to spill the pan of milk he was carrying, he moved forward step by step. In his other hand was the lewd stick. You could see by the way he sucked in his lip he wished they'd let him leave it home. He stopped in front of the goddess. There was never yet such a pair as those two gaping at each other since the world began.

Hugh Handsome was narrow and the goddess was wide. He was young and she was older than Cashel. I misdoubt he'd ever spilt seed in his whole life save dreaming maybe and she with her fringed part agape and her round belly teeming. He was dry as the stick in his hand whilst through the clouds of cow dung smoke she glistened with the butter they'd rubbed on her splintered cheeks and hams and along the inside of her thighs.

Hugh Handsome took the pan of milk and poured it over her till it run dripping down off the rows of her teats. Then he took the painted stick and shoved it in her with a look like he'd sooner be shoving his hand into the flames of the fire. You never heard such a caterwauling as there was then. They knew now the corn would be fat come harvest and the herds dropping calves like berries. They made lowings and moos, pig squeals and cock crows. Black Hugh got to his feet and cupped his mouth to give out with the blistering shrill cry of a bull in rut.

The end of it was the blessing. MacLennin, or Colman as he was now, hoisted his arms for it and a hush come over all of them there in the great hall. The druids with their gold sickles and the brehon lawmakers and the cow lords all hoisted their arms as well. You could have heard a sparrow break wind.

Hugh Handsome got down on his knees by the king's empty chair. Brendan held his two hands over his head like a roof with the thumbs together and Erc's ring shining on one of them.

"In the name of holy God and to the honor of Bishop Erc I bless thee Hugh, Lord of the Red Bulls and Cashel's High King," Brendan cried. His voice was high-pitched and unsteady.

Then he set the black heavy crown of iron on Hugh Handsome's head and with a wan smile the new Lord of the Red Bulls rose to his feet the first man of the new faith ever to rule at Cashel.

We left to go back to Jarlath's a day or so after. Maeve come for the goodbyes.

"Have done with your monks then, Bren," she said, pushing at his chest with her fist. "You was always handy with a wood blade. Learn a thing or two more at my school and you'll end up with a sack full of heads like the best of them."

Brendan would not look at her when he told her no of course but there was a crooked fluttery smile on his lips. It meant if ever he was to look any young honest woman in the face it would be Maeve because he had known her from a child and she had known Erc and was Briga's friend. It meant he had once turned himself inside out in a cave nearly, praying for the mercy of God not just for himself but for her as well. Maybe what his smile meant most of all though was how proud he was that all she did that night with Black Hugh in the king's chamber was wrestle him to the ground only.

"God's luck go with you then," he said. He give her Bauheen's brooch for a parting gift.

"I'll wear it to your wedding, Bren," she said.

We had come from Jarlath's two. We went back four. Crosan and Colman that once was Mac Lennin went with us. They each had their own reasons. King Hugh took hostage a pack of Black Hugh's kin so if Black Hugh ever made trouble for him he'd have their heads on poles before they knew they was off. It happened Crosan himself was one of them and not wanting to risk being lopped he let the air out of his bladder, tucked it under his shirt, and crept by darkness out of his hut to join us. We met by the same holly bush where Brendan got the spear out of the man's nipple.

Colman come because of his scorn for the new king.

"MacLennin will be no bard to a flounder-faced ninny like that one," he said. "Never yet was there a yellow-haired king would have used a stick like that on the Great Mother. With my own eyes I've seen them mount her like bulls. I've seen the hot smoke hiss from their bums while they was at it. I've seen their stones glow red as fire.

"Besides," he said, "I'm Christ's bard now."

Thus we started for home. When Colman twisted his foot in a rut we had to wait a whole day till he could set his great weight on it again. He passed the time learning psalms.

"Christ is my druid, I shall want for nothing!" he called up at the clouds.

"He cloaks me in a thick mist from the eyes of my enemies! He reads the secrets of my heart like the guts of an owl!"

The Gannet in the Wind

[XI]

W E found Erc at Jarlath's when we got back. He said he
knew we was coming from the flight of gulls. A gull has a
way of tilting her wings when she wheels and has lines
she draws across the air soaring and swooping that's plain
as words if you can read them. Erc could.

It was coming on Christmas when we got there. There
was cruel winds off the sea and frost deep in the ground.
Erc had a beehive to himself where he stayed mostly.
Jarlath let him keep a fire in it against the rule. He seldom
ventured out save every so often to clamber down the rocks
with Brendan and walk along the sands at dusk.

I've seen them the size of beetles from the tall cliffs with
the western sea stretching behind them like a dream. They
scarce seem to move at all till you mark how they've passed
by this spit of rock or that bend in the glittering shingle.
I've waved at them and they never saw. I've heard a monk
gathering samphire on the cliffs cry out to them and they
never noticed.

I first knew Erc was ailing by watching them like that
when they didn't know. It was the slow way he moved and

how he bent to Brendan's arm. It was the wavery line of his footmarks in the sand. I read it like the flight of birds. Erc would never have owned it but I saw there was a frost heaving under him would send the great heap of him toppling at last.

What did they talk of the two of them? Of Saint Patrick for one, it seems, and Erc did most of it. He showed Brendan for the first time the bell Saint Patrick had blessed and given him. He wore it around his middle under his shirt muffled so the holiness wouldn't all be rung out of it. It was high as from the tip of a man's thumb to that of his small finger spread and fashioned of two thin iron plates hammered into corners and coated with bronze to give it a sweeter tongue. Once there was many like it scattered all over but lots had been lost or broke or stolen through the years and Erc's was his dearest treasure. Patrick had three smiths just for the making of bells, Erc said. He laid his finger alongside his nose and winked, for it was thought by many the holy saint journeyed by himself.

It seems there was all manner of priests and deacons and bishops with him when Erc saw him anyhow, some of them his own kin from across the water. They moved over the land like the Heavenly Host, the pipers playing and banners bright against the green hills. He had a psalm-singer and a brehon lawmaker and a bell-ringer with him not to mention a cook, a brewer, and two waiters, Erc said. There was three women as well, one of them his own sister, for making nothing but vestments and altar linen. He had a bully with him with legs on him like tree trunks to keep him safe if there was brawling and to carry him on his back over rough ground. It was this same bully he later made into the great Bishop Mac Carthern, Erc said.

Patrick was an old man when he baptized Erc but Erc said you'd never have believed it to see him. He stained his hair dark with berries so there wasn't a whisper of grey in it. He bathed his face in chill spring water each morning and often at night slathered it with the whites of duck eggs to draw out the wrinkles. He had a whispery kind of voice like it was you of all the world he'd picked for telling the secrets of his heart to. Such a smiling blithe way he had with him, Erc said, he could have charmed a weasel out of his hole and back again.

Creeping along with most of his weight on Brendan, Erc told how he had been won to the new faith by him. There was a cruel chief name of Eoghan, an ugly small man that traveled some ways to see what manner of man this Patrick must be as had all of them talking about him in those days. Erc served Eoghan as druid, though only a young man back then, and traveled along with him. Patrick met them in a glade. He told Eoghan if he'd get down on his knees to honor God's unblemished Christ, he'd see to it he didn't go off empty-handed for his pains. All this Patrick spoke in his silvery voice with that face on him you'd never have guessed was an old man's face and Patrick laid his hands on his head and called down the dove of heaven on him.

Erc said when it was over you wouldn't have known it was the same Eoghan. The king was an ugly small man no more. His mouth wasn't twisted or his nose flat. His warts was all gone. When he got back on his feet he come up high as Patrick's collarbone whereas before he'd scarce cleared his ribs. Erc said he'd never have believed it without he saw it with his own two eyes.

That same day Erc give up the old faith. He broke his druid yew wand in bits. He crushed the white berries under his brogues. On the day following Patrick baptized him in a pool in that same glade and give him the bell. Patrick laid the bell in his hands himself, Erc said, and with his own hands closed Erc's fingers over it.

Besides Patrick, Erc spoke much of the sea as well to Brendan as they moved along the edge of it with their hoods over their ears and their cloaks flapping at their blue shins. Erc was a sea bishop in his time, taking mass to the bare stony islands in his curragh that slid light as thistledown over the grey hills of the waves. He told Brendan of monks that tossed their oars and rudders over the sides altogether and left it to the winds of Heaven to puff them wherever they listed with nothing save fish to feed on or gulls' eggs when they could find them. They carried a flask of holy water tucked up under the gunwales for luck. There was no desert for fasting and praying in like in holy times, Erc said, so they made the sea their desert. Year after year they drifted about on it some of them.

He told Brendan red martyrs was martyrs that shed red blood dying for Christ and green martyrs was them as worked grievous torments on themselves for their sins like Ita with her beetle. The ones that for the love of God give up home and kindred and every chance they ever had to be happy in the world at all, they was the white martyrs. But Erc said there was blue martyrs as well though they wasn't so named. They was the curragh martyrs. They had beards of seaweed. Their cheeks was all barnacled and their eyes blear with salt from scouring the blue storms of the sea for the peace of God.

Once I saw the pair of them perched on a humpback rock with the tide coming in and the spray flying. Brendan squatted on his heels. Erc stood behind him with one hand on the point of Brendan's head to steady him and the other stretched out toward the edge of the sky. Erc told how farther off than the sun's setting was Tir-na-n-Og, the Country of the Young. Nor age nor death has ever found their way there yet, he said, neither has tears nor rough laughter ever yet been heard there. Hy Brasail some call it, the Land of the Blessed, because it's the land of lovely brave women and men and singing birds. It's where you go to after you die if you've lived a decent life on earth. Erc told how the only one that ever went to it and come back was the bard Oisin that cantered there over the foam on a foam-color horse. Three hundred years he dwelled there and might be dwelling there yet if he hadn't taken it into his head to return to seek for the comrades he'd left behind him. The moment his heel touched the earth again all the three hundred years fell on him at a clap, Erc said. His white beard swept the dust at his feet.

Before Oisin died he pictured Tir-na-n-Og to Patrick. Erc told Brendan others have seen it since. Some have seen it glimmering and wavering in the depths of loughs. Some have seen it rise up out of the sea and have heard the chime of its bells carried away on the wind. Others have looked out from the western cliffs and found it floating over the water like a bright shadow. Gentle men. and handsome women lie together in the shade there without shame or sorrow, Erc said. There is no dying there, he said. The salt spray was wet on his stone slips. There is no nastiness there of any kind at all.

Erc didn't do all the talking though nor could he even if he'd wanted. He hadn't breath enough for walking by the sea and talking both. Brendan had a thing or two of his own to tell. We was in Erc's hut once. It was a raw day with the thump and ebb of the waves below and the curlew's lonesome cry. Me and Brendan was warming our fingers at the fire. Erc was laying on his slab with his shaggy cloak tucked about him and a skin over his feet. The fire was more a glow than a flame but Brendan's face was flaming. His skin was red and his eyes dancing. He talked like the words burned so hot in his mouth he couldn't spill them quick enough.

He told about Bauheen like it had happened that very day though he didn't picture the lewdness of the stone he'd taken his club to nor was there any need. There's plenty stones like it and Erc knew the kind he meant well enough. Brendan told it straight pretty nearly but when it come to other parts of our journey he let it boil out however it suited his fancy. He said he sat up all night with the woman that give us shelter the night of the storm. He said he coaxed her with Christ till when morning come she begged he'd baptize her and all her kindred with her and so indeed he did, he said, right there in the ditch around their houses that was filled clear to the rim with the night's rain. The truth is he slept the night through without so much as stirring. None knows it better than me that lay in the same flea-ridden straw with him and felt his snores hot on the back of my neck wondering if he'd choke to death on the bishop ring in his mouth. As to the tinkers and herders and bog women and fishers we met on our way, it's true he'd tease them with holy matters till some of them pestered him for more, but to hear the way he spun it out to Erc you'd have thought he won most of the people of the world on the way out and all the ones left over on his way home.

Erc loved it. He lay there with his eyes fixed on Brendan's face and the shadow of his smile black in his mouth. Partly I suppose it was to make Erc smile that Brendan told it like he did and the broader the smile the grander he told it. The old bishop raised his hands heavenward when Brendan got to the man with the spear in his nipple. The man was stone dead, Brendan said. His limbs was stiff. Only the whites of his eyes showed. Brendan said he spoke the holy names in the man's ear. He drew the blessed cross on the man's chest with dust and spittle. The color come back in the man's cheeks, Brendan said. He sat up. He opened his blue lips. He glorified Christ.

Maybe it was to glorify Christ Brendan told it like that, yet it was to glorify his own self as well surely. But I held my tongue. He took such joy in his brags and Erc was so proud of Christ and Brendan both I couldn't bring myself to wreck it. But for his own cunning Brendan said there wouldn't be a king of the new faith on the throne of Cashel. But for his boldness Colman would still be the bard Mac Lennin cracking men's legs over his knee for breaking wind in his presence. That much of it was true enough anyhow. I wish he'd made mention of Maeve's and Crosan's part in it though.

Brendan was made priest on Christmas eve day. Erc did it with Jarlath to help. Crosan and Colman was there in coarse wool cloaks with ropes knotted about their middles. You'd have taken them for monks if you didn't know they was only a bard learning the new faith from scratch and a clown being fed more of it than he'd ever bargained for before. Briga come too. She was already a nun by then and had a nun's shawl over her head. Her face was sour as green apples till when she smiled. Then it was like the sun of Heaven itself. There was a few herders and clods from the glens as well. They stood about the church door stomping their feet and blowing on their soiled fingers. They'd heard there was one being priested that day so they come to gawk. Some said he'd raised a man from death. There was snowflakes in the air.

Next to the crowning of Hugh Handsome the priesting didn't come to much. There was only a handful at it for one thing nor so much as a piece of gold finery among them or a horn to toot or any to throw their hats in the air and howl. Brendan knelt at the altar slab barefoot and barehead. He wore a white thin shift only. You could see his breath. Erc stood at one end of the slab and Jarlath at the other. The ringed stone cross was set between them. Erc leaned on his crozier so his jowls slipped sideways. Jarlath's mouth was clamped that tight his nose and chin all but met over it.

It was close to the longest dark night of the year. That's the night they say the old gods walk. If you're of the old faith you pour out child blood then for wheedling Crom Cruaich back with the sun again. King and people together grovel so tight to the frozen sod the gristle of their noses and the caps of their knees and elbows crack against it. It's the time the Dagda couples with the river Boyne after eating a ton of porridge from a hole. Women and men couple to the light of fires so the bags on the ewes will be full when the time comes and the corn stand high. The gentry slip out from their burrows under the hills then. They ply their deviltries best when its blackest. They keep their eyes squinnied. Their fingers is like parsnips.

Erc knew all these thing. Jarlath knew them. You could see the darkness of it in their eyes. You could see it biding its time in the shadows of the chill church. Erc was bent under the weight of it. Jarlath clamped his jaw thinking on it.

"I bear witness before the King of the Stars that the things of the world are no more to me than the sand of the sea or the leaves of the wood," Brendan said from his knees.

The holy oil was slick on his brow from Erc's fingers. Jarlath held the cross for him to kiss. It was the selfsame hour Christ was delivered of Mary. I never heard a tall tale I'd sooner have true than that tale. How the Light of the World come into the darkest night so there'd never be cause to fear darkness again.

A tear dropped off Briga's nose. Colman had his knuckle between his teeth and the dusk turned Crosan's cheeks blue as clay. Brendan touched the cross with his lips. Erc heaved up his hand to bless him.

Brendan rose to his feet trembling in his shift and each of the two old men took him in their arms in turn.

There was little more to it than that save the sound of the old gods whistling through a chink in the stones.

Erc died while it was winter still. Only that same morning he had been telling of Patrick again in his hut.

"Oh he was a lovely saint of a man, you see," he said. "I've told you have I not how he left two salmon alive in the well of Aghaghower? They abide there to this very day. One of them is great-grandson to the Salmon of Wisdom himself that swims in the Boyne and carries the sun on his back. Patrick was ever a giving man. He gave me a bell I'll show you one day. He blessed it first and latched my fingers over it himself. He always turned back the gifts they laid out for him on the altar. Haven't I seen him do it with my own eyes? What need may I ask had he of their yellow-backed cream and their wool headcloths and their iron pots that had his own bee-keeper if you please not to mention his own comb-maker and three fine women just for the sewing of altar covers? Once by mischance he drove his pointed staff through the foot of a woman at worship. He asked her later why she didn't cry out and she said she thought it was only part of the mass. How he did laugh telling it!" Erc said.

I think it was the only time I ever heard Erc laugh himself. He threw back his head and opened his wide mouth. It sounded like the sound of a man rolling stones in a cave.

They found him frozen stiff as salt cod the next day. He had scrabbled down the cliff without Brendan for once to walk along the shore. He must have stopped to rest because they come on him seated on the shingle with a rock at his back. He had his eyes staring wide open with his last sight of the sea froze in them. They buried him among the monks' graves just under the place he had waved Brendan and me goodbye the day we set out for Cashel. Brendan saw to it they laid his bell in the hole by him. Afterwards he spent three days and nights without food or drink in the same cave he prayed for God's mercy in as a boy.

There was dismal rain and hail showers all that winter with tawny floods in the brooks and full roaring in the rivers. Winds stripped the trees bare and roused the tides to a fury. The monks moved about sluggish and grumbling in their long cloaks. I was set to kitchen work mostly and keeping an eye on the sheep in their rocky pasturage. I kept the paths clear of ice where the monks trudged to prayers with their noses in their fists and their beards frosted.

Brendan mourned Erc till Jarlath told him it was ungodly. Jarlath was mostly bones by then and his mad eyes peering at you out of his cowl. He said Brendan should set his mind to heavenly matters more and Brendan did the best he could. He was on his knees all day and passed the all-night vigil at the altar oftener than his turn. He took on heavy penances. He wouldn't scratch save on sabbaths. He sat hours at a stretch on the backbone of a whale. You could tell his heart wasn't in it though.

Colman and Crosan might have cheered him but he saw them little. Colman they kept so hard at learning his psalms and scriptures and the holy matters of faith he scarce had time to piss he said. I'd see him humped over a leather-cased book in the scriptorium or copying something out with a crow quill. It made me think how he was when I first heard him out of my good ear bawling his song of the two Hughs with sweat running off him and squirting his goatskin into the back of his throat.

As to Crosan, Jarlath said he'd played clown long enough and set in to sober him. He cropped his clown topknot with his own hands. If a monk died, he had Crosan lay the first night with the corpse where they stowed them in a shed to wait burying. The corpses was merrier for company than Jarlath, Crosan said. They didn't blast your ears with scriptures the whole time anyhow. Once I found him puffing air back in his bladder behind the cookhouse. He said it was nothing unseemly because he'd placed three garlics in it in honor of the blessed Trinity.

When it come spring Brendan asked Jarlath leave to go home on a visit. He said it was long since he'd so much as set eyes on his parents. He wanted to take them a priest's blessing and give them tidings of their kinsman Erc. He said maybe he'd win more heathens on his way. It was fresh sights to fill his eyes with he wanted as much as anything I think but he said nothing of that. Jarlath give him leave anyhow and said I should go with him for safety.

We had a grand time making our way along the top of the headlands that look down steep onto the bays and creeks of the sea. There was cuckoos singing and a white haze mornings. Gossamers floated in the air or shimmered rainbow colors in the dew. Our cheer was like dew as well sad to say. At our journey's end it ended.

The house Brendan was born in was a heap of charred

wood. The palings about it was tumbled and broke. Finnloag's plow and stilts and yokes lay smashed in the ditch. The bones of his hounds was all scattered about together with Cara's churnstaff and the ripped coverlets and skins off their bed. It seemed Finnloag and Cara themselves was dead and gone with the rest. Cow raiders had sacked the place long since.

All this was on a narrow neck of land where the tide runs up on both sides pounding it. West by a little rises a mountain straight from the shore to a proud height. The top is more often than not cloaked in fog. There's a track twists up it along the path of a thin stream. Brendan climbed it with me. His eyes was still charred by what he'd seen and his mouth choked like the ditch.

The stream winds its way up far as a bog where it turns to marsh and the track ends with it. We could see down to the creek where there was a man putting out in a curragh. As we stood watching him the fog rolled slowly down on us from above. It was so heavy we couldn't see each other more than a few paces off. We kept in touch calling out. We went on climbing by guess only, setting one foot after the other and then stopping to make sure we wasn't about to pitch headlong down one of the fearsome gashes in the mountain's flank.

Sheep come bumbling across our way here and there and white-rumped wheaters circled about us. I thought it was a burying place we'd got to at one place but it was only tall boulders standing like graves. Higher and higher we went till we could feel the ground start to level off under our feet. I told Brendan it was likely we'd missed the summit altogether. We moved onward like blind men from there feeling to see was we starting down the other side.

All at once then the salt wind hit us full in the face. Through flying torn clouds we saw the summit cairn. There was a iron cross on top of it. Behind it the cliff dropped off sheer and terrible to the sea.

We didn't speak a word. The wind would have blown

it away if we'd tried. I see Brendan there yet with his beard whipped sideways and his charred eyes slits. His feet are set square. His shirt chatters and roars like a sail in a squall.

He told me it was then he vowed he'd scavenge the watery desert storms for the peace of God. He'd be a blue martyr for Erc. He'd outpatrick Patrick among the dingles and combers and heaves of the sea. If luck was with him he'd come at last to the Country of the Young where age has never come nor death either, the Land of the Blessed where lovely brave women and men lay about in the shade and all you've ever prized and lost is once more found.

[XII]

WHEN it come to bulding the curragh there was Brendan and me with me first and foremost for once. I helped my father build curraghs as a boy. He landed me with a stiff clout over the ears every time I bungled so I learned well. Brendan's brothers worked at it with us. There was a pair of them lived near the head of the creek where we did our building. Niall and Con they were, older than Brendan was. They looked so much alike I way always mixing them. They was cheerful skinny men with bowed legs like their father before them and black beards. They spoke little and wore their nails to the quick before we was through.

We tramped back to Jarlath's soon after our climb up the hill. Brendan told him what had befallen Finnloag and Cara. He asked would the monks pray for their souls for a full year of masses since they was slain with no chance to pray for their own it seemed. Then he told him as well how he had it in mind now to put out to sea for the glory of God. Erc himself had counseled it but a few days before his end Brendan said though the truth of it was all Erc did was speak of blue martyrs alongside Saint Patrick and all the other matters they chewed over on their walks. Brendan put the scheme to Jarlath so sudden anyhow that before the old man had time to think he said yes. Indeed he gave his blessing so easy I wondered was he light-headed from years of water and barley bread only.

Colman and Crosan begged Jarlath to let them go with him. Crosan said he'd slept so long with corpses he'd never blue his cheeks again or need to. Colman roared with delight at the thought of seafaring.

"O to sing Christ to the salt sweet waves!" he cried. "O to hear with my own ears the song of our lovely sailorman Christ whistled on the lips of the wind!"

Like a heifer in a fen, Jarlath found it easier to go forward with another short yes than backwards through a slog of no's so he give Colman and Crosan leave as well. Thus they too was among the curragh's builders.

Each had their own tasks. We used the heartwood of oak for the gunwales. For the hull and stringers we used fine white ash because ashes grow strong yet light from having to scratch a living off mountainsides. Con did the cutting and Niall the trimming or the other way round maybe. They sang at their work. Sometimes they talked to one another. It was so much like a pair of bullfrogs croaking even Brendan couldn't catch their meaning.

Crosan had the slenderest fingers so I set him to working with the thongs. I had him soak them in seawater first and knot them while they was still wet so they'd grip. He said it was like eels the way they slipped apart but he got the knack of it as last, sticking his fingers through the holes in the frame to catch their slippery ends. His muscles cried mercy from tugging the knots so tight, he said, but one after another he knotted them together till after weeks the curragh's wood bones was finally lashed so strong with leather that when he leapt up and down on the hull to test it, not one rib of it so much as whimpered.

I give Brendan the greasing. I told him the loathsomest work should be his for being the cause of it. Tallow and cod oil was what my ham-handed father used but others say wool grease is fitter for keeping out water so I set him to boiling up pots of it on the fire. He used a besom and rags for slathering the frame with and got himself so slathered in the bargain you could smell him a mile off. The leather stank and the grease was so foul it was enough to make you retch.

Colman and me did the hides. We coaxed a great heap of them out of Brendan's kindred. They'd most of them been stripped of their hair in lime pits already but there was some we had to scrape smooth with knives. I told Colman to dig a hole big enough to bury himself in, and when finally he got it done, groaning and sweating and rolling his eyes the whole time, we poured in barrels of water and oak bark we'd pounded to bits. You'd have thought it was good enough to drink the way it foamed up but Colman said it was bitter as dishonor and spewed it out. We soaked our hides in it to tan them and then hauled them out dripping to weed out the ones as had warble-fly holes or cuts from the scraping that would make them leak later. Then Brendan took his boiled grease to them.

I was handy from butchering and cutting up pigs all my life so I trimmed them alone. For covering the frame with them I needed Colman though. First we tried draping them on it every way we could think of to get them to fit but it wouldn't work. Heating them over red coals to try stretching them didn't work either. Colman tried thumping them into shape with a club but he only made holes. So we had to settle for stitching them together finally and that was hardest of all.

We used flax thread stiffened with black wax and more wool grease. You had to jab the thick hides with your awl first and then get the needle though quick as a wink before the hole vanished. We snapped needles. We ruined thread. We busted awls. Our fingers was raw and bloody. Then when the thread was through we had to tug it tight. Colman was best at that. He tugged till every muscle on him bunched like a bullock's and the flax cut into his hands. I had to dab him with wax so he wouldn't fester.

It turned autumn before we was done. The ground was thick with litter. Awls and pincers, scribers and shavers and crimpers lay about everyplace. There was grease puddles and wood chips and bits of hide. The green roof we'd set up for sleeping under was sere and yellow. The curragh lay bottom side up under the pale sky.

Then one day the time come round at last. Brendan crept beneath the hull with Colman and Crosan. I climbed onto it to fit a cradle for saving the leather when we got her right side up and skidded her. When that was done they heaved up under her and flipped her over.

It took all six of us huffing and puffing to haul her the width of the beach to the creek. Slender and shapely she was, long as four cows set nose to tail. Gentle as we could we tipped her till she slid of her own heft into the shallows delicate as a leaf. The water scarce stirred about her. It took a bit of time to step the masts then and set up the steering paddle while Niall and Con on one side and Crosan up to his middle on the other held her steady. The last thing was loading the two square sails. Brendan himself had painted them in red with a ringed cross.

Once they was stowed he gathered us together. He stood barefoot on the sand in his filthy shirt. He raised his arms.

"Bless then the work of our hands," he prayed. "Send winds to blow us safe to Tir-na-n-Og. Blow all our sins away as well like clouds. May holy Saint Patrick and Bishop Erc be with us on our journey and at our journey's end." He wasn't merry like you'd think with the work all behind him. His voice was unsteady.

Colman was ready with a song in her honor, but when Brendan said her name was to be Cara after his mother the bard was too shook for singing. He knelt among the rushes instead and sloshed his head back and forth in the creek to cool it.

It took a time to store her once she was afloat. Brendan wanted food and drink enough to last us forty days so there was much to gather. We stowed dry fish and parsnips. We stowed laver and dulce and hazels. Con's wife give us onions and a sack of flat loaves. We had water in skins and wine for mass. There was spare hides and thongs for mending and grease for dressing. Brendan had brought quills and parchments from Jarlath's. We crammed things wherever we could leaving scarce room to move without stepping on somebody. We fixed two pallets one by the foremast and the other by the mainmast with skins strung over them for shelter. Two could sleep in each if we lay head to toe and didn't thrash. Brendan had a flask of holy water Jarlath blessed for him. He tucked it up between one of the pallets and the hull though if you ask me it was most of it spilt or dried up by then.

We was only a day from setting forth when one or the other of Brendan's brothers looked up from stitching a loose skin and give a loud croak. We all looked up. Two figures was coming through the marsh. They was waving their arms over their heads and calling.

"Dismas and Gestas!" Crosan cried. "We're like Noah. We'll have two aboard of everything."

It was a pair of monks Jarlath named in jest after the two thieves nailed up next Christ. Dismas was a plump soft monk with brows and lashes too pale to see and a round pink berry of a mouth. His friend Gestas was a shorter man with a brown face and long arms. He was bald as an egg. They shared a beehive between them and Gestas tended out on Dismas like a pet heifer. He helped him over the ice to winter prayers. He saw to it he got his full share to eat. He comforted him when he was ailing or out of sorts.

Dismas was half dead by the time they reached us. He sprawled in the shade while Gestas fetched him water to drink and a handful of wet rushes to cool his brow. Gestas did the talking. They knew from Jarlath of Brendan's voyage. Above all things they wished to go along. The cold and damp at the monks' was driving Dismas to an early grave. The sea air would more than likely save him. If Brendan wouldn't take them, he'd as good as have murder on his soul. If Brendan would take them, he'd find they was a blessing. Dismas give a ragged sigh and rolled his eyes piteously.

It was plain to see Brendan didn't want them. We'd be cramped enough as it was with all the stores. But when tears started rolling down Dismas's round cheeks, Colman raised his eyes heavenwards as if even taking them would be better than this. Crosan said Dismas had flesh enough on him to feed us a month if we run out of pig. He meant no harm by it but it sent Dismas into such a fit he started chewing on his cowl. Gestas pleaded all the harder then and the end of it was Brendan relented. Thus it was six of us instead of four that set sail down the creek the next day and headed for the bay and the sea beyond.

A soft breeze was blowing when we hoisted sail for the first time. Cara tilted to it a little as she begun skimming along through the water. You could see reeds waving down at the bottom. Brendan had the rudder. The creek was wide and twisted its way through grasslands. We made hardly a whisper as we went. A grey gull flapped overhead like she was getting ready to dive but changed her mind. A pair of red cows looked up from their munching to goggle at us. There wasn't but a cloud or two in the whole sky.

When we entered the bay the wind flattened us nearly. The frame grunted and shook like a beast in pain. Brendan braced his whole weight against the rudder to hold us steady. Ropes come loose and flailed about. The sail went banging against the mast till Colman made it fast again. A stiffer gust yet almost blew him overboard. I added my weight to Brendan's at the rudder to keep us heading bayward but it was no use. The wind drove us back into the creek again where we fetched up into the marsh grass. It took us better than an hour up to our knees in the peat to shove us free. Three or four more times it happened that way before dark. We hadn't the strength by then to get her back on course. Even taking turns at the oars we found her too unwieldly to row against the wind. We ended by dropping anchor near the creek's mouth and spent the night aboard.

Brendan kept watch in the stern. When he saw I was awake he beckoned me to come. It was all I could do not to tread on somebody's face. For a while he was silent.

"Finnloag and Cara are alive," he said at last in a whisper.

I thought he'd lost his wits.

"Niall told me," he said. "I could have gone to them. They'd have come to me if I'd sent them word."

"Why didn't you, Bren?" I said.

"They'd have told me I was mad to sail like this. They'd have bade me stay," he said. "Now I'll never see them again in this world at all. It's a black sin on my head and I'll rue it the rest of my days."

I could hear the men snoring. Dismas had one white arm flopped out from the skins. You could hear the water clucking against the hull. There was a thin moon.

"It may be all for the best," I said. "You'll never know." He only shook his head and turned away.

It was cold comfort but the best I could manage. If it was to the glory of Christ he was setting sail, Christ would surely forgive him about Finnloag and Cara. Wasn't it Christ himself said with his own lips we're to hate our father and mother and follow him? But if Brendan was following only his heart's desire, who's to say how Christ would fancy that. I feared Brendan would never forgive himself in any case. Maybe that was the sin of it. I couldn't whisper all that to Brendan though nor did he look like he wanted me to. I crept back to my bit of space between Colman's great rump and a sack of onions.

What happened next was almost as quick to come as it is to tell.

Later that night a squall rose with gusty high winds from a new quarter. We slipped anchor and was in a fit trying to handle the rigging and stay afloat. Somewhere in all the howling dark of it I was pitched overboard. Even if they'd heard my cries over the din there's nothing in the world they could have done to save me in such a sea. Lucky for me we was still near shore. I floundered through the waves someway and washed up at last on the stony shingle. By the time the sun rose over the marshes Cara and her crew was long since gone.

That's how come I passed the first of Brendan's two famed voyages on dry land. As for Brendan, one thing at least he said would happen happened. He never did see Finnloag and Cara alive again in this world. They was both of them snug in their green graves well before he come home.

[XIII]

I'D have told the tale of it the way a ship sails if I'd been aboard. I'd have said this island followed that island. We met such a one here, such a one there. Here's what we spoke and what they answered. I'd have told the way the winds changed or there was no winds and listed the different seas and weathers. The sights I saw with my own eyes only are the ones I'd have set down. I'd neither have added nor taken away any or made them more wondrous than they truly was. But I saw none of it. I spent the years of Brendan's voyage back at Jarlath's. I butchered and chored for the monks. I wedded a woman that bore me a son. I grew some deafer in my bad ear. I wept some and laughed some. When I thought of it I kept one eye to the south for the sight of Brendan's red head bobbing up the track again someday if the sea spared him. That is my own dry tale of those years trimmed to pocket size. Brendan's wet tale must be left to Brendan.

He scratched it on his parchments as he went. Some of it he did aboard by the looks of how the crabbed lines crested like waves and the ink was blotted. Some of it he did weeks afterwards or more. Sometimes there's no way of telling if this come first, then that, or the other way round.

There's no way of telling either if it all fell out just like he says or if that's just how he wished it had. Maybe it's how he was afraid it had. Things get muddled after months at sea with nothing much to tell plain truth from fancies by. Nor is plain truth the only truth there is either any more than what you see with your two eyes is all there is to see. What follows is his parchments just as I copied them down myself, the same parchments as he used for spinning his soaring grand tales from for many a long year afterwards till in the end he burned them.

I listen to the waves separated from my ears by an oxhide that's less than a straw mat thick. The waves knead me to the shape of a wave. They mould me like water. The sides of the leather hull puff in and out like a bellows.

I could be Jonah in the cage of the whale's ribs as the great beast breathes his way through the deep, breathes me. I cry Jonah's cry out of the belly of Hell.

I am cast out of Thy sight. The deeps close me round about. I wear weeds for my hat. There are conchs on my feet for brogues. It is not little Gestas only that turns from me now in his sleep. It is Thou that turnest from me as well, my dear.

I shall never see Cara again that bore me. I shall never see Finnloag that whittled the cross I wear on a string. I might have brought comfort to their old age. I might have brought them a priest's blessing. I fled them instead on the feet of vainglory and self-seeking.

I that am vomit, bid the great fish vomit me forth once more on the strand of Thy good grace. Remember the hind Thou didst send to suckle me at her dugs. Remember the gold flame in the wood.

Pray do not forget, my dear, how Thou didst mark me once for Thy precious.

The surface of the sea is but the height of a man's knee short of our gunwales. There is nothing but sea. Even middling waves loom over us like blue downs. Thanks be to Christ Cara's hull cants at their approach. She lets them slide under her meek as lambs. All save myself that was raised by the sea go the color of cheese. They huddle and clutch at the gunwales as we rock to and fro. The mast whips the sky. The hull creaks.

Dismas is first to be sick. He leans so far out to empty himself that Gestas takes him by the ears to keep him from going overboard like poor Finn. You'd think he had emptied himself of his chance for Heaven as well as his dinner the way he weeps. The others are not far behind him. When I tell them to breathe fresh air, Crosan casts me a bloodshot eye. What other course have they, says he, with the fresh air blowing in one ear and out the other. The only other cure I can offer is chores.

There are ropes to coil and spare halyards and sheets to sort so they won't tangle. There's such a clutter of stores in the waist you can hardly stir without skewing an ankle. I set them to stowing it all shipshape wherever it best fits. They lash down the water skins. They lay the oars trim along the center of the hull. I make sure the anchor's on top. You need tidiness to hold onto in a stormy world. A monk needs the lauds and prime and tierce of his tidy prayers. A woman's needs her cups lined up straight on the shelf. Is it not why Thou madest light the first of all things, my dear, knowing we'd take fright else with every-thing formless and void and dark on the face of the deep as well as within our own faces?

Their heads are as dark against the heaving sky as the heads on the walls of Cashel. They're as wrapped, each one, in his own thoughts as they're wrapped in their cloaks. Even Colman is silent.

He is the little dove I fashioned Thee out of the bard Mac Lennin when Thou wast my stout right arm in the making of the right Hugh king.

It is to Thee my thoughts soar like doves now. If I should forget Thee, let my hand wither. Let my wagging tongue cleave like barnacles to the roof of my mouth.

Night watch.
Rain dripped down my arm the whole time holding the crosspiece of the rudder. Rain soaked the skin roofs over the sleepers' heads. It blew in on them harder than spray. Dismas whimpered and whimpered. The sails grew sodden and doubled their weight. When dawn came at last, Gestas pointed to them.

"If it please you, Father," he said. It's Father rather than Brother or Bren since I got priested. "I don't fancy at all how the mast is bending, look you. One good gust could snap it."

He was right. I had him and Crosan doff sail a bit and tie the nether edges down so they wouldn't swing so hard to our rolling. How I could use Finn with his nimble fingers!

Did you make it to shore, Finn? Did you drown? God rest you either way, old friend.

The wind slowly moved to another quarter. Puffed us north along the coast. The far shapes of hills in view. For every ten lengths we sailed forward we lost a length slip-ping sideways light as a bladder. We made so little stir as we went we all but capsized a gannet dreaming on the swells. We tipped her hindside up before she knew we were on her. Such a squawling and flailing as she sought the sky in her dudgeon!

"*Christ's luck to you, sweetheart!*" Colman cries. "*Happy be she that wings where the wind wills knowing it blows fresh from the mouth of the King of the Clouds! Happy be she that leaves it to God where her feathers fly her!*"

It was the closest he'd come yet to a godly song since the monks had him. Colman thought it unworthy the way he spat to leeward right after, yet *Thou speakest straight to my heart through his words even so. Thou teachest me we must cast ourselves on Thy mercy alone.* I gave thanks for that lesson along with our meal that night. We find ourselves sticking to stray blobs of grease from our last slathering. Everything tastes and stinks of it.

Some fifteen days out the wind dropped. We came on two men hauling in nets. Their curragh is like ours save for the stern cut off square. They bent to their sculls as soon as they spied us and came skimming over.

Could we use some crab then? they shouted. We'd hardly had time to say yes when a glittering gay rainbow of the creatures came flying through the air at us. One of them caught hold of Crosan by the thumb as he tried to keep it from scuttling into the bilges. He got some peat glowing in the firepan anyway and boiled us up a mess of them in a pot of brine.

Beached Cara for a touch of earth again. Roamed the blessed sod a while. Bright with buttercups. Violets. Great slabs of rocks with purple gentians growing up between the fissures. Rain pools in the hollows of them filled with cloud.

Wind dies. Hours of waiting. Dismas and I pray for a breeze. Crosan whistles. We row out to find if there's any stirring farther off. We're four oars and five to man them. We row past sight of land. Gestas wraps Dismas's blistered hands in rags. Even a fillet doesn't keep the sweat from Colman's bulging eyes. Not a breath blows.

It wasn't Dismas for once who started weeping. It was

me. I didn't know the tears were coming till my eyes filled with them. It wasn't want of wind that brought them either. That would be mended soon or late. It was the sadness of things altogether. The sadness of birth as well as death. The sadness of the sea. The other men caught it from me like yawning. Save Crosan the clown. He stretched his wool cap down over his face and started cockadoodledooing and flapping his arms.

Then it was I thought again of Colman's song.

"Fear not, brothers," I said. "God is our helmsman. Hoist the sail.

"Ship the oars and stow them.

"Ship the rudder and stow it.

"We'll wing where the wind wills like the gannet."

I see their round eyes and wet cheeks still.

They thought me mad, my dear, and so I was. But I do believe it was with Thine own holy madness.

Sure as there's fish in the sea, come evening a fresh breeze blew and carried us off with it. For weeks now there's been no dearth of it.

Glory to God.

We eat each second day. We drink in sips. No fish. It's Crosan says we should fish instead for birds.

Stump-tail fulmars follow us in hope of slops. Crosan fixes a flake of our last cod to his hook. He trawls it astern with the stone off so it will float. The fulmars peck and squabble till one of them gets it and starts soaring off. She pays for her greed. The force of her own flight catches the hook in her bill. Crosan hauls her in. We pluck and grill a few of her sisters the same way. But they grow wary in time. We fast again. Our throats are parched. We talk in grunts.

* * *

A rocky high island. The cliffs rise straight as the walls of Cashel. Streams flow down them like silver tresses. The men are desperate to catch some water from them as we draw alongside. They manage only to lose a pot overboard. I tell them God will provide us with drink in due time as he provides wind. Pilgrims we are, not plunderers I tell them. They think me mad enough already.

We spend the whole day circling for a break in the cliffs. I make them drop sail when we find it at last and bless it. I make the holy sign fore and aft, port and starboard, so others after us may find it easier. I see them eyeing each other sideways. They're hot to start foraging.

The rock rises sheer on either side. It is ten times the height of our mast or more. The dark water is deep as the walls are high. With the wind cut off the silence is deeper yet. The plash and drip of our oars is the only sound.

There is a dog to greet us. She is a merry small dog dancing in the sand. When we gather her up one after the other to embrace her, she turns to a mad tumble in our arms. How she licks the salt from our cheeks and ferrets our beards with her chill nose in a fit of welcome! I think there isn't one of us without a catch in the throat. She's the first warm-blooded creature we've seen for weeks. She skitters up a path in the dunes. We follow after. She looks back over her shoulder and laughs as loud with the glee in her eyes and her tongue dripping as ever a man did slapping his thigh and cackling.

Surely too she has cause for laughter. We are a sight to see with our hollow cheeks and cracked lips. We're so stiff in the joints from weeks of crouching we can hardly stand upright.

Gestas has his arm about Dismas. Crosan and Colman walk so stooped they all but trip over their own fingers. The dog leads us along the top of the cliffs. A path winds its way inland. We come at last to a square stone house. There's smoke coming out.

It's the second time you saved my life, Fiona. The first was showing me the shape of your name in the eyes of Bauheen the way Finn explains it. The second was sending your gay small sister to lead me the way. Thank you, my honey, my garnet-eyed lovely grey mist of a hound that was the joy of a heathen king. Thank you for the house and the man in it.

We never learned his name. His face, though, I got by heart. The timid round eyes. The mouth shriveled to a slit by years of silence.

He said nothing to us. He took us into the house and warmed water. He bathed our feet. They were foul from the bilges and ragged from the rocky climb. He brought us a basin of silver for washing our hands. He served us at his table with the whitest loaves I ever saw and with roots of great sweetness. Though I never saw a cow, he brought us milk. He held the pot to our lips like a chalice, each of us in turn.

When we tried to thank him, he laid a finger across his mouth. His lids were heavy with shyness. He showed us where there were niches in the walls to sleep the five of us and many more. He set out wool covers for us. He showed us by signs that we were to take our night's rest while he stayed by the fire to keep it alive for our comfort.

It was far into the night that I woke to find he'd fallen asleep himself. He had his hands folded under his cheek like a child. The fire was flickering just enough to see by dimly. Had Fiona been there keeping watch, it would never have happened then as it did. She would have needed only to raise her head. The evil creature would have quailed and run from the fierce kindness of her eyes.

It leapt out of the shadows, a twisted black shape no higher than a hound. Spinning it went through the glimmer not making a sound. The silver basin we'd washed in was on the table, the firelight swarming soft as gold bees on its silver sides. The creature circled it with its black arms. It tilted it this way and that to cast the sheen of it at the

*niches where the men slept. One of them raised his head.
It was Dismas.*

*The creature made fun with him. It dazzled Dismas's
eyes with the basin till his eyes themselves went silver.
His whole face came slowly awake as I watched. He sucked
in his mouth to a small O. He raised his pale brows staring.
His nostrils swelled and shrank like gills. He reached out
one fat hand toward the basin. His bare arm was white
as suet.*

*The ceature threw back its head and howled with mirth
yet made no more sound than a man stepping on a beetle.
It must have cast a charm on me then, for I fell asleep. Had
you but been there, Fiona my heart, you'd have nudged it
into the coals with the moist black nob of your nose.*

*When we woke the next morning, the basin was gone.
It seemed I was the only one that noted it.*

*It was then the shy man spoke at last. In few words and
many signs he told us how he came to be on the island. He
was the last of a company of monks that had built the stone
house eighty years before. I'd have thought him no more
than half that old. His face was mostly eyes though, and
eyes change little with the passing of time. He and his
brothers had followed the way of silence. Year after year
they never broke it save with the singing of songs and
praying. Not a single word passed their lips otherwise, he
said. When my men started clucking and chattering their
wonder, I raised my hands at them for marring a silence so
long in the making.*

*He was the last of them, the shy man said. He dwelled
there with only his dog for company. I wondered if she followed the way of silence as well. Never once did I hear a
sound out of her. When her master finished, he lowered his
eyes to show us he wouldn't speak again for another eighty
years. Then he passed among us and kissed us each one
in turn on the brow.*

*Dismas was last. When he was kissed, he clapped his
hand to his brow as if the kiss was fire. He fell to his knees*

*wailing. Reaching up under his cloak, he drew forth the
silver basin. The black creature came leaping out of his
cloak as well. It opened its mouth as though it was being
crushed under a wheel. Its cry was shriller than the gulls
over our heads as it fled.*

*Dismas bathed the shy man's shins in tears. The shy
man signed him with the cross. Then he made his farewells
to us all without uttering a word.*

Gestas cradled his friend's head on his shoulder.

Crosan held his forked arms to the sky.

Colman buried his face in his hands.

*Just before she turned to follow her master into the
house, Fiona, the small dog whispered your name in my ear.*

*Full daylight. Fog on our cloaks. Fog on Colman's great
bush of a beard. Fog on the shawl Crosan clutches under
his chin coughing. Droplets of it glitter everywhere. We
are all of us robed in pearls. We are all of us kings. We
are all of us sinners.*

*Forgive me, Finnloag, my great shame the day Erc came
with his questions and I knew you couldn't answer a one.*

Father and mother, forgive me breaking your hearts.

*Help me forgive you for packing me off in a stranger's
arms before I had words to cry mercy even.*

Gestas slaps his brow like a man stung by a bee.

*"Mary, Mother!" he cries. His eyes are starting out of
his head.*

*There's a sound of great sighing, then a rippling. Not
six paces off our bow rises a black sleek hill of skin. Water
runs off it and eddies away. It wallows by us three times at
least the length of the Cara.*

*Dismas hides his eyes and squeals. The monster heaves
and sighs again. It sinks like a mountain with a sucking*

and braiding of water all about. It surfaces again a way off. It breathes into the air a tower of mist.

"Canst thou draw out Leviathan with a hook?" I call out from Scripture.

They've all got their hands clasped under their chins praying.

"Out of his nostrils goeth smoke," I call. "Who can open the doors of his face?"

Dismas squeals the louder. Does he think the doors will open wide to gobble him for a thief?

I think of a psalm to comfort and quiet them. The fog muffles my mouth. The sea is flat as a floor. I sound like I'm chanting it in a room.

"O Lord, how manifold are Thy works," I say. "Yonder is the sea great and wide wherein are things creeping innumerable."

Crosan claps his hands over Dismas's mouth so he won't deafen them.

"There go the ships and Leviathan whom Thou hast made to play therein," I say. "The Lord shall rejoice in His works."

I lay my hands on Dismas's quaking shoulders.

"He's only at play, my darling," I whisper in his ear. "Rejoice with the Lord."

He uncovers his eyes and gives me a look wet with beseeching.

There are scores of them about us now, some no deeper than the height of a man. Down through the water you can see the shadowy vast shapes of them. There's a hissing of air from their lungs when they rise to breathe. Sometimes as many as a dozen come up at a time. There's a deep-drawn sighing all about us. Perhaps they take us for monsters ourselves in our monster-shaped boat. Perhaps they are right.

Some by being blind and witless. Some by sin. Some by only dying like Fiona, like Erc, and breaking the hearts of the ones left behind as easy as Maeve cracking stones with

*her spittle. By a single toss of their mighty tails the mon-
sters below could shatter us to pieces. And by one thing or
another as we move through the deeps of the world there's
hardly a day goes by we don't shatter each other to pieces
as well.*

[XIV]

GESTAS is nothing but grumbles.

"What are we using for ballast, Father?"

"Water," say I.

*"Stones would be better. There's more life in stones," he
says. "Why don't we sail to the wind, Father?"*

"Brother, we're lucky she'll sail at all."

*"To the wind would be better," says he. "We should
never have shipped the rudder if you ask me."*

*"Rudder or rudderless don't matter a scrap when you
haven't a notion in the world where you're going," says
Dismas.*

*He flounces when he pouts. His flax beard goes all curls
in the damp. It turns his round face rounder still.*

*"You've a lovely pink mouth, Dismas," says Crosan. "It
puts me in mind of the pink hole under a white ewe's tail."*

Gestas takes hold of Crosan's nose in his fist and twists it.

*Crosan snatches the rag Gestas ties under his chin for a
hat and tosses it overboard.*

Dismas clucks through it all like a setting hen.

*"I'd sooner be back at Cashel teaching King Hughie to
tup," says Colman with a lewd sign. He's baling the last
blue wave out of the bilge.*

*"I'd sooner my head was stuck on a pole than chase after
will-o-the-wisps in a ship of fools," cries Dismas.*

*"It's not will-o-the-wisps," say I. "It's the Land of Fair
Hope we're chasing after."*

"You'll be after catching the wind in a net next," says Dismas.

"Can it be you had a mother like the rest of us, Dismas?" I ask. I bite my tongue then to see him look so stricken.

He purses his lips at me.

"Will she be dead then?" I touch his hand by way of asking pardon.

His eyes well up for an answer.

"It's your mother we're chasing after as well," I say. "She'll be there on the green shore with the others waving her shawl when she spots you aboard. Saint Patrick himself will be by her. You'll see. And Cuchullain as well. And all our greatgrandmothers."

And Bishop Erc too. I stop just short of naming him for fear I'll start welling up myself before them all.

And Thou as well, sweet Christ? What a grand sight Thou wouldst make standing in the rushes with Erc on Thy right hand and Dismas's old mother on Thy left, Thy brow crowned with stars.

The men sit there riding the swells thinking each on his own mother perhaps. Their heads are bent, their eyes lowered. They do not see what I do.

Far off a vast whale hurls itself free of its wet world. Glittering from the depths it springs time and again toward the sky. Each time it tumbles back again, great fans of ocean soar and shatter.

Maunday Thursday.

We beach on a wool isle. You can hardly see the ground for sheep bumbling and nudging. They part before us like the sea before Moses. Short horns. Long fine wool. There are boulders the size of churches. There are peat bogs and sheets of fresh water the sun glances off of. Shearwaters and whimbrels wheel over our heads.

Colman takes the rope from his waist and ties a fat ewe

by the horns. She follows him meek as you please. I tell him for Maunday Thursday there must be a lamb though. They must find one spotless.

Crosan whooshes and flaps his arms to turn them. They stream past Colman in a flood of white wool. He lets several loose for the black patches on them. Several for speckles of grey or lop ears. The one he finally finds he brings me in his arms. Its delicate small mouth is agape but dumb. It makes no struggle. Its milky legs hang motionless. Its eyes are filled with mirth.

Gestas does the butchering and skinning. Dismas does the roasting. Through all of it I turn my face. When the time comes though, I bolt my tender charred share as wolfishly as the rest.

We sleep huddled close by the red coals. Dismas mumbles of his mother in his dreams.

Good Friday brings a blue bright wind. Scarce a good Friday for Thee, Thou Lamb of Heaven. Life seeps from Thy death like blood from a wound. It's the carefree laughing life of slaves set free. It's the same darling life I told by the river to Bauheen's kindred and baited the hook with to catch Thee Mac Lennin in the trough at Cashel. O sweep like a summer wind through this wintry world, my dear, that the hearts of the heathen may grow Gospel green at last.

A shepherd brings us a basket of bread he's baked under stones and a flask of wine. He bows to me. He says they're for Easter mass. He says there were monks here before us. Dismas titters at the way he speaks our tongue.

I help the shepherd to his feet and kiss him. Christ himself has puffed us here to celebrate his raising on these rocks, I say.

The shepherd looks at me with wizard eyes. Not on these rocks but on those, he says. He points to another isle

*not far off. How does he know? Before we set sail for it he
brings us meat and drink enough to last till Pentecost.*

*Crosan makes "Thanks to you" come forth out of a ram's
lips.*

The shepherd winks farewell.

*A pool lies among the stones blue as an eye. It's a small
isle of wet rocks. No sod or sand. While the others draw
the Cara to a safe berth in the shallows, I clamber ashore.
I feel the rocks rock under me, but I make no mention of
this. I have no wish to frighten them.*

*We will spend Easter eve afloat at our prayers, I tell
them. We'll have mass on the rocks at daybreak. They sleep
like rocks themselves. I sit in the bows and watch the moon
glint white in the flat pool.*

*At first sunlight we tuck up our cloaks and wade ashore
through the shallow surf. The shepherd's loaf serves as Thy
white body, his wine for Thy dark blood. A choir of wings
flutters over us. I feel a fluttering behind my eyes as well.
Perhaps it's the wine. We've been fasting three full days.*

*"O jubilate! O jubilo!" cry the five of us to the wind.
Our beards blow free.*

*Clown Crosan picks stones off the beach. He juggles
them grave-faced.*

*"They blocked him in his grave with stones like these.
They might as well have used eggs," says he.*

*He follows their curved path through the air with his
eyes.*

*"Whoopsa! Now you don't see him, now you do!" he
cries. "Fresh as dawn rose he. There's no such ugly thing
at all as death for them as have their sunrise life from him."*

He lets the stones fall to his feet in a heap.

*"Huzzah for clown Christ!" cries he. He tosses his hat in
the air. "Huzzah for our precious lovely zany!"*

We all throw our hats in the air save hatless Colman.

"O kittiwake Christ!" cries Colman. "Peck Heaven open wide, dear heart, to all that yearn for Thee!"

We light the fire for our feast afterwards. We are feeding it driftwood when the isle rocks again. This time it quakes so under our feet it sends out waves. All but me fly back to the curragh in terror. I fail and fall by the pool filled with sky.

The pool is an eye. It is the eye of the black great whale we took for an isle. It's on his hump we've set our fire.

He roars in torment and shakes again mightily. The pool of his eye weeps snails. He roars like waves in my ears.

"JASS! JASS!" he cries. Just is it? Jest is it? God is just? God is jest?

"CONE!" he cries. Is it come *he tries to say with his whale's tongue? Come to me ye heavy-laden?*

"YUSS!" he hisses over me like the tide. Yes is it? Yes? Yes is the start of all things? Yes is the end of all things?

I wake on the Cara where they carried me in a swoon. They are ringed about me looking down. Their mouths are pinched. Their eyes aghast.

"Fear not," I tell them. One by one I touch their beards for comfort. "It wasn't an isle at all. It was a fish. It was the first and foremost of all the whales. He is forever trying to bring his tail to his mouth for the glory of God only he can't because of his great length."

Crosan presses my hand to his lips.

"His name," say I, "is Jasconius."

Or is it God is jest? And just death is all there is? The words are hellish in my heart. I'm feverish still though days have passed. We're at yet another isle. A white bird comes flying from a huge tree of birds. The sound of her wings is like a handbell. She perches near me on the prow. She stretches her wings for joy.

"You and your sisters, where do you come from?" I say.

She cocks me a mild eye. She opens and closes her bill.

The men are ashore scouring for eggs. There's every kind of bird I've ever seen.

We entered the isle by a stream scarce wide as the Cara. They towed her in with ropes. I stayed aboard too feeble to tow or walk even.

The plump fulmars are the Crosans of the clouds. They loop and glide in rings above me. Other kinds skim the waves on stiff wings. Others dive for fish. Others battle. The one on the prow is white. She wears a grey mantle and a black pert cap.

"Well, and we come from the Country of the Young, your worship," she says, bending a yellow knee.

"Is it fair as they say?" I ask.

"I should think rather fairer," says she.

"Tell me of it," say I.

She preens her breast.

"There's a lough in it that's grand for healing they do say," she says. "If you dip to the bottom with a long pole, you come up with a wondrous black muck. It will make you young if you're old, you see, and well again if you're anyways ailing. If you've lost a limb it will grow it back on you quick as a lizard tail."

"Were you ever to Cashel?" say I.

She stretches forth one wing. "It's full of nasty heads," she says.

"That's what I was coming at," say I. "Your black muck then. Would it grow bodies back on the heads of Cashel, think you?"

"I was myself once a head on the wall there," says she. "Winters was worst. My eyes froze hard as stones, would you believe, whilst I still had eyes. One time a boy clouted me off the wall with a stick. Before they set me back again, there was already a pair of black beetles raising a family inside my skull."

I put my hand over my mouth.

"I'd led a good enough life though, you see," says she. "I saved my old uncle once when a bull treed him. The god-

dess got my firstlings every spring though what use she ever found to make of them I never knew. So now I dwell in Tir-na-n-Og with the other blessed souls. Every once in an age or so I come here with my sisters. We warm our feet on the rocks mostly. There's little else to do."

"Will I ever see your country for myself?" say I. My heart is thrashing inside me like a caged bird.

She takes quick steps sideways on the gunwale as if she fears I'll try to catch her in my hand.

"I venture you won't be breathing your last for a while yet. You look hale enough to me," says she.

"I don't mean then. I mean now," say I. "Will the winds carry me there in this curragh, think you? Will I find Erc?"

She flicked her wings and was just opening her bill to answer when Dismas came splashing through the water with eggs. It scared her into the air.

Dismas thinks I'm out of my head with fever again babbling at birds. He breaks me a pair of his eggs in a bowl and feeds me.

The men have the flux. Colman's is worst. When the sea is heavy, he groans on a pot wedged amidships. The rest of the time he hangs his great bum over the stern. He shakes his fist in the air, crying out, every time a cold wave slaps him.

Far away, islands hang in the air over the sea. Some of them hang upside down it seems. Gestas says he saw a druid once turn a whole meadow of cows upside down so the milk streamed out of their teats like rain.

We can see our breath. Dismas says if a woman breathes in a man's breath she'll be with child.

Crosan tells Dismas he'd best keep his mouth shut then. He says we're cramped enough just the five of us.

Hail showers. High winds. Lowered the mainsail. Reefed up the foot. Please God the thongs hold. Colman took down the mainsail and almost went overboard.

Bilges awash. Took turns bailing.

Lines holding crossyard to mast gave way. The stitching worn through from the rolling. Crosan took a needle and awl to it in the thick of the gale. The thread whipped from his hand.

Northern course now. It lays our starboard bare to the rollers. We breathe brine. Our bedding's turned seaweed. We drag ropes to slow us. Someone says we should drag Dismas.

Yesterday forenoon a brown and white pippit struck the sail and slid down stunned. Colman picked her up and sheltered her under his cloak. He is a large creature to shelter such a small one. He blew warm breath on her. When she was strong again she sat on his head.

She spent the night on the skin roof over the sleepers. I took comfort in seeing the shape of her there during my wet watch.

By dawn she was stiff and cold in death. The wind bitter.

We sink into deep troughs. The swells loom over us. They sweep in on us heaped to the height of high hills by the wind blowing counter to the current.

Gestas is at the stern. Cashels of water rise behind him. Trickles slither down their foamed grey battlements. His head soars against the clouds as the swells beneath us swell.

Each time we heel to the wind, the waves pour in. They

swish and swash in the bilges unbalancing us. We're half mad bailing.

I poke holes in a sack of wool grease and dangle it over the side. It quenches the crests astern a little. Christ have mercy.

We'd have gone down surely if Dismas hadn't remembered the spare hides. They were stiff and awkward with cold, but somehow he managed to lace them together with thongs. He had only one hand to lace with. He held on for dear life with the other as we bucked and tossed. Waves poured in on him over the stern. His pink mouth was puckered to a whistle. His flax beard was sodden. He got it done at last someway. He got a sheet of laced hides lashed over our stern so when the breakers crashed down on us there, they struck the sheet and rolled back into the sea.

We all of us owe Dismas our lives thereby. Even Crosan owns as much. "You may kiss my bum if you like," he says, offering it him. Dismas flicks it with his thumb and finger making a sour face, but you can see he's pleased.

Days later, in a crystal hill, we offer thanks to the King of the Waves for sending us Dismas to save us.

The hill was high as a peaked mountain. It was circled with a net of meshes wide enough for the Cara to pass through. The net was silver and stood out from the hill a ways like a great skirt.

The hill was blinding in the sun. It sparkled and gleamed frost white. Deep within it showed crystal and emerald. A fierce blue-white glinted up from the ledges of it deep beneath the water. There were caves in it and crags down there.

"Let us row in through one of the meshes," I said. "We will behold for ourselves these wonders."

We spoke only in whispers from then on.

The water was clear as air deep as we could see. We could see to the nethermost footings of the hill. We could see where the silver net rose from the sandy bottom. Shafts of sunlight through the water lit it. Three days we spent marveling at it in perfect stillness.

On the third day we sculled our way into a high-roofed chamber. The walls were many-faced. The sun cast flakes of light through them like snow. The air was soft and chill as winter. We found a window giving out on the sky. On a ledge beneath it was a chalice and paten of the same crystal as the hill.

"Lord, Thou are just," I prayed. "All else is jest."

Dismas flushed with pride when I tendered him first over the others the blood and flesh of Christ.

[XV]

STRONG winds and hail kept us four months on a flat shore feeding mostly on a dead whale we found beached.

Inland we found water and roots enough to stock Cara afresh when it came time to go.

Forty days out we sighted Hell.

He was full of smoke with clouds on his summit. He was shooting flumes higher than himself. They were falling back down on him sending such a spray of sparks and embers the air all around was ablaze and I feared for our sails. One of his flanks was cracked open. There were gold wide streams of fire seeping out of it. They slipped slow as mud over the crags and made a fierce seasnake hiss when they reached the water. Clouds of steam rose up and went steaming over the surface. All the while there was the sound of monstrous bellows blowing and a great booming and thumping like a thousand smiths. It was toward midday but you'd have sworn it was dusk.

He was hurling lumps of burning slag into the sky.

Bigger than the Cara they were and white with heat. One fell close by our bows. The sea boiled and foamed like a pot where it struck.

The demons were worst of all. You could hear them howling their fury on the wind. You could see them fleeing in flame down the cruel flanks. Some of them gathered shaggy and black on the shore. They flung blazing coals at us with tongs. They called out their names and the names of torments too terrible to tell. They called out our names. You could feel the floor of the sea quake fathoms below us. It churned the dark waves.

As Erc died with the sight of the sea in his eyes, I came close to dying with Hell in mine. A lump of burning slag fell so close it almost foundered us. We heeled so sharp half our stores went overboard. The foremost roof of skin caught fire. Colman and Crosan tried to beat it out.

I thought the shriek at first a demon from the island. It was Dismas. One sleeve of his cloak was in flames. Flailing it through the air only flamed it brighter. Gestas stumbled through the bilges to reach him but came too late. More fearful of fire than demons, poor Dismas leapt into the fiery sea to put it out.

The last I saw of him was the sodden sponge of his flax beard. The hair on his head was burning.

Joseph, Mary, pray for Dismas. Thou knowest he was feckless and fat. He was foolish as well and a thief. Lazy he was, making gruff Gestas a handmaid to pick things up if he dropped them and help him over ice if there was ice. But Gestas found something dear in him, it seems. Maybe Gestas had sharper eyes in his head than ours.

Maybe the best Dismas ever did with all his years of monkery was win the heart of his friend. Maybe the best Gestas ever did was lose his heart to Dismas.

Forgive the one. Comfort and succor the other.

Gestas is nearer Hell now than ever he was at its very

shores. He sits in the bilges with his brown bald head in
his hands.

Have mercy on the pair of them. And on us all. Amen.

Sailed south seven days. I thought at first it was a great
bird flapping on a rock. The rock was whale-size. It lay off
a spit of shore. When waves struck, it ran with brine. When
the waves ran off, it glistened.

As we drew closer I saw it was a shaggy man. He had
bird droppings on him he sat that still. Before him was a
pair of forked irons hammered into the rock. A sheet of
coarse sacking hung between them. Sometimes the wind
blew it away from him. Sometimes it lashed him with it
about the face and eyes. He made no move to shield himself. He sat mostly naked on a slub.

We were of no mind to speak to him. Dismas's hellish
end was fresh still. Gestas sat huddled in the bows like a
carved man. He hadn't spoken a word since it happened.
He hadn't taken so much as a drop to drink or a crumb on
his tongue. There was the thin shadow of a smile on his
lips. It was worse to see than if he'd been gnawing on his
arm for grief.

We passed within hailing of the rock but none of us let
on we saw the man. His eyes were shut just then against
the sheet's lashing. Perhaps he didn't see us. We all of us
hoped he was only a troubling dream. We hoped he would
be gone when we looked again.

We sailed on till he was almost gone indeed. Then the
wind dropped and the current bore us slowly back. Colman
roared we were ninnies not to ply the oars. I reminded him
of the gannet and the mercy of the wind. If we were willed
to see that rock again, it wasn't for us to seek another
course. We were thus willed indeed. The current did its
work well and took us almost under the man's nose. The
sheet of sacking hung quiet as our sails. The man peered
at us under heavy brows.

"*God's peace to you, brother,*" I said.

Colman and Crosan raised their hands in pale greeting. Gestas did nothing. For the first time in days, though, his eyes were fixed on torment other than his own.

I thought the man must be a lunatic the way he gobbled and stammered. His eyes rolled about in his head. His tongue wobbled like a crab claw in a hole as he tried to get a greeting out.

"*Pardon my boldness,*" said I, "*but I've never seen a living soul in such a fix. Is it some penance you've set yourself? Have you been banished to this rock for some grievous fault?*"

His hairy chest heaved. His beard shook.

"*P-p-p-paradise!*" he finally said. "*This rock is paradise next to where I dwell mostly.*"

It took him far longer to say it than me to tell it. He kept halting to untwist his tongue and keep his eyes from popping out of their sockets.

"*Hell-ell-ell-ell,*" he said. "*My home's in Hell. Perhaps you've seen it. Day and night I b-b-b-boil in a pot. Only on sabbaths and the great fea-ea-ea-easts am I let come here. They'll drag me back when the sun sets. Sometimes they turn me on a spit and baste me with oil so I won't burn up and end my torment.*"

"*For the love of God, man!*" Colman cried. "*What was your fault.*"

"*The kissing of a friend by moonlight,*" the man said. His words came trickling soft as tears. Gestas's face went white.

"*Surely a man may kiss where he loves and not be damned like this,*" said Crosan. He'd seen Gestas's face as well and his words I thought were as much for him as the other.

"*You mark these iron forks?*" the man said.

We all nodded.

"*The night after they carried my friend away, I used*"

them for hanging my cookpot over the fi, the fi, the fi-fi . . ."

"Fire," I said. I wished I hadn't. I could as well have set fire to his naked feet the way he whimpered. I saw a man tormented that way once. At first he howled like a wolf. As they kept at it, though, he could have been an infant gurgling at his mother's teat.

"At sunset the fiends will come for me," the man said. "Save me if you be my friends."

One corner of the sacking flapped in the air. The man took it in his hand.

"I gave it to a leper one day when I was kee-ee-eeper of my friend's poor store of things," the man said.

"If that's a crime," Colman said, "then sweet is sour and turds are sausages." He thumped his fist on the gunwale.

The water lapped between the man's rock and the Cara. His tongue got so overheated twisting round his words he let it hang out of his mouth for a little like a hound.

"Sla," he said. "Sla-sla-sla." His eyes rolled back white. "Slab!" he choked out at last. He pointed to the one he was sitting on.

"Before I knew my friend even," he said, "I used it for patching a hole in the road. How could I foresee he'd tread upon it someday on his way to death, to dea-dea, to death-th-th-th. The death I brought on him myself."

A gull hovered low and dropped a chalky splat in his hair. He didn't even notice it. Crosan's face went black with trying not to laugh, and to my shame I felt my own doing the same. It was the awful grimness brought it on. The harder we tried to quell it the harder it was to quell.

The man got off his slab. He came and knelt on the rock's edge nearest us. He cupped his mouth with his hands and tried the best he could to whisper.

"I'm Ju-ju-ju-ju. I'm Ju," he said. His eyelids fluttered. His nether lip sagged. The spittle hung from it in strings. He pushed his fists against the rock till they bled.

"Judas," he said. "I'm Judas." We had to cup our ears

to hear. "*As to my friend, I can no longer shape my lips to speak His blessed name. Of all my torments, that's the most fiendish.*"

Of a sudden Gestas sprang to life. He tore his hat from his head and flung it in the bilge. He spewed with rage.

"*The fiend is God himself!*" he cried. "*What's the moonlight kissing of a friend set next his filthy cruelty to you! This cursed rock! The shit of birds!*"

His face burned so hot the spittle sizzled on his chin.

"*Betrayed your friend, did you now? Betray my bleeding bum! What's that beside how God betrays this bleeding world for sport each bleeding bloody day? Hell and his fires has no crueler torments than the way he buggers us that serves him best. What's friends and gentleness to him? What's broken hearts? What Hell is worse than life itself?*"

He worked himself into such a fit, that brown small man, he suddenly went limp.

Judas was crouched on the rocks still. Colman, Crosan and I were like frozen men. Gestas raised his fist and shook it at the sky. He was now so feeble, though, he could almost as well have been waving at a friend.

"*Thou holy bleeding God,*" he said. "*I piss for spite into your lovely eyes.*"

A minute or two or an hour? A year perhaps? Time stopped. The whole world held its breath. The sea was motionless. The birds in the sky were still as painted birds. The sun paused in its setting.

"*They'll soon be coming for me now,*" the man said. "*I pray you, save me.*" He held his hands out to us as far as they would reach.

None answered him. Perhaps he was a dream indeed, Or we were dreams.

We hoisted sail to catch what little breeze had risen. Soon he was no bigger than a warble fly upon his rock. The heavens burned behind him.

* * *

Tir-na-n-Og at last.

Green trees waving. White sands. At the mouth of a sea cave a small girl and boy play. They are bare but so young as to be smooth and shapeless. The water stains them blue as the sky. They lie on their bellies in the shallows kicking up a froth. They have golden hair. When we hail them from the curragh, they look at us with terror in their eyes.

It's four monsters they see. We are burned black by the sun and matted. You can't tell our clothes from our flesh we've worn them so long. All but Gestas. Gestas has taken to going about naked. He no longer does chores or bails. He takes no watches. Sometimes he crouches hours in the bilges cupping water over his head. He hasn't spoken a word since Judas. Save now and then to Dismas.

This Dismas is a cloth that Dismas himself was wont to use for mopping his face and such. Gestas has stuffed it with dulce and stitched it up. He cuddles it close to him in the dark of night. He speaks to it in whispers. If there's ever some special sight, he holds it up to see. He rocks it to sleep. I've heard him singing songs to it.

The round small hams of the girl and boy flash gold as their hair. Into the trees they scamper fleeing us.

We set foot on the Country of the Young. Our feet look yellow as a bird's. They are puckered and spongey from months of soaking. The nails are curved thick and long as talons. We follow stiff-legged the path the children took.

The handsome brave women and gentle strong men await us surely. They lie together as Eve lay with Adam before the serpent came. Erc sits against a boulder resting his head on the moss of it. Patrick has a bell in his hand lulling him. He swings to and fro on a low-sweeping branch. I see my little bird again. She has changed her grey mantle and black cap for a snowy gown. On her head she wears a crown.

"There's more to the world than just green things growing every whichway," she says. "Women and men, the

beasts even, we'll all of us grow to something grand in the
end if the crows don't get us."

"Ah but it's a world of crows, you fool!" Gestas will tell
her.

"There's the crows to be sure, my dear, but I'd sooner call
it a world of crowns," says the bird. "One day we'll all be
wearing them if the Glory of Things has its way with us."

There's a clamor of voices from deep in the trees as we
make our way through them. There's the smell of cooking.
Gestas has gone ahead to find what it is. When he comes
back, his face is twisted in dark mirth. With his finger to
his lips he beckons us to follow. Light as a fawn he leaps
through the ferns. He shows us where to crouch so we can
peer out hidden.

There's a clearing crowded with people. There's a fire
going. They're roasting a whole ox. They have it on a spit
so unwieldly it takes two men at either end to turn it.

The tongue hangs shriveled and black out of the ox's
mouth. There are two scorched holes where his eyes were.
The tassle at the end of his tail is in flames. Smoke curls
out of the flap of his pizzle. The drool and grease of him
flare in the red coals as they crank. His hide is blistered and
steaming.

There's a ring of flat stones about the fire. On each stone
is a head. They must have shrunk them in lime and are
drying them. Some are no bigger than a man's fist. Most of
their faces you can't see for the length of their hair.

I run back through the trees blinded. The others are at
my heels. The tears sting worse than salt.

We come out on the beach again. Colman throws his
arms about me to keep me from swooning. Gestas is bent
double cawing and cackling. He's leaping about pointing
at something for me to see. Crosan is trying to block my
view of it holding out his cloak to either side.

There in the sand by a sheet of sky-color water are the
gold bodies of the two children that fled us. They are playing at coupling.

The Cloak on the Sunbeam

[XVI]

BRENDAN come home to the light of torches. Con and Niall spotted the red ringed cross of their brother's sails skimming southward and raised the kindred. So it seems they was all lined up at the mouth of the selfsame creek he'd left from where I'd been pitched overboard. Brendan Creek they've come to call it in his honor. The high hill we climbed there in the fog is Brendan Hill now.

They was perched on the rocks waving their torches about in the dusk, huzzahing and banging pots as the curragh come close. They'd all thought he was long dead. Con and Niall doubtless threw their arms about him and croaked froggish welcomes none understood but themselves. Maybe it was just then they told him the deaths of Finnloag and Cara while he was away. Maybe they didn't think of it till later.

There was five full years of deaths for him to learn. The one struck him hardest after his mother and father was Jarlath. Jarlath died of fasting as much as anything I think and we put him in the stony ground next Erc. There Brendan could pray for the souls of the pair of them without shifting his knees even. The death that struck him least was my small son's. Brendan never saw him nor knew he was at all till after he was no longer. Nor was there many to know him the few months he breathed the air of the world before he coughed himself clear out of it. He was no bigger than a hare hardly when that time come though already he had something of my wife's way of smiling or so I thought. We named him Brendan.

Somewhere in all the fuss of torches and huzzahs Gestas run off. He made no farewells nor did any of them see him flee into the dark. He went naked, it seems. They found his ragged cloak in the bilges later. They didn't find his stuffed cloth Dismas. He must have grabbed it to his bosom with one hand as he clambered over the rocks with the other.

Crosan and Colman went back with Brendan to Jarlath's. A fat monk was abbot now name of Lugh. That was fine by Crosan for he reckoned Lugh's tastes run less than Jarlath's did to sobering clowns by bedding them with corpses. Lugh indeed was a blithe-hearted man and took such pleasure in it once when Crosan showed him the face he'd painted on under his shirt again he had him say the Jubilate through its lips one morning at lauds. I think Crosan would have gone back to clowning at Cashel save he feared King Hugh would take him hostage and thus threw in his lot with the monks again. Colman did likewise for he told me there was nowheres else he felt safe from the horrors he'd seen of Hell.

"Those demons, Finn!" he said. His eyes stared aghast out of his great face. "You should have seen how they hurled slags at us. And the torments they work! They roast you on coals with oil so you can't burn up altogether. Hotter and hotter they make them till smoke comes out of your pizzle." He vowed he would stay with the monks and get himself priested.

"I ask you, Finn," he said. "What's the fame and power of a bard set next the heavenly treasure a priest heaps up saving sinners from agonies the like of that?"

I think it wasn't so much to save sinners those agonies as to save himself that he turned priest though why he believed a man less ripe for Hell if he was tonsured I never learned.

The Hellworthiest thing I ever did myself, I think, was leave my wife to follow Brendan when he took it into his head to go off again after a few months. We'd lost our own small Brendan by then nor was she in a way to have another the women said, so I hadn't that hope to keep me by her. Besides she was after me day in, day out, to give up slaving for the monks that was little better than slaves themselves. She said I should seek out my father again for heavy-fisted or not he was honor-bound to further me. She said I should soon have a herd of my own as well as a proper house to keep her in. She was right perhaps. We might both of us have been happier if I'd done her bidding. I'll never know.

She stood in the door of our hut on her skinny legs. She had her shawl drawn tight over her ears. It was a bitter day. Brendan was with me. He kept his eyes to the ground. He said nothing. When I reached out to her, he give my cloak a tug from behind. I didn't take her in my arms then like I'd meant. I only took her wet face between my hands and shaped the word farewell on my lips without a sound.

Maybe it was because Brendan failed to find the Blessed Land that he took it into his head to pick out and bless some bit of land himself. He wanted to start a company of monks of his own anyhow, and Lugh told him there was none better fit to counsel him than Abbess Brigit. She had a great house of many monks and nuns together to the east of Jarlath's. There was a bishop name of Conleth helped her run it. Lugh said Conleth was a worker in metal and had taught his monks the craft as we'd see for ourselves if we went. There was gold shrines in Brigit's church, Lugh said. She had a screen of silver fixed down the middle as well for keeping nuns and monks apart. You could see such a screen was meat and drink to Brendan. So was the dream of having one as grand himself some fine day.

We traveled to Brigit's in a horse-drawn car Lugh loaned us. Brendan was by way already of being known for his journeying and the wonders he'd seen and thus not one for hoofing it any longer like we did to Cashel when we was boys. He carried his parchments in a sack and read me from them on our way. Parts of them set the tears running off his cheeks. Others got him baring his teeth in mirth like a horse being bitted. It was the closest he come to giving me glimpses of his heart since he went away. He was ever one to keep such matters to himself and after he come back from his journeying he was more so. His face had the look of a closed door. Inside I think there was crueler, lovelier memories of all he'd seen than any he ever told afterwards when folk come from far and wide to hear him. His looks was changed as well. His beard was grey-flecked now and the hair on his head gone to straw from the sun. He was gaunter about the cheeks. There was furrows between his brows when he smiled.

Brigit's place stood on the edge of a wide grassland where she grazed and bred horses. Some said she loved them more than the blessed saints of Heaven. She was older by then than Brendan's mother ever lived to be yet she was still riding and racing. We saw mares and geldings feeding as we come by in our car. We saw shaky-legged foals and stallions prancing about haughty as sin. They all had glossy proud coats on them bright as sunlight from brushing and their silky tails streamed out behind them when they run. Their stables was grander than the nuns' houses.

It was the stables we stopped at first looking for Brigit. An old apple-cheek nun had a gelding on the end of a long line running him in circles. Mother Brigit was off tending the holy fire with twenty of the sisters, she said. She told us the fire was kept burning ashless year after year to the glory of the Queen of Heaven. She drew a cross in the air over all of us and the gelding as well. There was sisters kept it blazing night and day with their bellows and fans. Faggots for feeding it was piled high. There was a tall hedge all about it and none ever let in beside the nuns but chaste women.

When she was done with the gelding she give him a flick over his rump with her willow wand. Then she hitched up her skirts and showed us to the chamber they kept for guests. It had many windows giving out on the grasslands and the horses. There was a sun painted on the ceiling. It was a gold round sun with a woman's face in the midst of it and the rays flowing out from it like a woman's gold hair.

We cooled our heels there an hour or more till Brigit come at last. We heard her puffing around the corner before she showed in the doorway. She was a smaller woman than I'd pictured. Her face was flushed and damp still from the flames. Over one arm she had a cloak dripping with wet though outside the day was fair and blue as could be.

"I'm forever catching fire, you see," she said. "And they're forever putting me out."

You could smell horse on her. Her hair was a fright and there was ashy smudges on her cheeks.

"This will be for keeping you waiting," she said. She took a cross from about her neck and tossed it to Brendan. She said she'd wove it out of rushes that was strewed on the floor when she was telling the Gospel once to a dying heathen. "Just before he leapt the dark ditch," she said, "I slipped Christ's bridle on him, the Holy Mother be praised."

She asked our pardon for not showing us her fire. Men was not allowed in to it.

"Look you," she said, "whether you're tasseled like a

133

stallion or cleft like a mare matters not a bit in the world
to God." She pointed to the sun on the ceiling. "Howsomever I keep them both at different tasks even so. That way
each honors the mystery of the other better and their own
mystery as well. My nuns puff their womanhood to a blaze
with their bellows. My monks hammer out their manhood
supple and strong at the forge. And all the godlier the
sport for each when they come together, you see."

Her eyes danced like fires in her leathery bit of a face.
When she turned them on Brendan he didn't lower his
own for once.

"Higgledy piggledy, woman and man," she said, clap-
ping her hands. "Is God either one of them, think you?
Neither if you ask me. Or both. To my way of thinking
God's more like the sun for the sun both brings forth like a
mother and pierces deep like a father. Yet it's greater than
either, look you, the way it draws all creatures under
Heaven to its blessed light without raising so much as a
thumb. Would Lough Dern itself was filled to the brim
with beer so all the women and men in the land could drink
to God's fiery grand glory!"

She dabbed the sweat off her brow with her sleeve.

"There's them that holds I spend too much time in the
saddle for a nun. Doubtless it's so," she said. "Howsomever I'll tell you this if you care to know. I never canter
more than the length of this room, my dears, without
turning my mind to Christ and his holy Mother."

When it come time for Brendan to ask her counsel on
starting his own company of monks, I said I'd go back to
the stables. It seemed fitting the great abbess and the great
sailor be left to themselves. Just as I was at the doorway
though she grabbed hold of me by the shirt. She took a ring
off her finger and pressed it in my hand.

"That's for remembering Brigit by," she said. She
winked one of her blue eyes at me. "A rush cross for your
friend and a ring for you so you won't feel slighted."

134

I showed it to the apple-cheek nun when I found her again. She was feeding the gelding off the flat of her hand.

"Ah well, she'd give you both her two legs only she needs them for praying on," she said, "not to say for clenching with over ditches so she won't get throwed."

The nun told how Brigit drove her own father clean out of his wits nearly the way she had of giving anything away she could lay her hands on. She give away food and drink to any that asked her or even if they didn't. She give away the clothes off her back and the cows out of the meadow. At last he all but drove her from the house to be shed of her. Now she give the nuns' butter and cream away till they'd none for themselves. She give the brogues off the monks' feet and the precious work of their forges. She give away her own horses even though they was dearer to her than eyesight, the nun said. When Bishop Conleth brought a cloak of gold cloth home with him from Rome, it went off on the back of the first ragged soul as come begging.

"Faith, she'd give Heaven itself away if she could," the nun said, and I wondered if that wasn't indeed what great abbesses was for.

I didn't see Brendan again till dusk. They fed us on porridge and yellow cream then, just the two of us, in the same guest chamber.

"I'll tell you something to pop your eyes," he said. His own eyes popped as he told it.

"You'll remember that wet cloak she had over her arm?" he said. "Well, after you went she said she'd best hang it to dry whilst we talked. There wasn't any place I could see for hanging it though so I said I'd go out and spread it on the grass for her if she liked where the sun could get at it. 'Ah but there's no need of that,' says she. 'There's sun aplenty in here.' So there was, Finn. There was a broad gold beam of it coming in through the window just by us. Now listen to this," he said. He leaned closer to me over his porridge and spoke in a hushed voice.

"She took her cloak and this is what she did," he said. "She went and laid it out over that sunbeam as easy as you'd hang your hat from a tree. May Christ be my witness."

His eyes was wide with wonder.

"She laughed when she saw how she'd struck me in a heap," he said. " 'Give it a try yourself then,' says she. 'You'll find how easy it is.' So I tried it. Three times I tried laying my cloak next hers there. Three times it fell." His face was gone pale.

"Finn," he said, "I saw nothing to match it in all my voyaging, and so I told her."

When Brendan started his own company of monks at Clonfert not long after, he did it for Erc. He did it for Jarlath. He told me once he thought of Gestas as well when he did it. He said he wanted to make up for the terrible curse that crazed man cried out against God after Dismas drowned. Surely he did it as well to the glory of Christ.

But the fierce labor he put in it for months on end. The way he coaxed men to break their backs hoisting timber and stones. The herds and flocks he begged off small kings roundabouts. The journey he took back to Cashel to see if King Hugh would spare him silver and gold for the vessels of mass as indeed he was happy enough to do remembering he'd never have wore his crown at all but for Brendan's doing. The way he gathered monks from over the whole land, and would-be monks, with promise of a new godly rule he made for them himself. Right or wrong my own view is this. Brendan would never have worked so hard if he hadn't the notion tucked at the back of his red pointed head that someday God in his glory would reward him for it all by letting him hang his cloak on a beam of the sun like Brigit.

To my way of thinking the reason he picked Clonfert for his monks with its green rolling meadows near the river

Shannon was that Clonfert is as far from the sea as any place you can find in the whole land.

[XVII]

SOON as he finished with Clonfert he built another not far off for Briga and her nuns. There was no stopping him. Much he built with his own hands and me there beside him to help. For a roof to Briga's church we put up a carved ash frame like the Cara's for luck only thatched it in place of hides. Brendan himself painted the ringed red cross on the wall behind the altar stone.

He was more his old self with Briga then anywheres. He got her into a fit of laughing telling how Maeve spit the stone in two and jabbed thorns into the runners' feet. He made no mention of how she uncovered the truth of Black Hugh's blemish though or the heads on the wall or any of that nastiness at all. Briga didn't learn the death of Finnloag and Cara till Brendan told her but he didn't tell her he'd sailed without seeing them or how their house was burned by raiders first. The two of them wept bitter tears over it. I saw them standing by a haycock with their heads on each other's shoulders.

More than anybody Brendan could make the smile shine out of Briga's cloudy face and Briga more than any could soften Brendan. He told her his voyage like it was all fair weather. The gold children on the shore. The birds. The whales sighing and spouting like old milkers in a blue meadow. You'd never have known to hear him with her he was on his way to growing a temper to match the fiery redness of his beard.

More often than not he kept it tethered but it slipped loose sometime if things come on him unawares. We was having porridge one day with the sisters when one of them

137

asked could she play him a song. Before there was time to fit the wax balls in his ears she had her small harp out on her knee holding it with one hand and plucking it with the other. She was a young slender woman with dark lashes on her cheeks. She'd scarce started playing when Brendan brought his fist down on the table so hard it knocked his porridge to the floor. Tears leapt from the young nun's eyes like he'd slapped her.

He all but died when he saw what he'd done. He tried telling her the best he could how ever since he'd heard the music of Heaven as a boy praying in a cave he'd vowed to hear no earthly kind. He said it was the archangel Michael himself come to him in the shape of a bird and drew his beak across the wattle of his wing to play. The sisters' eyes was big as wheels. Even the young one forgot her tears to hear anything so wondrous godly.

Briga was there to see him the time he brought tears to the eyes of a lough. We was sitting on the bank and Brendan angling for trout in it. A bully come up with a spear of straw in his teeth and told Brendan there was no strangers allowed to take trout from that lough save himself and his kindred only. Surely they wouldn't grudge just one or two to a poor priest and his sister a nun at that, Briga said. She looked to make light of it that way but the bully was a heathen. Nuns and priests was nothing to him if he'd so much as heard of them even. Strangers was strangers, he said. He knocked his leg with the fat ashplant he carried and rolled the straw to the other corner of his mouth.

For Briga's sake Brendan only mumbled something and drew out his line at first. Just as we was setting out to go back to the sisters with our empty basket he stopped on the bank though. Loud enough for the bully to hear from the far side he called a black curse down out of Heaven that there be nothing with fins swimming in that water till the end of time. Nor has there been, Briga says, from that day forth.

"They do tell another worse still, Finn," Briga said. "Perhaps you'll remember how an ox got into a one-eyed man's field when there was nobody watching? How the one-eyed man for spite knocked the poor beast over the head with a rock and dropped him? Well," she said when I nodded I remembered, "seems Bren searched the man out in a red fury. Finn, he was never seen again in this world." She lowered her voice then to a scant whisper. "To this day there's a one-eyed weasel in that same field though. You can see him for yourself if you've a mind to. He does nothing all day but run back and forth through the gorse wringing his hands and calling on the sky for mercy."

Brendan said the first mass in Briga's church once we finished thatching the round roof. He fed Christ to the nuns like they was all of them his blood sisters not just Briga. He called them by their right names—Eithne, Riga, Gormlai, and so on—as he laid a crumb from the loaf of Heaven on each of their pink chaste tongues. When it was time to go back to his own monks afterwards Briga bade him farewell.

"You make a grand priest still for all your sailoring, Bren," she said. "But remember how you saw the mount of Hell blowing sparks out its top. Don't you be doing the same out of yours, mind!"

Brendan took her chiding to heart I could see from the way he kissed her. When she kissed me her great nose and mine got tangled and we all three cackled together there on the steps of the new church.

Brendan netted far more monks than Jarlath ever did as the years went by though never perhaps as many as Brigit. He kept count by scratching a mark for each on the walls of his cell. His rule was not as hard as Jarlath's. The monks could have a fire if they was ailing. They was allowed bundles of straw for their beds in place of bare slabs. There was fish on the table more often. Maybe it was remembering the hardness of life at sea softened him some. But the hours of prayer was every bit as strict together with the night vigils and the singing of masses for the dead.

There was hard penances as well. For any loss of seed at all you wore cold iron a full month. Even a small lie cost a week of fasting. Striking another was forty days. There was no meat save for guests. There was no beer ever.

They come to Brendan part for his rule I think and part for his tales. He never tired of telling nor them of hearing. There was an island growing grapes big as apples, he said. There was such a sweetness in the air you could let it fall at night like dew and gather it in the morning like honey. There was days with no nights to them at all week after week and the sun always warm and gladsome overhead. There was an island of mice the size of sheep, he said. One of his crew was gobbled by them in his sleep so there was nothing left of him but a heap of gnawed bones. One sea they sailed was so curdled there was men grazing cows on it. There was a tree growing out of it so thick with birds you couldn't see the branches.

The island he loved telling best was a holy island. There was one choir of boys in blue, another in white, a third in purple. They sang to the glory of God day and night without pausing to wet their throats even. The abbot was a saint had hair on his head white as milk and a shining silvery face. Rush lights on the altar come alight by themselves each dusk. Brendan told how he saw it with his own eyes. On feast days and sabbaths there was always fresh loaves though none could say who baked them or brought them.

After they left that island, Brendan said, the Cara shone at night like the moon. Her sails and ropes was strung with stars. The three score men he had aboard come to love one another like brothers. They stopped all their spatting. If food run short they'd chop off their fingers and roast them for each other like sausages. Later all their fingers grew back. Brendan said all he had to do if it got rough was chide the waves and they laid flat for him. He said one of the monks fell overboard in a storm once and he walked dryshod through the foam like heather and saved him.

He'd stand in a circle talking and talking and talking. Sometimes he'd do it out on the grass if it was fair. The monks and monks-to-be would gather around with the scholars and copiers and builders. Maybe there'd be a nun or two from Briga's for good measure and who knows what-all else by way of bullics, soakers, bog folk and the like. Often there was heathens come as well. Sometimes with his eyes open, sometimes with them closed, he'd spin out his wonders through his great teeth.

Then after he got through a pack of them he'd always end up talking of the King of the Stars and the Waves. He'd never have made it home without him, Brendan said. We'd none of us ever make it home without him. He was himself our home and our peace, Brendan said. Even the heathens went misty about the eyes when he talked like that. As to the Prince of Light, you had only to touch the hem of his cloak to be healed, he said, and there wasn't a one of us wasn't in need of healing one way or the other. Following after him was the grandest voyage of all, he said. There was a swarm of stinging gnats had all of us swatting and scratching while Brendan was going on like that one summer eve. He bade them be gone for the love of God and just like that they was either gone or we was so lost in the glory of his words we forgot them.

Brendan was forty-odd or so when he was shook worse than any time since he found the shrunk heads and the children playing in the shallows at coupling and knew it wasn't Tir-na-n-Og at all. He'd started three or four other companies of monks by then. Much of his time he passed traveling between them. He'd done so much building over the years his hands were thick with callouses from heaving and hammering. His eyes was red-rimmed and sore from stone dust. He'd stopped keeping count of his monks on the walls of his cell for the walls was full. He'd come some way toward cooling his hot temper. Then come one wild autumn day.

He kept a small curragh in the Shannon nearby for fishing. The salmon was thick there and plenty of trout in the streams and loughs. There was tales of raiders thereabouts just then so he took it into his head to send a monk to keep the curragh out in midstream where none would be like to take it. The one he sent was one Malo by name. He was a black-haired pale wrathful man. Brendan picked him part because he'd be better than most at scaring off raiders and part just to be rid of him for a time. Perhaps he hoped to chasten some of the wrathfulness out of him as well.

Then one noonday a storm come up. The thunder shook the ground under your feet. The rain whipped you sideways and frontways and all ways. The fields was flattened and the limbs blown off trees. A priest come running up to Brendan to send for Malo off there in the Shannon so he wouldn't be drowned. He was just such a young sickly cow-eyed priest as Brendan had no great love for at the best of times. He kept plucking at Brendan's sleeve and praying for mercy on Malo long after Brendan had already settled in his heart to grant it. The next thing Brendan went mad.

"If you've that much pity, you ninny, go drown in his place yourself and be damned!" Brendan shouted.

He meant nothing by it other than a way of stopping his pestering, but the priest took it to heart and run off through the storm to obey. By the time the storm ended Malo was back looking like he'd swum the whole way under water and the priest off in the Shannon guarding the curragh in his place.

The next day I went with Brendan to find him.

The curragh was washed up in the reeds. Part of her hull was stove in. The oars was gone. There was no sign of raiders. The river was all churned up mud-color. White birds pecked at the carcases of fish the storm had tossed ashore. The priest was floating on his belly a little ways downstream. His cloak had got caught on a branch.

Brendan stood up to his shins in the water. He took the priest by the scruff and lifted him enough to see his face.

It was swelled like bees had stung it. It was the color of whey. Brendan let him down again into the water. The way he bared his teeth you'd have thought he was smiling if you didn't know better.

"Finn, I didn't even know his name," he said.

"Beothacht. That was the priest Beothacht, Bren," I said. I hadn't known it myself. Malo had told it when he come back.

"Goodbye curragh," Brendan said. He give it a push with the toe of his brogue. He couldn't seem to get his mouth closed right. "How did you say his name was, Finn?" he said.

"Beothacht," I said.

"There's a name for you," Brendan said. He was looking up at the sky like he was wondering what the weather might turn to next.

"He hadn't the voice for mass," he said. "It was a bleat of a voice. He sung mass like a sheep bleating."

A current had started turning the priest around. Fearing he might be carried downstream I took him by one foot and pulled him onto the bank. Brendan stayed where he was. The water went eddying about his white shanks.

"Would you say he was twenty yet or what?" he said.

"Twenty perhaps," I said.

"Always ailing," he said. "They say he was always fussing his teeth ached."

"Ah well, teeth," I said.

A school of salmon shot past. Big-tailed and glittery they was. They flashed by Brendan close enough to touch if he'd cared to. Watching them go by got his mouth closed though not like he usually closed it. He sat down then.

He sat right down there in the river. The water rushed up at his shoulders and gurgled about him. A red cow on the far bank turned a round eye on him. Over his head the sky looked like it had never known a storm since the world begun. He stayed there the rest of the day with his face in his hands. The breeze lifted his hair sometimes. The water floated his shirt out about him. Sometimes I thought the sounds I heard was him and sometimes the river. I took him what comfort I could, but I was never much comfort to Brendan. You need somebody bigger than yourself to comfort you. Maybe he never had a comforting friend.

I went out and squatted by him in the water. I laid my hand on his shoulder and talked straight into his ear when he didn't seem to hear me otherwise. I told him it wasn't his fault about Beothacht. You might say he'd as good as held the poor soul's head under water with his foot sending him off in a storm like that. Yet you might say as well he never thought Beothacht would take his angry words to heart if he thought at all in the heat of saying them.

Brendan give no sign he heard me anyhow. The muddy water sucked and spun about us. If all they say is true, I said, drowning like that would only get Beothacht to Heaven the sooner. Think how glad he must be to be rid of his aching teeth once and for all.

I left him sitting in the river. I lugged the priest to drier ground. I pulled his cowl over his head so we wouldn't have his poor swelled face to haunt us. I straightened his cloak about him and crossed his hands over his chest so he wouldn't lay there without honor. There was midges in clouds over the river. The red cow and her kindred was slapping flies with their tails as they browsed on the other bank. They was drunk on clover. They raised their drooling chops from time to time to call a drowsy blear-eyed moo at us. I laid down not far from Beothacht after a time and fell asleep. It was dusk when Brendan woke me.

On our way back that night we come upon a pack of gentry.

Brendan was sopping wet still from the river and his teeth rattling. I had Beothacht on my back. His white legs flopped in front of me, the rest of him bobbing about over my rump. Lucky for me he was bony and light for a priest. There was moonlight enough to skin a hare by. We was picking our way along the edge of a bog when they was suddenly on us.

There was one old one so swag-bellied she could hardly stump along. The way she rocked back and forth as she went you thought she'd tip over surely. She had a brown greasy face and sagging lids she could scarce see under. There was another no higher than your hip with a great bladder of a head. There was another fishbelly white. He had the staring round eyes of a fish as well and only two holes where his nose should have been. He had unfinished ears. Maybe there was as many as a dozen of them all told. They lurched along beside us plucking at our cloaks and waving their arms about.

I couldn't make a run for it with Beothacht on my back. Brendan could have but he stayed by me. We tried to shove them off. It was like shoving off moths. One of them tried to slip a finger in my mouth. One of them kept snatching at Brendan's parts. There was a few of them behind me doing something nasty with Beothacht. I could feel the heft of him shift about from their handling.

They was chattering away at each other in some gentry gobble no mortal soul could understand. It sounded like they was chewing on snails. Brendan caught one of them on the side of the head with his fist. That was when they started using words we knew. They used them on Brendan.

"Bugger! Child-sticker! Wife-stealer!" they skreaked out at him. "Pizzle-puller! Dung-eater! Frigger of bulls! Cow-sucker."

They was leaping all about us grabbing and sniggering.

"Liar! Dupe! Sham! Quackster!"

One naked one blocked Brendan's path bending double and speading his cheeks at him.

"Sore-head! Mulligrub! Hellhound!"

They gathered up lumps of muck from the bog and threw at him.

"Swaggerer! Braggart! Gaud! Prig!"

He slogged on grim-faced. His cloak was a wreck from their filth.

"Turd! Puke-mouth!" they hurled at him. "Sloth! Do-nothing!"

They grabbed and held him by his arms finally. He made no struggle to escape them. His face was milky, his head bent back. I could have set Beothacht down and battled them off for him. He shot me a look said no.

The fat one with the heavy lids had lagged behind. She caught up now and waddled out in front of him. She could have been the goddess they wheeled in at King Hugh's crowning. Squat and smirking she stood. The other stopped yammering. Slowly and never looking away from Brendan she stuck her thumb up in herself. Slowly she pulled it out again. She wagged it under Brendan's nose.

"Killer!" she cried. The others crowded round echoing her. Killer! Killer! Killer!

I rushed in on them in a fury flailing Beothacht's stiff legs about me like a club. They run off screeching. They was gone quick as they come. You could see their pale rumps tumbling through the bog. You could hear the sucking of their feet.

Some of the gentry are fair as stars in the sky. The People of Dana some call them. They have bright soft hair and slender hands. They are gentle-spoken. Those that night was rotten as death though. Maybe it was the smell of death brought them out from the dark houses they dwell in under the hills.

[XVIII]

THE monks fussed over having to bury Beothacht without Brendan there. Briga come trundling in her cart too late to find him. He was gone by lauds two days after the drowning. He fled to Ita like a stag before hounds. I went with him. Another trailed him in the shadows.

Ita was all he had left for mother and father with his own both dead together with Erc and Jarlath. He had doughty strong women like Maeve and Brigit still. He had Briga. He had me. But there was none of us could fill so much as a corner of the empty place the dead left behind them save Ita. She was the one Erc carried him to from his mother's arms. She was the one he learned hurley and angling and praying from and the one Erc come and plucked him from that winter day in the smoky hut. She was the one bade him see a bit of the world before he was priested. It was Ita waved him goodbye with Erc to one side of her and Jarlath the other. That was the last time he'd seen her indeed though he carried her in his heart all the years after even so.

She was living in the shadow of Sliabh Luacra with her nuns like she always did. She couldn't walk save with two sticks and someone behind her lest she stumble and fall. She had two or three of the fairest young sisters ever with her and they vied for the honor. She was merry company besides even though she was fuddled in her mind off and on. She might say there was a bearded small man in a pointed hat making long bacon at her from the corner when there was none there at all. She might take you for your great-grandmother or place her brogues on the wrong feet. But she herself half knew her own fuddlement. Maybe that was how come toward the end of her days her face was always cobwebbed with a vast smile. You scarce saw her eyes any more for the wrinkles of it. The whole world seemed to have her always on the edge of laughter and her own daftness most of all.

There was no more hurley or angling or swords for her in her last days. But she played much at chess.

She played it with a blind man name of Mahon. He couldn't see the pieces on the board but knew where they was from the feel of them. Ita could see well enough but was so nearly deaf as a turnip most of the time he talked to her with signs. Hours on end they'd keep at it with their kings and bishops. Mahon had thin hair and a tall brow. You'd never have known he was blind his eyes was that clear though he did get to batting the lids at times like he'd got sand in them. He was the one told me what happened when Brendan and Ita first met after all those years. He was the only one there. But before that meeting there was the ruckus over Malo.

The only reason Malo was living at all was Brendan had sent poor Beothacht to drown in his stead. It wasn't for love of Malo he done it though. Malo himself knew that well enough. Malo was a thorn in Brendan's foot same as in everyone's. He was a cruel-tempered man that was always picking fights. It was a bitter jest to Malo his life was saved by a man couldn't abide him. It was a bitter shame to Brendan to think if it wasn't for his temper poor Beothacht would still be bleating mass and Malo the one in the early grave he deserved if any ever did.

Just before we left Clonfert for Ita's this Malo come to him at the church door. He crooked his knee to Brendan. He pressed his lips to Brendan's hand though he knew it for a custom Brendan much misliked. Brendan was pale and rattled yet not just from Beothacht's death but from his set-to with the gentry. Every foul word they flung at him left a bleeding wound. Every nastiness they charged him with he took to heart. He stepped through the church door feeling shook and lost. The bell was jangling in his ears. The monks was hurrying by him and staring. There was nothing he craved more than to leave Clonfert quick as he could. Yet there was Malo on his knees and holding his hand kissing it so he couldn't get past.

"Holy Father, how can I ever thank you for the saving of my life?" Malo said. His face was twisted into a smile. "What did I ever do to deserve your love?"

Brendan couldn't speak even. He muttered something in

his beard and tried to retrieve his hand. Malo hung to it like a lobster.

"If only poor Beothacht was here as well," Malo said. He dabbed at his dry eyes. "What a lovely-voiced stalwart young priest he was surely. How it must have broke your tender heart to lose such a one."

You could see how he relished each time he give his skewer another twist. His eyes was rimmed with black lashes. Though a clean-shaved man his jaws was blue where his beard would have been if he'd had one.

"I pray the Queen of Heaven each night to make me just such a sweet-tempered sailoring saint of a man as your worship," he said. He covered Brendan's hand with fresh kisses.

I all but pulled him off finally and Brendan reeled away to make ready for leaving Clonfert.

Ita's was a good ways south but he settled on not taking his cart and pair. For penance he walked barefoot instead though there was many a brambled rocky stretch to bloody him. He wore nothing against the weather but what little was left him then of the saffron wool shirt Cara give him as a boy. It hung in rags about his hairy thighs. He made sure I had food enough in my own sack but said he'd manage himself on whatever he could forage. I knew he planned to make a black fast of it long as his strength held. We'd just set off on the southward track out of Clonfert with our tall staffs when once more Malo was upon us. He come racing from behind all out of breath.

"Holy Brendan, take me with you!" he cried. There was such a passion in his voice I wondered if this time he was in earnest.

"Let me be your body's servant," he said. "I owe you my life."

Brendan raised his staff. I thought he was fixing to strike him. He believed Malo was mocking him. The blood rose dark in his face and he sucked air. He didn't strike though.

He only placed the end of his staff square on Malo's chest to hold him off.

"I am a foul sinner, Malo," he said, "and so are you." The quiet of his voice was fearsomer than anger. "Pray mercy on your own black soul," he said. At each word he give Malo a little shove with the staff. "If you've any breath left over then, pray mercy on mine."

He looked a true simpleton standing there barefoot in his rag of a shirt but there was an air about him would have quailed a bull. Malo said nothing more. He just stood in the track with a queer look on his face as Brendan and me wound our way over the first green hill.

I knew he was trailing us. Day after day I'd hear a rattle off in the bracken or see the high grass bend when there was no wind to bend it. Once at night when we was sleeping in a gully with our heads pillowed on each other's shoulders I saw a shadow pass among the trees. If Brendan saw anything he never said nor did I speak of it to him. He had troubles enough.

He scarcely spoke at all the whole journey. Over and over he must have run through how in a red fit he sent Beothacht to his death and the loathsome way the gentry used him. There wasn't a foul sin they charged him with but he believed he'd already done it in his heart. I could have told him we all have hearts made the same way but it probably wouldn't have comforted him much. Sometimes if I woke in the dead night I'd see him on his knees. His feet got so tore and scraped he took to walking on the edges of them bow-legged. If he put anything more in his mouth than a swallow or two of ditchwater I never caught him at it. After such a fashion we reached Sliabh Luacra at last.

The nuns told us the best time for seeing Ita was when she was fresh from her noon sleep. It was then she was clearest in her head, they said. We sat under an oak near her cell waiting for word she'd woken. At our backs Sliabh Luacra rose shaggy and proud into the sky. At her feet there was squirrels chattering. Ragged-winged hawks floated in rings about her head. Suddenly then Malo come. He stepped out from among the oaks. He blinked his eyes in the sun. Brendan looked so little shocked he must have known the whole time the man was following us. Maybe he was just too weary to make much of a stir at anything. Malo himself looked about to drop.

He squatted down on his heels. We none of us spoke. He kept his eyes on Brendan. There seemed less of mockery in them and more of bitterness.

"My life's like a hook in a fish's maw," he said. "For years I've tried to spew it out." He was peeling a stick with his thumb as he spoke. "When the storm come up over Shannon, I prayed I'd drown."

The eyes he'd fixed on Brendan was dark as sloes. He broke the stick and tossed it aside.

"I've this to say then," he said. "You gave me back a life I'd have retched long since if I dared. So now that life will be a curse on you as well as me. The rest of your days I'll be to you like a limpet to a rock, Brendan. It's the Hell we both got coming."

Just then a young freckled nun come out of Ita's cell. She made Brendan a reverence and told him the holy mother was set to see him. Fair as a lily she stood before him with the shadows of the leaves dappling her. Brendan made her no more of an answer than he had Malo. She reached him her hand to help him up. He seemed a man dreaming the way he took it. He went on his sore feet after her like a clubbed ox.

Mahon said Ita didn't speak when Brendan first come in. She was in her bed. They kept a heap of skins over her even in summers for the chill was in her bones. There was a rood on the wall over her head. A chessboard lay on the floor at her side. Mahon sat in a corner waiting for their game. He told me what happened like he had eyes to see it. They say the blind have their own way of seeing.

Her face shone like a star, he said, her eyes as hid in the wrinkles of her smile as her words in her throat. She sat up

straight in her skins when she first saw Brendan. She
reached out her arms. He come over and perched on the
edge of her bed. You'd have thought he was still the wisp of
a boy she once dandled on her knee the way she greeted
him. She run her bent fingers through his hair. She touched
his lips. Neither spoke for some time, Mahon said. Yet the
very air was loud with words unspoken.

Brendan told her everything in the end, Mahon said,
though how much of it Ita could hear was hard to know.
She made chirp sounds now and then. Other times it was
more like she was crooning. Once in a while Brendan
would break off talking. Perhaps she was showing him then
what she thought of it all. Her wrinkles would deepen here,
soften there. She'd make small shapes in the air with her
hands. She'd cluck her tongue.

Mahon said Brendan was so stirred when he told her of
Beothacht his voice broke altogether. He told her of Malo
as well. He told her the terrible words Malo had just then
flung at him. He told her of his meeting with the gentry.
It seems there wasn't a grief from Erc's death on he didn't
set before her like the bishops and pawns on the board at
her side. The question was could she hear him at all.

When he got to telling her his voyage, it was plain she
heard. She started speaking herself then. She had him telling her the storms wave by wave nearly. She made him
count every burning slag for her shot out from the summit
of Hell. She clapped her hands together to hear how the shy
man's dog whispered Fiona's name in his ear. She laughed
aloud at how Colman and Crosan floundered about in the
tumbling wool river to catch them a spotless lamb for
Maundy Thursday.

There was no end to her questions when he got to the
whale Jasconius. She couldn't catch his name so Brendan
shouted it into her ear much as he'd himself first heard it.
"Jass!" he called, then "Cone!" then "Yuss!" When Ita got
it at last she said it over and over. Jasconius! How he must

have leaped when the fire was lit on his hump, she said. Was they all scared silly? Would he ever manage to get his tail in his mouth to the glory of God did Brendan think? How it must have gladdened the holy heart of Christ to hear his Easter raising sung on the back of such a noble creature as that. Had Brendan come at last to the Blessed Land he was seeking then, she asked him. Mahon said there was a deep quiet. Then Brendan said no.

It was dusk by the time he finished. Mahon could hear the crickets' sad song from the marsh. Then Ita spoke a bit herself for a change.

"Bren," she said. "You've given me back for a while what it was to be young. May the garment of Christ cover you for that. These ears have heard more than they have for ever so long. Maybe it's because there was more worth hearing. I must have been looking the other way when old age crept up on me. I never saw it coming anyhow. Else I'd have taken to my heels and outstripped it maybe. I thank the angels every day for sending me Mahon. There was never a man could steal a bishop or a tower from under my nose like him and blind as an oyster at that. Praise God for the sisters as well. If it wasn't for them I'd have long since laid down in my grave and happy enough to do it when the time comes round though I'm in no great hurry. But it's you, Bren, that's warmed my heart most this day. I'll not soon forget. There's one thing I wish to tell you in return for all you've told me. There's three things I wish to give you."

Mahon said he could tell from the sounds that Brendan moved up closer to her on the bed to hear her better. Her voice was weak.

"Bren, I want you to have a second go at Tir-na-n-Og," she said. "I want you to go for Christ and also for me. Perhaps I'll be there myself by then singing like a bird in a gold tree and it will do me good to see you. Only this time you're not to take some leaky featherweight boat of hides. You're not to leave it to the lunatic wind to blow you where it pleases either. Go make yourself a proper boat of wood. I've seen them in my time. They've got a deck of honest oak caulked with tar. They've anchors of iron and stout wove sails. Take a *rudder*, Bren! This time set you a course true west by the sun. Keep to it then. Take plenty of monks as well not just a bard and a clown and a pair of zanies. You'll need them all surely before you're done. Do like I say, Bren, and just see if you don't reach your heart's desire in the end. Your monkeries and schools back here will manage very well while you're off. Don't fret about them."

Mahon heard her breathing hard like she did when she was wearied.

"As to my three gifts I'll be short and sweet," she said.

"First off, I give you Mahon. May he bring you the comfort he's brought me. He can't tell a hat from a hedgehog but you'll be glad of him anyhow for they say there's no place lonelier than the waves."

How did Mahon take to being given away like that? He never said.

"Second," she said, "I'm giving you a penance to keep you in mind you're a sinner and ninny just like the rest of us for all your grand deeds. To that end you're to take this Malo as well."

Mahon said he wondered if Brendan would cry out at that but he was still.

"Third and last," she said, "is for strengthening your heart against hard times to come."

Mahon couldn't see what she did but guessed it from the murmuring soft sounds. Brendan saw well enough but only long years after told me of it. It seems she reached in her shirt then and took out her breast.

Was he struck blind, that monkish man? Did he start back in terror? Did she have to tickle his cheek to get him to take her? If there's angels keep watch over us like they say, did they stifle their mirth with their wings or dab at their tears at the sight?

He let her suckle him anyhow. With none but a blind man to watch he took milk from her teat. He said it was rich and sweet as Heaven.

The Land of the Blessed

[XIX]

I didn't get pitched the second time. It would have been more than a curragh's fall to the water if I had you may be sure. A prow high as a cliff she had with a stern to match. She had a single stout mast amidships and a wove sail you could have wrapped the church at Clonfert in. There was a bank of oars it took ten on either side to man and a hull and deck of honest oak like Ita said with place for stores and sleeping below. Brendan named her Bishop's Joy after Erc. It took most of a year for him and his monks to pound her together and caulk her.

We sailed from Brendan Creek again only with fifty aboard instead of the six there was the first time till I went overboard and made it five. There was mass on deck before we weighed anchor instead of just Brendan barefoot in the sand praying. Soon as it was done he was a wreck shouting orders and racing from port to starboard. There was no red cow in the watermeadows to watch us go. The monks was all fussing and sweating. Two or three was puking over the side before the sail took the wind even.

The only one of the Cara's crew aboard was Crosan. He'd

caught such an ague from the chill at Lugh's he stopped combing his hair in a topknot. He said his coughing only shook it to pieces anyhow. He rarely painted a face under his shirt anymore either. He was so bony and hollow-chested by then he said it was less a face than a death's head and scared people out of their wits rather than set them cackling. He come along because he hoped the waves would cure him. Brendan tried coaxing Colman to come as well but Colman by that time had his own company of monks that lived with him in a warren of caves under a hill. He said it was to keep safe from raiders but I always thought it was for fear the slag-hurling demons from Hell was after him yet. Niall and Con come this time. So did Mahon that was Ita's farewell gift to Brendan. And Malo as well of course that was the penance she set him. All told they was the ones Brendan knew best of the fifty till a week or more out he found there was another yet.

It was a yellow-hair monk that stared at you with blue eyes over a sackcloth bandage tied over his mouth. He said it was a penance for lying. I think Brendan knew from the start it was Maeve though he didn't let on. It wasn't till we was well past turning back she come in secret and told him. He threw up his hands and feigned surprise. He chided her for playing him false. But when she pled the bandage was a true penance for the lie she told as to why she wore it he could no longer hide how pleased he was to have her as shipmate on the lonesome sea. Crosan warned him he'd best not chide her overmuch lest she spit a hole in the hull and drown us entirely. So there was nothing for it but to keep her, he said. All he asked was she tell none save ourselves she was a woman.

There was more than a few aboard the second time that knew seafaring better than Brendan. More and more as the weeks turned to months it was them he gave the helm to. A far cry it was from the days on the Cara when he was the Moses of every blue mountain that heaved them skyward and when after he shipped the rudder it was him alone as

knew how to catch whatever the wind God sent them in his
mercy or his sport as the case might be. From Erc he knew
a thing or two. He knew how to fix a course by the stars by
night and the sun by day. He could read which way was
which from the mast's shadow and the flight of birds. Every
once in a while he'd go straddle-legged across the tilt of
the deck to counsel the helm on such matters. But mostly
he gave it over to others. He told them to keep true west.
The rest was theirs to figure.

Many an island we passed on our way and many an out-
landish shore but there was no stopping to gawk at wonders.
Maybe by then he'd seen wonders enough to do him. Maybe
he knew there'd never be any to match the ones had grown
more and more wondrous over the years as he dropped the
jaws of the world telling them. We'd cast anchor to forage
and take on water. We'd shelter from storms and such. But
that was the end of it. West was the only wonder he sought.

I'd see him sitting on a coil of rope maybe or hanging his
hand over the stern staring at the wake. He could as well
have been at Clonfert at his prayers or milking a red cow
for all he saw of where we was. I think it was his hopes he
saw mostly. It wasn't the waves or the puking monks or
Maeve making like she was a monk herself or Con and
Niall patching the sail. It was the shores of Tir-na-n-Og
at last. He was searching for them that might be standing
there waving their torches to welcome him, calling his name
out at him over the gold sands. Beothacht might be among
them if he'd found it in his heart to forgive by then and
had spewed out all the Shannon he'd swallowed. Might Ita
herself be there by then like she said? Maybe he was most
of all searching to see could he spot himself there. He was
peering to find how he'd look washed clean of all his nastiness like Mac Lennin in the trough at Cashel or Bauheen
and his kindred in the river's bend. The tumbling glittery
wake was his own face perhaps with all the griefs washed
from it, all the hurts and knocks and foolishness.

One way he passed his time was learning chess from

Mahon. If the weather was fair and the deck not awash they'd sit with the board between them. Mahon would show him the way each piece moved.

He said towers moved straight forward or sideways as befitted the straightness of towers and Brendan told him of the straight tall towers of Cashel with the king's chamber at the base of the tallest and a silver gong in it to ring if the king was thirsty.

Save for pawns, Mahon said, the king was weakest of all. He could move anyway he wished but only a step at a time. Yet he was the dearest piece even so, Mahon said, for the whole game hung on keeping him safe. Brendan told him Christ too is just such a king in his weakness, meek and lowly of heart and like a sheep dumb before its shearers. It's ourselves above all we must keep him safe from, Brendan said, for with our dark ways we're ever bringing woe upon him.

"A bishop sweeps all before him but mind you slantwise only," Mahon said batting his lids. Brendan said nothing to that but I knew well enough the bishop he was thinking of. He was thinking of the track that runs slantwise down the steep cliffs to the sand. He was thinking where they found him grey as stone with the sea froze into his eyes.

"As to queens," Mahon said, "there's no way they can't go and no end to their power hardly at all."

Brendan thumped the deck under him and threw back his head in mirth.

"That's Maeve for you!" he cried. "That's Brigit! That's Ita as well though she's old as earth." He might as well have said the goddess too though he didn't. I thought of her power to bring man crawling at her caked feet and offering her their firstlings regular as rain.

"It's women rule the world like queens," Brendan said. "There's no doubt of that surely."

Mahon held one of the horse-head bullies up before him then.

"Ah well, they're ourselves I see," Brendan said. "Part

man, part beast. We've no more sense between our ears than a horse if that even. We're greedy as swine. The lewdness of goats is ours and the sloth of a dog by the fire. We're cruel as wolves with our nasty temper. Not even the hawk in his soaring can match us for pride and haughtiness."

"They can move only crooked," Mahon said. "They leap any pieces that stand in their way so long as there's a clear place to come down on at the end."

"May Christ in his mercy make straight our crookedness then," Brendan said. "May he forgive us the ones we leap like muck in a ditch. May he lead us at last to the peace of a clear place."

Mahon taught Brendan chess and Brendan in turn was Mahon's eyes when it come to getting about. If he saw Mahon feeling his way along someplace he might fall or get hurt he'd leap to his feet whatever he was doing to save him.

"I am the cloddish pawn," Mahon said. "It takes a man with eyes to move me."

Brendan saw to it Mahon's pot and cloak and stick was always left where he could find them. He kept him by him always. Sometime he'd read him from his parchments.

Malo seemed to take to Mahon too or as much anyhow as that bitter man could be said to take to any of us. If Mahon was stumbling about the slippery deck and Brendan for some reason not about, Malo would offer him his shoulder to guide him. One day when he slammed into the mast I saw Malo bring him sops soaked in brine to staunch his bleeding. Sometimes the two of them would sit and talk. They made a queer pair. Malo had the blue lean chin and sinewy frame of a stalker. Mahon was pale and thin-boned as a harper. His blind clear eyes had the look of a man listening to tunes even if all it was was the flap of the sail or a monk tossing slops into the sea.

If ever Brendan come upon them, Malo rose and left without a word. Once when Brendan called his name after him, Malo turned on him. "Why don't you call me Beothacht?" he said. "It was him you drowned for me."

"A man must be crazed to hate so," Brendan said to me.

"He hates you for saving his life. He said so himself," I told him. "It's his own life he hates most."

"I hate it as well, I fear me," Brendan said. "Ita's penance is only sinking me deeper in sin than I was already."

Besides Malo to trouble him Brendan also had Maeve. He was ever afraid the monks would find there was a woman aboard. If that should happen, he said, half would be scandalized clear out of their wits and the other half tempted to uncleannness and lechery. She told him she'd see to it none of them ever guessed the truth. She hadn't been chief of the war school for nothing all those years. She'd stomp about the deck on her stout legs and talk rough and gruff as any through her bandage. She hauled sail and handled rope with the best of them. Indeed there was more man in her I think than in some of the monks themselves even if they had beards on their faces and was decked like men elsewhere.

Every time one of them made water over the side in full view of her though Brendan died nearly. To ease his mind she always made a great show of looking somewheres else when it happened and when she had to make water herself waited till dark.

We never saw the crystal hill where Brendan thanked God for sending them Dismas the time he saved them from the storm with his stitched hides over the stern. We saw slabs of it lurching and dipping all around us though. They made a growling sound when they struck up against each other. Some was a white snowy color and some glittering blue. Others was grimed all over with dust. They was the size of curraghs the greater of them and it got to where they was so thick about us sometimes we was afraid they'd crush us. Once Brendan had monks perched up on the gunwales kicking them off with their brogues so we could pass through. Another time we was trapped a whole day in a

glittering great meadow of them. Con and Niall got off
and scampered about flapping their skinny arms and kicking out with their bowed legs like a pair of crows till Brendan hailed them back aboard for fear they'd slide off and
drown.

Crosan spent hours on his high perch on the mast. There
was a basket fixed there and he said it made him feel snug
as eggs. It spared us the sound of his coughing besides.
There was times he got going at it so hard it turned his face
black nearly and his eyes streamed tears. Maeve took to
clambering aloft to take him honey for it but Brendan put
a stop to that. I believe he feared some monk might chance
to look up her cloak as she went and get himself an eyeful.

I wondered did the monks burn for women ever, the
strapping young ones especially with glossy pelts on their
chests and their stout arms. I wondered did the old ones ever
give thought to the children they might have got if they'd
wed. Did the boys and girls they might have fathered ever
go skittering through their dreams pulling at their beards
with their small fingers and laughing and calling them
foolish names? I thought of my own boy some. I wondered
what manner of man he'd have growed to be if he'd growed
at all. I thought of my wife. I thought of how Brendan gave
my cloak a tug whilst I was telling her goodbye at the door
of our hut.

Crosan was on his perch one day with a shawl tied over
his head. All at once he set in to hooting and pointing till it
got him coughing and he had to stop. We all run to starboard. Off in the waves a spout of water shot into the sky.
Slowly a hump-shape big as Bishop's Joy rose up flashing
sunlight in our eyes. We all of us froze.

It wasn't just the size of the monster froze us. It was
knowing he come from another world than ours entirely, a
shadowy world fathoms beneath us. There's great monsters
moving about lazy and soundless as clouds. Wonders are
hid down there the eye of no mortal man has ever seen
since time began. We all knew the sea belonged rightly to

him and we was only trespassers on it. Next to him we was the size of gnats.

He heaved a windy deep sigh that stopped even the monks in their babbling. Slow as he'd rose in sight he sunk then.

When he rose again it was close enough to touch with an oar if any had dared. His head was crowned with green weeds and barnacles. His nether lip, long as our mast was high, hung in a huge sulk. Far back near the crook of his jaw was his lashless eye. It was small as a foal's. It was staring at us.

"Jasconius!" Brendan cried.

He reached out his arms to him over the side. He'd have taken and hugged him if he could. The tears was streaming down his cheeks. His lips was parted over his teeth.

"Christ be with you, Jasconius! May Heaven be your bed" he called loud as he could till his voice broke.

It took him a moment or two till he got it back. The monster seemed to be listening. His ear was a hole you'd have had a hard time fitting your finger in a little lower than his eye.

"I'd have known you anywhere, my dear," Brendan croaked.

"And so would we all," a voice behind him muttered. It was Malo's voice. "We've heard you tell of him till we could puke."

It was like somebody broke wind at mass. Jasconius waited a moment or two. When he sunk it was like he sucked half the sea down with him. It went all slick and moiling where he'd been.

Mahon and me went to Brendan after. He sat in the stern with his head in his hands.

"There's one he hates more than his life even or than you," Mahon said.

Brendan raised his eyes to him.

"It's Christ he hates, Brendan," Mahon said.

"Hates Christ?" Brendan said. He said it in a whisper like was he to say it aloud the sea would swallow us.

Mahon's lids went fluttery as he nodded.

"Why is it me he mocks and torments then," Brendan said.

"Because you're the closest to Christ of anyone he knows perhaps," said Mahon.

"To take Christ's blows for him, Bren," I said. "That's a grand honor."

You'd have thought I'd blasphemed the way he clapped his hand over my mouth.

"Why would a man hate the fairest in Heaven?" Brendan asked. "Can you tell me that?"

"If you like I can tell you," Mahon said. "It's not a tale to bring good dreams though."

"Play chess instead, Bren," I said. "You've had hate enough to last you this day surely."

"Tell it me, Mahon," Brendan said.

Mahon had the look of listening to a tune as he spoke. His glance was at the sky. His head was tilted sideways a little.

"Malo's boy has hair black as Malo's only tumbled and thick like wool," Mahon said. "He keeps a brindled hare named Og. He gives everything names, even the pots on the shelf. He has a sister something smaller. She's fair like her mother. She was born with a twisted foot and limps. She has her mother's way of shutting her eyes when she laughs. Her mother has braids down to her waist."

Whatever the tune Mahon was listening to there must have come sourness into it the way he bent his mouth.

"One day a man of the new faith comes by, a gentle-tongued man with a feather in his hat and a taking way," Mahon said. "He sits on a rock evenings when milking's done and the people gather round to hear him tell them Christ. It's the gold lazy days of the year when harvest's not quite upon them yet. There's time on their hands for

164

trading tales and all such as that. They're pleased with the man well enough, some more some less. He makes them laugh. Now and then he'll bring tears to an eye or two maybe. But when all's said and done Malo is the only one of his kindred to take Christ to his heart. He told me it was like it would be if suddenly a blind man like me had eyes in his head so he could see with. The whole world was that fair he could hardly bear looking at it, he said. Even men he had grudges against seemed fair. Even the muck on his brogues. Even his own face looking up at him out of the water trough. So he let the man baptize him in a stream and his wife and children with him. The kindred told him he was a ninny to do it. Harvest was all but on them, they said. It was no time for bartering old gods for new. But Malo went and did it anyhow. A day or so after, a fire started. The flames of it raced through the tall corn on the back of the wind. The kindred laid it all to Malo of course."

Mahon made his lips into a shape for whistling but no sound come out. Brendan had his chin in his hands listening. The grey swells rose and dipped behind him.

"What they did was this," Mahon said.

I remember he raised his brows like I've seen copying monks do when they come to a blotted line. He spoke slow like he was trying to puzzle it out as he went.

"They wrapped his wife's long braids about her neck and strangled her with them," he said. "They ravished her first though. Every last one of them, even her own brothers and father for they feared for their own necks if they didn't. Her daughter tried to flee but they caught her easy enough with her twisted foot. They pitched her into the dung pit and held her under with their forks till that was that. They saved the boy for last. They found him in a tree cuddling his hare. They brought him down where Malo could see. They cut off his parts and stuffed them in his mouth. What they did next Malo didn't see because while they were doing it he broke away and fled."

Brendan lurched about so sharp I thought he'd spotted

Jasconius again. He was puking over the stern.

"Malo came to live with your monks for spite, Brendan," Mahon said. "He's after wrecking as much as he can of Christ's peace for wrecking him.

For long days after, I think Brendan's only voyaging was away inside himself. Such wonders and Hells as he may have seen there he never spoke to a soul nor wrote out on any parchments as I ever come on. Crosan spent hours at a time in his nest. Maeve turned her face the other way whenever a monk aimed himself into the waves. Brendan had set aside his rule against meat for the voyage so we had pigs aboard. They dwelled in a pen on deck and grew so mopish with all the tossing they lay about groaning mostly with their flaxen-lashed small eyes shut tight. I think they was glad enough for it when one by one their time come for butchering. Con and Niall helped me string them up to bleed.

One of the ravens we kept for scouting land died with one black wing hanging out of her cage. Crosan said it was boredom pure and simple killed her. He said like as not it would get him next.

I think it was chess much as anything saved Brendan. He moved his towers straight and his bishops slantwise and leapt about crooked with his horse-head bullies like Mahon taught him. A light touch or two of his slender hands was all it took Mahon to know where each stood before he moved one of his own. Month after month they kept at it.

One time Mahon's king slipped from his fingers and went skidding over the wet deck. Malo chanced to be near and saw. He jumped up to fetch it for his only friend and took such a skid himself he might have tumbled into the sea if Brendan his enemy hadn't grabbed him. Malo grabbed back before he knew it was Brendan he was grabbing. For a moment they stood there wrapped in each other's arms. But for Jasconius I saw no wonder all those months to match it.

The winds grew warmer at last. Save for mass the monks

took to going about in their drawers. The waves turned greener and softer. They had purple shadows in them. There was fish the like of which we'd never seen. A monstrous one give us a terrible fright chasing us. It was only a flock of merry silver creatures though. Their arching backs as they raced beside us was what we'd thought was deathly coils.

Then the day come at last when one of the ravens flew back with a bit of dark leaf in her mouth. Brendan crooked out his arm for her to land on. He could have been Noah the way he closed his eyes and cradled her against his cheek. A tear or two run down. It wasn't long after we sighted land.

[XX]

T H E Y was carrying baskets of fruit some of them. There was gold ones and red ones from the size of your head down to apple or grape size heaped in shining leaves. There was yellow ones shaped like horns. They was brown-limbed women and men both with feathers in their hair or flowers. Some was bare. Some wore aprons of it looked like moss or skins. They was waving their arms. The breasts of the women was daubed chalky. The men was pricked blue about their mouths and thighs. Their calling was like birds calling.

I doubt they looked queerer to us than we did to them wading ashore from Bishop's Joy. There was the whole fifty-odd of us with Brendan out front holding Finnloag's cross high before him. It was warmer than summer. The air was moist and heavy. You could smell the fruits and flowers in it. The water was a color between green and blue. It had lavender streaks in it and went tawny toward the shore. It was so close to the same warmth as our bodies you scarce felt it for water. Down to the sandy bottom it was clear as air.

A few of the monks had their cloaks tucked up around their middles but most left them aboard. They was bare as the brown heathens nearly save for soiled breech cloths or shirts that was hardly enough to cover their shame. Crosan had his cloak in a bundle on top of his head. The fat monks had paps on them like women and puckery great hams. There was hairy monks and smooth monks, squat ones and tall. Save for their leathery faces and necks and burned arms they was all of them pale as cheese.

You'd have thought they was lunatics the way they carried on. They filled their cheeks with sea and sozzled each other. Some threw themselves down as they reached the shallows and thrashed about with their arms and legs. They made all manner of hoots and cackles. Brendan and Mahon was the stillest of the lot, Brendan with the rood in his hand and Mahon behind him with his hands on his shoulders.

Soon as we got to the beach the heathens swarmed about us. They felt our garments and made chirping sounds. They run their fingers down our milky backs and squeezed the soft undersides of our arms. They opened fruits and held the sweet meat of them out to us on the flat of their hands like we was horses. Sometimes they reached the fruits out and touched our lips with them. Women made dove noises into our ears. Some knelt to dry our feet with their hair. Calf-eyed children with black shining hair danced a ring around Con and Niall. The brothers stood huddled together peeking out at them through their bony fingers. A slender grave-faced man with shells in his ears come and bowed down low to me from the waist. You'd have thought I had the power to bring rain.

Soon as they found Mahon was blind they made a greater fuss over him than any of us. They hung flowers about his neck and shoved fruits in his hands. They run their fingers through his thin hair. They licked their thumbs and touched him about the eyes with them. Poor Mahon stood there all the while not knowing what in the world. Brendan did the best he could to tell it all to him over the ruckus. He kept them from picking him up and carrying him off in their arms anyhow.

When the king come they showed him Mahon first. I never saw a kinglier man. He would have looked grand sitting in purple and white on the throne at Cashel. He stood a head higher than Brendan that was the highest next him of any of us. He wore only a bit of apron below his navel and nothing behind at all. His hams was full and hard as a stallion's. He had circles of pearls about the ankles. A chain of shells hung low on his chest and fish-tooth bracelets on his arms. The feathers of his hat was dawn colors. His nostrils swelled to a great size when he breathed in through them. His eyes had a faraway stately look to them like he was alone someplace watching the moon rise instead of crowded about by his kindred flirting and fooling with a pack of half-daft monks.

He reached out and placed his two hands on both sides of Mahon's neck just below the ears. Poor Mahon fluttered his lids worse than ever thinking they was fixing to take his head off perhaps. Brendan shoved his way between them. He wore a harried lopside grin. The king took a step or two backwards. Brendan went a step or two backwards as well taking Mahon with him. It was like a dance.

"Christ's peace to you," Brendan said.

He could have been talking to a man in a tree the way he had to look up. Mahon took shelter behind him.

Every last one of us held our breath waiting for the king to speak. Not even Brendan an anointed priest and friend to Jasconius the whale looked a match for that tower of a man in his feathered hat. One wave of his hand and he could have had the heads off all of us. His nostrils swelled in and out. His bracelets rattled when he placed his hands on his hips. The stillness went on till he broke it.

"Ta!" he said. It could have been somebody thumped down hard on a hollow log.

Mahon's fingers tightened on Brendan's shoulders.

169

"Ra!" the king said.

Brendan opened his mouth to make him an answer. He had his head tipped to one side a bit and his eyes closed trying to think of what answer it would be I suppose. Before he thought of it the king spoke again.

"Ta! Ra!" he said. He come down hardest on the Ra! You could have driven a yoke of bullocks through his smile.

Tara was it? To hear a name like that from home on a heathen's lips was such a shock all Brendan could do was stand there gaping.

"Ta! Ra!" the king said again. He pointed at Mahon behind Brendan's back. "Ta? Ra?"

Brendan shook his head no. He meant just to save Mahon from whatever the king had in mind to do with him I suppose but the king took it for an answer. He spoke to a toothless small man at his side. His words was like branches rattling in the wind. The small man chattered back at him like a squirrel perched in the branches.

This time the king pointed to Brendan. His long finger come so close to him Brendan could have touched it with his tongue.

"Ta? Ra?" the king said yet again.

"Tara," Brendan said. He held out his hand. The king clasped it in both of his and worked it up and down laughing and wagging his head about. All about the two of them the brown people showed their lovely teeth and clapped softly with their fingers cupped. Seeing how the wind lay the monks all joined in.

The king caught Brendan under the arms and raised him off the ground easy as a fork of hay. Brendan's head was in the sky. The king turned him slowly around so even the ones farthest back could see. They all called out what seemed the only word they knew in the world.

"Tara!" they cried, waving their flowers. "Tara! Tara!"

The king led the way off the beach inland. Brendan and

Mahon went just behind him and the rest following. We stooped under leaves broad across as shields. We passed by silvery tall trees with no branches to them at all and nuts growing on top the size of a man's head. Some trees was twisted about others like they was wrestling. Some had white waxy flowers hanging from them. Close by our path was green spikes growing sharp as spears and ferns higher than the king's head even. I saw a bird with a painted lobster-claw of a bill on her greater than herself. I saw small birds flittering about like sparks from a fire. Over our heads was a crimson one with eyes round and mad as Jarlath's. Her tailfeathers hung to the ground nearly. She cocked her head and opened her beak at us. Inside you could see her black dry tongue.

There was a brackish pond by the side of the track with a thick-barked tree floating in it among the lilies. We was just passing when it come alive. It swung open a great mouth with rows of teeth in it straight as a comb. The roar of it was like the fires of Hell. The monks all froze in terror. The creature was full half the length of our mast. It had eyes on top of its head and a wicked snout with smoke curling out of it. The next thing it slid up onto the far bank and went racing off on stub legs dragging the heft of its scaly tail behind it through the muck. Maeve let out such a shriek I thought for sure the monks would know her for a woman at last. They was all too caught up shrieking themselves though and throwing their hands in the air to mark it.

We was an hour or more tramping through the forest. The monks kept silent mostly listening for some new monster to rush at them out of the thick leaves or drop from overhead. There was serpents big round as a man's arm strung through the branches. You could see thin flames flickering from their maws. The heathens that was with us kept silent as the monks. There was little to hear save the padding of our feet. The green warm air curled the monks' beards. Sweat poured down them. Those as hadn't doffed their cloaks doffed them now. You'd scarce have guessed they was the same men that was years slipping over the ice to matins with their blue noses wrapped in their cowls and blowing at their fingers.

Crosan was huffing and puffing near me. He fixed me with a red eye. "If this be Heaven, Finn," he said, "please God they find me unworthy."

We come at last to a clearing. The feathers in the king's hat nodded and swelled like gold clouds when he raised his arms high to halt us. There was a ring of blackened stones about a heap of ashes. A pot hung over it on a hook. There was a gutted deer strung from a pole by its hind feet with its tongue lagging. Cages was scattered about. Some had birds in them. Some had beasts I knew from home like coneys and weasels but there was others the like of which I never dreamed. They had watery eyes staring at us and bright whiskers and tails dangling through the bars. They fussed when some of the monks poked their fingers at them or made lunatic faces at them but they seemed so used to humankind otherwise they paid us little heed at all. There was fruits and nuts in their cages. There was shells of water to drink from.

In the midst of the clearing was a high fence of peeled palings. It was built in a circle. There was a door in it hung with straw matting. The king put his mouth to it. "Tara!" he called. After a time he called again. "Tara!" It seemed queer he didn't just pass on inside but stood there cooling his heels instead. He had scars cut in patterns on his cheeks. He had curved heavy lips. The monks was whispering among themselves like it was unseemly to speak louder. When the king placed a finger over his mouth they went still as stones. He flattened his ear against the straw mat listening. Then he pointed at Brendan to go in. Brendan took Mahon by the hand and showed me I was to come as well.

Inside there was a hut on poles. It had a fern roof and a porch along the front. There was wood stairs up to it.

Herbs in bunches and dry flowers hung on the porch walls. There was a perch with a green bird on it scraping at her beak with one claw. There was a plank table cluttered with all manner of oddments, jugs, a cup or two, bird skulls it looked like, a heap of yellow horn-shape fruits. Several rough stools was placed about it. Overhead there was shells hung on strings. They was flat and round and made a dainty sort of clinking when the air stirred them. It was all of it such a clutter we didn't see at first one of the stools behind the table had somebody in it.

He was an old small man bare from the waist up. Below he wore a grass skirt covering his knees. He had skins on his feet. His hair was snowy and reached to his shoulders. Around his neck was two black sticks fastened with a pearl where they crossed. He was leaning on his elbows staring at us. His chin jutted out like the sharp end of an egg. He had one eye screwed up and a wry twist to his mouth.

"And what manner of half-naked mad creatures might you be then?" was the first words he spoke.

"Holy Mother of Christ!" Brendan said. It's a wonder he could say anything at all. We was all three dumbstruck at the sound of our own tongue coming out of him.

"Ah so you're Christ's, are you?" the old man said. "Though I might have known if I had my wits about me. They're mostly Christ's that find their way here."

Brendan started toward him, his mouth open.

"That find their way to . . . ?" he began. His voice broke on him.

"To Hy Brasail, you ninny," the old man said. "Wherever else do you think you've got to?"

Brendan swooned at the sound of the name and I swooned myself nearly to think we was there for sure. He lay at the bottom of the porch steps with his mouth pushed crooked against the earth. He looked like he'd fallen out of a tree.

You'd have thought it was some clown's stunt the way the old man cackled. He come down off the porch like a

clown himself with his grass skirt and bandy legs. Me and
Mahon dragged Brendan into the shade and the old man
fetched some water in a skin. When he slopped some of it
on him, Brendan opened his eyes part way. He looked clear
through us like we wasn't there at all. Then he closed them
again like he'd moved from his swoon into a deep sleep.

"There's always a few carries on like that at first," the
old man said. "Best leave him be till he wakes or he might
croak on us."

Mahon was groping about trying to pull Brendan's cloak
over him better. The old man saw it and come around close.
He placed his thumbs in his ears and waggled his fingers
at him. When it was plain Mahon couldn't see a thing the
old man stuffed a fist in his mouth and all but fell to the
ground at the jest of it. Mahon should stay there and keep
an eye on our friend till he waked, he said. Soon as he said
'eye' he could hardly get his fist back quick enough.

Poor Mahon was pale with wonder. He'd heard we was
at the Land of the Blessed but had only his ears to go by.
The old man could have stood high as a tree for all he knew
different. He might have held the seven stars in his hand
and a two-edge sword coming out of his mouth like the
holy gospel.

The old man screwed up one eye again and fixed me with
the other. I was rolling with sweat and mucked to the knees
from our tramp through the forest.

"You come along then," he said. "I always have me a
bathe about now. You could use one yourself from the whiff
of you."

Brendan was dead to the world breathing heavy. Mahon
was crouched next him his face pinched with fright. We
each of us had a thousand questions to ask. The monks was
outside waiting on us to come back. There was no telling
what the king had in store for any of us. But I'd no wish
to rile the old man lest he work some mischief on us. I let
him take me by the beard like a goat and lead me off through

another doorway in the back of the palings so the ones out front was none the wiser. To the end of my days I will never forget the place he took me to. It was only a short ways through the trees and soon as I saw it I knew we must be in Hy Brasail indeed.

It was a small half-moon of a cove with piles of rock at either end to shelter it. The rock was grey and honeycombed like children made it dribbling wet sand through their fingers. There was white rollers coming in over the shallows. They was that bright in the sun they almost blinded you. The breeze blew them sideways and crossways and every whichways. Now and again they run into each other and sent riffles racing along the line of the shore. I never saw anything to match the blue of it. Yet it was no bluer than it was green and went gold more where it touched the beach.

I never before thought the sea a friend. She brings us fish to be sure and brine to boil them in. It's true she sometimes chuckles and lisps against the hulls of boats. On summer nights along the shingle I've heard the soft hiss she can lull you to sleep with. I've listened in the dark to the slow measures of her dance. But more often than not she roars and pounds like a demon. She breaks ships over her blue knees like faggots. She hurls her wrath at the sky. She's a desert like Erc said. She's a deep grave to Dismas and as many others as there's grains of sand on her shores. A haughty cruel queen she is and mad as the maddest flirt of the gentry.

There of all places she was a friend though. The old man knew it right enough. Maybe it was the old man made a friend of her. He took his shirt off anyhow and stood to his shins in her naked as Adam before his shame. His buttocks hung in folds. The breeze tossed his snowy hair about his shoulders. He waved at me to follow him.

I waded up to my middle in the surge of her. She boiled all around me. I let her take me then. I arched back into her. She bumbled and nudged me. She swung me about. I lay in her cuddling arms belly up for a time. Then I flopped belly down. I let her drift me along that way with my fingers trailing the sandy bottom. When I raised my head to breathe she come pelting me with her soft combers. When I tried to ride on the back of one she pummeled me all over and teased me with drowning. The taste of her was sweet on my tongue. My eyes welled and stung with the salt of her. She foamed and tumbled about me. Yet only a little ways out she was nothing but green soft swells. The old man was bobbing among them like an onion. He raised his hand at me.

"Cantate Domino!" he called out. He was afloat on his back with his toes in the air.

"Benedictus es Domine!" he called again as a swell heaved him skyward.

The king and his heathens was gone by the time the old man and me got back to the clearing. The monks was still there waiting for Brendan to come out. They was lolling about in the shadows and playing with the beasts in the cages. Some was asleep. They'd none of them dared venture into the forest again for fear of monsters. Soon as we appeared they come crowding about us. They couldn't believe their ears when the old man started talking to them in their own tongue.

He was a monk same as them he said. He was one once anyhow though so many years back he'd lost the count. Tara was where he come from he told them. That's why they called him Tara. It was the only word he ever spoke to them they could twist their heathen tongues about it seemed. Now they called their own king Tara as well. They called all kings Tara. As to the old man's true name, he said, he'd long since forgotten it.

He told them the heathens would doubtless be back soon bearing them food and drink. They wasn't a bad lot when they wasn't paring the skin off their enemies' heads. He showed them with a finger on his own head how they did it. They cut down to the bone all the way round from back to front. Then they took you by the hair and pulled your scalp off like a hat. The old man give his own white hair such a tug it jerked him off his feet nearly. They dried it over the fire afterwards, he said, till it looked like a parchment. Then they hung it from a pole. He got so stirred telling about it to the monks he went jigging around in his grass skirt screwing up his eye at them.

He took us back in through the palings then. Brendan was wide awake. Mahon and him was sitting side by side on the porch steps. He had his cloak wrapped about him tight though it was warmer than summer. His face was sticky pale. He seized me by the hand.

"Hy Brasail?" he whispered. "Is it true then?" It was like he feared if he said it aloud he'd blow it away.

Tara heard him nonetheless.

"There's not a doubt of it in the world, my dear," he said. "Who should know better than me that's been here longer than any living soul?"

Brendan give a sigh worthy of Jasconius. Tears wobbled in his eyes.

"They'll all be here then, the blessed ones?" he said.

"If there's any missing," Tara said, "I'd have heard of it surely."

Brendan's hair was as damp from his swoon as was mine yet from the cove. It looked like he had scarce strength enough to hold up his head. You could see he was all ablaze inside though.

"Might you have chanced on an old dear friend of mine, I wonder?" he said. "He was bishop in his time and worthy of this blessed land if any ever was."

"There's bishops here thick as maggots," Tara said. "Toss a rock in the air and chances are it will brain one of them."

"Erc," Brendan said. Short thought it is for a name he

drew it out to a psalm's length. "It's Bishop Erc I mean."

"That will be a fair-haired slender bishop, I believe," Tara said.

Brendan shook his head. The furrow between his brows deepened.

"Ah but of course now," Tara said. "He'll be more of a stout dark man if I'm not mistaken."

"A stout dark man indeed," Brendan said. "The very one!"

"That's him sure as rain," Tara said.

"You've seen him then?" Brendan said. He would have staggered to his feet and gone looking for him then and there I think if Mahon hadn't laid a land on his arm to steady him.

"Only yesterday as ever was," Tara said. "I wonder might you be the one he told me to keep an eye out for."

"He spoke of me, did he?" Brendan said.

"How did you say your name was?" Tara asked him.

"My name is Brendan," Brendan said.

"Isn't that the very name now?" Tara threw his hands in the air. "He told me you'd be like to turn up here one fine day."

"Did you hear that, Finn?" Brendan said. "Only yesterday was he speaking of me."

"Easy, Bren," I said.

"Will you take me to him then for the love of Christ?" Brendan cried.

Tara had wandered over to where he could reach up to the green bird on the porch. He stretched his finger out and the bird nibbled at it with her hooked beak. "Take you just where, is it?" he said ruffling at the green breast feathers.

"Why to Bishop Erc," Brendan said.

"Ah well, there'll be plenty of time for that," Tara said. It was the bird he was speaking to more than Brendan. "He'll be all the gladder for waiting a little, won't he just, my chickabiddy?"

"He was baptized by Saint Patrick himself," Brendan said.

"You don't say so now?" Tara said. He winked one eye at me. "And wasn't I talking to the holy saint myself within this very hour?"

"You were talking to Saint Patrick?" Mahon said with great wonder. He turned in the direction of Tara's voice but his stare shot off just to the side of him.

Tara waved his hand back and forth in front of Mahon's eyes. When he saw they didn't so much as blink he bent double with mirth. He didn't make a sound doing it though so Mahon never knew.

"It's better than talking to myself anyhow," Tara said. "I live all by my lonesome, you see. I'd go silly in the head if I didn't have Patrick for blathering with now and then."

He caught up a bit of his skirt in either hand.

"All by my lo, all by my lo, all by my lo lo, lo-lo, lo," he sung. He twirled about a few times in front of us.

Brendan looked so pained and fuddled there on the steps I did what I could. "You've been here a long time then, Father?" I said.

Tara left off twirling and come back to where we was. His face wore a grave look. The flesh of it was all puckery like a hand that's been soaked in water.

"There was twelve of us when we started. We was the same number as the twelve of our holy King Christ," he said. "Sad to say I'm the only one left."

"Died did they then?" I said.

I held my breath waiting on his answer. Mahon and Brendan held theirs as well I could see. Death wasn't supposed to have found its way to Hy Brasail any more than tears or cruel laughter. Erc said so often. Every child knew it.

Tara screwed up his eye and give us a fierce look out of the other.

"Gobbled," he said. "Eat up. Every mother's son of them save Tara."

179

Mahon made the sign of the cross. Brendan lowered his eyes and shook his head slowly.

"It's a terrible thing surely," I said.

"Well but it's the way of it, you see," Tara said.

He went back to the bird again. He put up his hand to her. She reached out one foot and laid it on his wrist. Then she scrambled sideways the length of his arm till she come to his shoulder. The sun was on her there. In the light of it the green of her was so green it made my head ache. She cocked one round eye at us and opened her beak.

"Oremus! Oremus!" she cried. Her voice come out clear and human as you please. She could have been saying mass back at Jarlath's. "Laus tibi!" she cried. "Tara!"

Tara reached up and petted the top of her head with his finger. She caught a bit of his wrist in her beak.

"What think you, my honeykins?" he said to her. "Shall we show them what happened to the eleven then, God rest their poor souls?"

Brendan staggered when he first got to his feet but steadied himself. He took Mahon by the hand and the three of us followed Tara around the back side of the hut. Tara had the green bird on his shoulder still. Tucked partly in under the hut was a pen big enough to hold a sow and her farrow. It had a low roof on it. The bird flapped off Tara's shoulder and settled down on the thatch like it was home. Tara hunkered down near the door and craned his neck to peer into the shadows. He clucked with his tongue. He made a scratching sound with his fingers against the side.

"Oremus!" the bird cried. "Oremus!"

I thought I could hear something stir inside. It might have been just something inside my head though. I could hear Brendan breathing short where he crouched next me. I could smell him as well. The sweat was sticky in his beard and the hair of his chest. The afternoon sun was gold and slanted in low at us. There wasn't a wisp of air moving.

Some clean bones was laying about near the pen. Tara picked one up and keeping back far as he could reached out and wagged it back and forth at the dark door. There was a rumbling and scraping inside. Tara looked back over his shoulder and give us a wink. The pen shivered. Tara sprung back nimble as a coney.

It come padding out on tawny great paws. The skin on its belly hung so loose the folds scarce cleared the ground. Its stones in their sack swung like a pair of charred apples. It was that lean the shadow of its haunch bones made it look like the hindquarters wasn't fixed to the front at all. You could count every one of its ribs. It carried its thick tail stretched out behind with only the end curled. Its rheumy eyes sagged so you could see their red lining. Its small ears was ragged at the edges like mice had been at them. It come out of the pen far as the rope round its neck let it. The look it give us was sleepy and cross-eyed like an old soaker. It eased itself down on its bony rump with its hind legs sprawled out on the dirt to either side and its forelegs planted stiff between them.

"Raised him from a kitten we did," Tara said. "Many's the time I cuddled him in my lap and let him suck on my finger."

He picked up a stick and rubbed the beast's withers with it. It closed its eyes and give its grizzled jaws a swipe or two with its tongue.

"His name's Para," Tara said. "Para's his name and he's his daddy's best old sweetling isn't he just?" He ruffled the hair on its belly crooning at it.

When it yawned you could see most of its teeth was gone. You could have got your head inside its jaws.

"Para's the short of Paraclete, you see," Tara said.

Brendan's eyes filled with horror. "You named him for the Holy Ghost, Father?" he said.

"He's got eleven holy ghosts tucked away in his tum somewheres," Tara said. "If there's a fitter name I'd be pleased to know it."

"Para!" the green bird on the pen roof called. You'd have swore it was Tara's voice. "Para! Para!"

"When he was a baby he was gentle as the Lamb of God himself," Tara said. "He'd lay curled up sweet as you please at mass. He'd have us all in fits the way he chased his tail about. The brothers took turns feeding him out of their own hands. There was never monks had them such a darling since the world began. It was only after Bora he turned nasty." He frowned and jabbed at the dirt with his stick like it was Bora he was jabbing.

"Bora was a round foolish man though holy as you'd ever want like the rest of them," Tara said. "He cut his hand one day skinning poles for the hut. The smell of it brought Para snuffling at him quick as a wink. So what did Bora go and do? Would you believe he reached out that selfsame hand with the fingers all over blood and chucked Para under the chin with it? Well and he pulled at his whiskers with it and all but told him it was his dinner. The next thing Para had the poor ninny's whole hand in his mouth gnawing at it. And didn't fat Bora howl though? You should have seen the brothers catching hold of the beast's tail to pull him off till he made a snatch or two at them as well. How they did run for their lives then! We all of us ended up in trees that day I'll tell you. You'd have thought we had tails ourselves."

Tara cackled at the memory of it till the tears went running down his cheeks.

"When Para was done there wasn't enough Bora left to stuff a chink in a wall," Tara said. "It was his first taste of monk, you see. From that day forth it was catch-as-catch-can for the rest of us."

He tickled one of the beast's ears with his stick and it took a sweep at it with a paw the size of a cabbage.

"Some he got sooner, some he got later," Tara said. "By the time he got round to the last few brothers he was stiff in his joints as they was nearly. He'd lost most of his chompers by then besides. I think it was their own fright mostly as did for them though he had his share in it as well.

The only reason he spared me I think was so he'd have one of us left over to care for him in his old age. He's a lazy old nasty puss, aren't you now my darling?"

Brendan and Mahon was standing side by side listening to him. They was about of an age but you'd have taken Brendan for the father he was that furrowed. I remember thinking maybe it's what we see in this world makes us old before our time and it's only the blind has smooth brows like Mahon's.

"Watch now!" Tara said. "Watch what a clever holy puss he is!"

Brendan and Mahon raised their heads. The beast was laying on the ground half asleep now. Tara shoved it in the ribs with his foot. It opened one yellow eye and looked at him. Out of a pouch at his waist Tara took a bit of raw flesh the size of a child's fist. He waved it about as near the beast's muzzle as he dared come. Para paid it little mind at first. Once he got a good whiff or two of it though he give something between a snarl and a groan. After a couple of tries he pulled himself up to where he was sitting on his haunches. He had one forepaw planted farther front than the other so he tilted.

"Upsa!" Tara said. He held the flesh over the beast's head.

"Upsa!" the green bird called in Tara's voice. "Laus tibi!"

The beast stretched his neck about this way and that way. He closed his eyes down to slits. When he opened his jaws to snarl his whiskers spread out stiff. Such teeth as he had left was mossy and broke. Tara was jerking the flesh up and down over his ears. Finally it worked.

With a lurch Para raised his forequarters off the ground. He was sitting straight up from the haunches now. His eyes was on a level with Tara's just about. His forepaws was dangling at his belly.

"Oremus! Oremus!" Tara cried. He was dancing about

on his toes calling on us to watch. His skirt was rattling about his white puckery shanks and his snowy locks flopping.

"Pray for it! Pray for it!" he cried.

The beast made a sideways shuffle on his rump. Then he did what he was bid.

He closed his eyes chaste as a nun. He hung his shaggy great head. He crossed one paw on top of the other. I could hear the rumble of it gathering deep down inside him like thunder from far off. It was enough to make your flesh crawl. Then he opened up wide and roared forth a prayer they must have heard on the far side of the world. If I was God I'd have dropped everything else and come running.

The way he went at the flesh Tara threw him afterwards I couldn't help thinking of poor Bora.

The monks had been waiting outside all this while. It was dusk by the time we went out to them. The king had sent all manner of food and drink for their dinner like Tara said he would. Brown women was padding about on their bare feet serving them. They was all having them such a time they hardly marked us when we come out through the palings. Crosan tried speaking to Brendan as he passed by but Brendan was so set on where he was going he didn't mark him even.

I remember Brendan standing in their midst with the sky over his head. It looked bigger than I ever saw it. There was a few stars already. I remember the branchless silver trees and the bare breasts of the women. I remember the green soft feel of the air and the smell of it. It put me in mind of the time Brendan spoke to Bauheen's kindred under the hazels and told them how all their nastiness had washed off in the river.

You could hear the monks catch their breath when he told them we'd come to the Land of the Blessed. It was like leaves stirring in the breeze. I think they'd already guessed it. Why shouldn't they guess it with the women there to fan them if they looked flushed and baskets of fruit at their elbows and tart wine in gourds? But when Brendan come out and said it you could have heard the grass grow.

His words didn't come tumbling out like they usually did. His face didn't go red as his beard and the front monks wasn't sprayed. He spoke slow and hushed. He picked his words. He kept his eyes lowered mostly. He told them Tara said he'd seen Bishop Erc only the day before and promised to take him to him when the time come. He told them about the green bird that prayed like a man. He told them how Tara was the last of twelve holy monks that dwelled there once. He told them on that very day Tara had been speaking to Saint Patrick. He made the sign of the cross when he said the name and most of the monks did the same. It was like any moment Saint Patrick himself would come out through the palings with his crozier and his bell.

There was things Brendan didn't tell them as well. He didn't tell them Tara's way of cackling or the things he cackled at. He didn't tell them how he'd held his grass skirt out to the sides and done a few turns. He told them nothing of Para named for the Holy Ghost nor what become of the other monks. Most of all he didn't tell them how in the land where death has never found its way men went on dying it seemed the same as ever.

Mahon and me went back with him to sleep in Tara's hut when he was done. Tara chanted us a psalm or two before we laid down. He give us each one his blessing with his hand on our heads. There was an oil torch burning. His face was lit up by the flame of it and it glinted in the pearl on the cross about his neck. If you had only that sight of him to go by you'd think for sure there was none in the Land of the Blessed more blessed than that one old man with white hair to his shoulders and his eye screwed up.

Saint Patrick come about dawn. Tara woke us with his finger to his lips and told us. He took us out. The sky was just growing light enough to see by. There was a heavy dew. The leaves was dripping with it. There was the cry of birds from the forest. Tara led us through the door me and him had slipped through on our way to the cove. That's where we found him.

Saint Patrick was hunched on a low branch. He was eating a piece of yellow fruit with the skin hanging off it. He had sorrowing lovely eyes. His feet was black and long-fingered as his creased hands. He was covered in red hair from head to toe. Only his face was bare and his leathery small ears that stuck out. He drew back his lips and give us a fierce smile. He chattered something at us in a tongue we didn't know.

There was another yellow fruit laying on the ground just under him.

Even as we was watching he reached out with his long red tail and took a hold of it.

[XXI]

"T A R A was only having sport with us, Finn," Brendan said. "When the beast wrapped its tail about the branch and swung back and forth by it, didn't he laugh though?"

I suppose when he danced around in his grass skirt he was only having sport as well. And when he was telling how poor Bora got himself gobbled I suppose the tears that run down his cheeks was from sadness. I didn't have the heart to say it to Brendan though. He wanted so much to believe Tara was right about how we was in Hy Brasail. And who was I to say we wasn't? I'd have said no bird in the world could speak Roman till I heard it with my own ears. I'd have said no brown bare man could look as grand as the king. Save in Paradise could there be such a cove as the one I bathed in? So all I told Brendan was if I was him I'd ask

Tara to take us to Erc like he said. If we found Erc we'd have one answer. And if we didn't find him, we'd have another. So Brendan went and asked him.

"He's a bishop you say?" Tara said. "Bishops are thick as fleas here. I've all I can do keeping my beasts fed let alone gadding off after every bishop comes along." He was fussing about among his cages when Brendan come on him and cross at being pestered. "Go ask the king's wizard why don't you. He's a clever dried up nut of a little man. Perhaps he'll find your precious bishop for you if he's here like you say at all."

Brendan was hurt being talked to in such a manner, most of all by the one his hopes was pinned on. But he didn't want to chide him for fear the old man would say further things yet to make him fear his hopes was vain. So he went off heavy-hearted but meek as you please to do like the old man said. He didn't take to the idea at all though. It didn't seem fitting to seek counsel from a wizard on any such holy matter nor for the abbot of Clonfert to beg favors of heathens that pulled the skin off their enemies' heads like hats.

It took Mahon to talk him over finally. "If you want to clear a path for a bishop," Mahon said, "you sometimes have to sacrifice a pawn or two."

It was his pride Brendan had to sacrifice but he tried to do it proud as he could. Instead of skulking off by himself to find the wizard while nobody was watching, he fixed on making a grand show of it. He took the whole lot of us with him.

He had all the monks bathe themselves first. I led them to the cove where Tara had taken me. Monks by rule are not to look at their own bodies bare even much less anybody else's but you'd never have known it to see them that day. How they did scramble about in the white fleecy surf of the shallows! There was parts of them jouncing about in the sunshine they'd kept hid for as long as they'd had them nearly. Nor did it cost them any more shame than it would a pack of children. If they was led to lewd thoughts you'd never in the world have guessed it watching them. They rubbed themselves all over with sand and washed it off. They scoured their clothes in the brine and laid them on the honeycomb rocks to dry. They soaked their beards. They scrubbed their hair and shook it in the sun. You'd hardly have known them for the same men at all by the time they was done. They didn't look cleaner only. They looked haler and rosier and fuller of life. They looked ridder of their sins than any I ever saw baptized. Maybe it was the Country of the Young after all, I thought. There wasn't a monk of them didn't seem like he'd washed off four or five years along with the dirt.

The way Brendan got them lined up in twos then they could have been headed for easter mass. Brendan himself marched at the front. He held his cross before him like he did wading ashore from Bishop's Joy. He had Tara at his side to show us the way. We sung psalms as we went. It didn't sound like much though. With all the cries and chattering and rustles of the forest going on about us we could as well have been crickets.

The king was sitting cross-legged under his shaggy straw roof. He wasn't wearing feathers or shells or fish teeth like the day we beached. He didn't need them either. Even bare you'd have known him for king. He was leaning forward from the waist with his knuckles on the ground. A young woman knelt beside him. I never saw one lovelier in all my life. She had a pot she was dipping her finger in to paint chalky patterns down his back.

Soon as he saw us winding our way out of the trees he got to his feet. Straight and tall as a tree himself he stood waiting. Next to him, any other king I ever saw looked like a bit of gristle you might pick from your teeth after dinner. When he clasped Tara to him in greeting the old man's head come no higher than his nipple. Even Brendan seemed frail and small in his arms.

Tara knew their language. It was a chirpy fluttering

kind of speech off the end of the tongue mostly. He told the king Brendan wanted to see the wizard. The king told the young woman to go fetch him. He had bullies standing about with spears in their hands and they drew aside to let her pass through them into the shadows of the king's house. Tara screwed up his eye and told Brendan she was the king's daughter. If any man touched her by chance even he'd have his parts snipped off quick as a wink. He thrust his fist in his mouth to stifle his cackling. In a moment she come back out again with the wizard.

The wizard walked all crouched over with his arms swinging out to the sides like a crab's claws and his eyes rolling about in his head. He was loaded with strings of rattling shells. He had bones through his ears. He had a tail fastened behind him like the one Saint Patrick picked up the fruit by. I thought his apron was made of parchments till I saw the fringe was black hair. They was human scalps dried over red coals like Tara said. The wizard's face looked like it had been dried over red coals as well. There wasn't a tooth in his mouth. He went and crouched before Brendan swaying from side to side and rolling his eyes up at him and his shells all chattering like teeth.

Brendan didn't blink even. He looked straight at the wizard and spoke to him in our own tongue like the wizard knew it. His words come out slow and steady. He asked would the wizard take us where the souls of the blessed dwelled. The wizard carried a knobbed stick in his hand and made rings over his head with it to cast a spell on us. It was Brendan's words cast the spell on us though.

Up to then it was only Brendan searching for the souls of the blessed. Now it was all of us. There wasn't one of us didn't show it waiting there for the wizard's answer. Our beards was still damp from the cove. Some of us was plump, some lean. There was clever ones among us and foolish ones both, merry ones and sour ones. Different as we was though you could tell we each had the same thought. Each was thinking of some blessed soul he'd be every bit

189

as glad to find as Brendan to find Erc. I saw Malo near me biting his lip. Was it her with the long braids he was thinking of? Was it her with the twisted foot? And who for Crosan I wondered. Who for Mahon and would he grow back sight in his eyes for seeing whoever it might be? I knew the one it would be for me anyhow. Had he grown since I last saw him? Would he know who I was to him even?

Tara chirped the question to the wizard a second time in their heathen tongue. The wizard was still crouched before Brenhan working his bare gums like he was chewing the matter to shreds. They made a queer pair, Brendan red and moist with the cross of Heaven about his neck, the wizard brown and withered in his apron of men's scalps. The wizard was humming. You could scarce hear it at first. Then bit by bit it could have been a hive fixing to swarm.

He clasped his hands in front of his chest. He tugged at them harder and harder like he was trying to pull them apart without unclasping them. The veins on his neck swelled. His face went black. His eyes turned to slits. You could just see the whites of them. There was a sound like nuts dropping on a roof. It was the sound of his bones popping. You could see them at it under his skin.

His shoulders popped. The bones in his back popped and in his arms and wrists. The toes on his feet bent up. He thrust his head down between his thighs so far it come out topsy-turvy behind him. It seemed like his hips must pop out of their sockets. I thought he'd tied himself in a knot no wizardry could undo. Then all at once he sprung free of it his shells in a frenzy.

He spoke first to Brendan in a high-pitched lilting voice like he might be singing. He rolled his eyes and waved his knobbed stick about. Then he spoke to the king. The king's face was very grave. He listened with care to every note of the wizard's song. When it was done he paused a while before he bowed his head to the small man crouched there before him. Then he called to him the young woman that had been painting white on his back. He slipped his arm about her waist and nodded at Tara. Tara was the one that give the wizard's answer to Brendan.

"He says he knows where the blessed dwell right enough," Tara said. "He don't have time to take you there himself. He'll be changing himself into a blue toad soon to make sure the rains come. But he's leery of you. He believes you're a wizard like him. So he's got the king to loan you his daughter to show you the way. Perhaps you'll find your bishop after all. Or then again perhaps you won't."

I thought for a moment Tara was fixing to do his dance again the way he took hold of his skirt in both hands. Instead he crossed his eyes and dropped Brendan a bandy-legged little reverence. Brendan scarce so much as marked it. His eyes was misted over. His lips was parted.

All this time the wizard stayed crouched at the king's feet buzzing. Then all at once he leapt up and sprung into the crowd of monks. He darted first at this one, then at that one. Here he plucked at a beard. There he poked at a belly. He made weird faces like he was changing into a toad already. He made wild noises. He beat on the ground with his stick. The monks stumbled all over each other getting out of his way. Suddenly he give a great sideways leap that landed him square in front of one of them. It was Maeve. Before she knew what he was about, he snatched the cloak clean off her. Under it she was bare as birth. Her paps was milky pale. Her belly was round and soft. She was doing as best she could to cover her shame below.

The monks' eyes started out of their heads. They was looking at a woman bare. Many of them was looking at a woman bare for the first time in their monkish lives. That was itself enough to drop their jaws. But it was more than that. They believed they'd seen a wizard make a woman out of a man as sure as ever God himself did out of Adam's rib. It was like making wine out of water. It was like walking on the waves dry-shod. It was more wondrous than the wonder of the loaves and fishes even. Any doubts they had all went at once. This must be Hy Brasail indeed. Such holy wizardry could mean nothing less. All the months of storms and puking hadn't been for nought after all.

The next thing they was so busy dancing about and hugging each other and crossing themselves and praising the King of Heaven they clean forgot about Maeve. She snatched her cloak back from the wizard and wrapped herself in it. She fled to Brendan for shelter.

The two of them stood together like a rock. The jigging monks was the tide that dashed in about it. Maeve buried her face in Brendan's shoulder. Brendan wrapped Maeve in his arms. You couldn't tell which was his red beard and which her yellow hair hardly. Their eyes was closed. Their cheeks was wet. Save Briga she was the only woman Brendan ever held till then. Surely he was never to hold another his whole life long. It was the greatest wonder of them all that day. To my mind it was the holiest as well but the brothers was all too busy praising God to mark it.

Now she was known for a woman Brendan had no choice but to take Maeve on his journey in search of the blessed. Was he to leave her behind with the monks there was no telling what lewdness she might stir them to, he said. There was no telling either how much he wanted her with him for comfort but that he did not say. Mahon he took because there was no other he trusted to care for him. He'd have died sooner than own it was also because he'd come to need Mahon as much by then as Mahon needed him. He took Malo because Ita had given him Malo for a whale spine to sit on and a beetle under his shirt. He took Crosan because Crosan was dying.

The clown had no flesh on him hardly. His eyes was bright with fever. There was blood in his spittle when he coughed though he said it was only another of his clown's stunts. He swore he could just as easy make piss come out of his ears. Brendan remembered what the grey-mantled bird on the island told him. She told him in the Country of the Young there was a healing lough with black muck on the bottom. She said it could grow bodies back on the heads of Cashel. Perhaps it could mend Crosan as well then. So he got the king to give us a litter on two poles we could use for carrying him should he grow too weary for walking. And me he took to help with the carrying I suppose. That made six of us all told.

There was also the king's daughter. Etain we called her after the King of Tara's young wife in the tale, she that was changed to a butterfly by a woman jealous of her beauty. She could have been a butterfly indeed the bright-winged way she skittered ahead of us through the dark forest. She wore her long hair tied loose at her neck with always a flower or two in it. Her breasts was bare. Her feet and hands was slender. Brendan wouldn't look at her when she come near to show us how we was to go next even. To her we was all of us clowns. She laughed herself to tears at the queer tongue we spoke. She covered her mouth with her hands the way we went and hid ourselves to make water.

She led us through meadows of rustling waist-high grass far as the eye could see. She led us by shallow loughs filled with sky. Tall-legged birds white as clouds fed in the rushes. Lizards big as a man dozed in the slime. There was places the vines grew so thick we walked in a green dusk though it was midday. Creatures chattered and scolded over our heads as we passed. Some had long tails on them like Saint Patrick's. Some had nether parts gaudy as sunset. There was trees hung with silvery moss down from their boughs to the earth nearly. When Crosan was in his litter once, Etain gathered some for a pillow and slipped it under his head. He clenched his fist into a bit of a face with the end of his thumb thrust between the knuckles for a tongue. He made it tell her thank-you without moving his lips. She covered her face with her hands and twittered like a swallow.

Another time Crosan got to talking with Maeve about Cashel. He told her of the yellow-haired kings he'd served there. He said it was the dust from all the stale jests he'd told them had him coughing his guts out now. He said he should have left sooner than he did. Why had she herself left Cashel he asked her then. I remember still the answer she gave him.

"To find if there's a God at all," she said. "I was raised with everybody around me forever saying there was. Ita said it. Jarlath said it with every other breath. The way the monks all creep out to their prayers on cruel winter nights is a way of saying it. Who but God could get them doing such a daft thing? Yet I've never seen so much as the print of his shoe myself though I've looked sharp many a year."

I wondered was it her searching for God's shoeprint had given her her staring blue eyes. Maybe it was not finding him that give her her look of never-ending surprise.

"Perhaps he'll be waiting for us where we're going. Perhaps he won't," she said.

"My dear," Crosan said, the sweat running down his withered cheeks, "don't you see Christ his true son dozing there beneath that tree?"

"It's only Malo," she said in a soft voice. It was plain the fever had addled his wits.

"It's Christ," Crosan said. "Did you ever before see a face with such sorrow in it?"

As to me I'd have said bitterness and hate; maybe Crosan saw deeper than me to the soil they grew from. Malo stirred in his sleep as we watched him.

Some while later we stopped for the night near a spring. There was hardly a breath of air. Rose-breasted white birds come floating back over our heads from feeding in the marshes. Crosan was laid out on his litter with his cloak folded under him. Save for Malo they was all off foraging. I was starting a fire should they bring anything to cook. Crosan's eyes was glittery. He called to Malo to fetch him water from the spring. When Malo held it to his dry lips, Crosan took Malo's hand in his and kissed it. Malo drew it back like he'd been stung.

Crosan reached out and touched Malo's cheek with his finger.

"Tears leave tracks like a snail," he said.

"All mine dried away long since," Malo said.

"My dear, I know," Crosan said. "I know." He took a sip of the water. Some of it went dribbling onto his chest. "Surely thou hast borne our griefs," he said. "With thy stripes we are healed." He run his fingers along the stripes of Malo's frowning brow.

Malo caught my eye where I knelt by the fire. He shrugged.

Dusk was gathering in the limbs over their heads. A few stars had come out. Crosan's voice was scarce more than a whisper as he raised one hand to them.

"Scattering thy glory up there each night. Sweeping it away again each morning," he said. "It's weary work."

Malo's laugh was like he broke a stick over his knee.

"Weary as death," he said.

Maeve brought back a pair of coneys she'd brained with her sling and I roasted them. For drink we had the juice of yellow fruits Etain gathered. The moon was up. A bit of a breeze freshened. Mahon grew merrier at night. He said in the dark we're all of us blind. It made him less lonesome. He sung us a song or two of home in his thin voice. Etain tried working her tongue around our names. "Brin-oon, Brin-oon," she said. And "Crow-sin" and "My-low." Brendan bared his teeth to the moon with the rest of us. He even forgot he wasn't to look at her. The firelight flickered in her eyes. On her mouth the fat glistened.

I slept a ways apart from the rest of them on a pallet of ferns. Far into the night I was waked by something brushing against my cheek. I thought it was grass or some winged creature maybe. When I looked I saw in the moonlight it was Etain. She was kneeling at my side. It was her long hair I'd felt. It hung untied. Shadows parting at the hollow of her throat was all she had for covering. Her eyes was berry-dark. She was gazing down at me. Not a word passed her lips nor mine either. There was no need of any.

I don't know how long it was we stayed that way. After a time I raised my two hands and took her face between them. I can feel the cool soft shape of it yet. Slowly I turned her head from side to side. Slowly then I turned my own. She made a small whispery shape with her lips to show she understood. Then she brushed my eyes shut with her finger-ends. I didn't open them to see her go.

Had Brendan chanced to wake and find me with her it would have wrecked his faith we was in Hy Brasail where all is chaste and shameless. That's why I told her no. He might as well have tugged me by the cloak again. It wasn't the worst thing he did in his whole life surely. But if there's a day of final judging like they say, it's a deed he'll have to answer for no less even though he was snoring by the red coals when he did it and never so much as dreamed how dear a price his old friend paid to save his peace.

Our way ended at a great river. It was so broad you could scarce make out the far side. It was wrinkled and green and fast-flowing. Even if we'd had a boat we'd have been swept out to sea surely before ever we got across. We lined up on the bank like gulls.

Brendan called Etain to him. He asked her in signs what we was to do next. This time she was the one to lower her eyes. She had no more idea than blind Mahon. She'd brought us far as the wizard told her. The river was the far edge of the only world they knew. Whatever place we was seeking must lie beyond it. It was for Brendan himself to turn wizard now if we was to go farther. He sank down on his heels and looked out over the water.

There was no man-eating giant cats on the far shore or old addle-wit monks. They'd never strangle a woman there with her own hair or drown a child in dung or lop heads. Bravery and loveliness ripened there like fruits. The air was fresh with honor. Forgiveness glittered like dew on the grass. He'd never see it for himself now. You could tell from his eyes he knew it. You could tell from the sag of his shoulders and the way his hands hung slack.

Yet maybe in his heart he was just as glad for the river even so. There was something in the look of him made me wonder anyhow. He looked less like a man defeated than a man with a load off his back.

Suppose the King of Heaven himself was waiting there with all the others to welcome him? That would be nothing to sneeze at surely but could it be Brendan fancied more just the whiff of Heaven you get in the salt breeze sometimes or the glimpse of it in a whale's eye? He was always one for teasing the heathens like that anyhow. He'd give them a peek through the pearly gates every now and then but never knock them silly with the whole grand glory of it at a clap.

Suppose the King of Heaven didn't welcome him at all? Could it be Brendan feared he'd curse him for his sins instead and send him off to a rock in the sea like Judas or the fiery mountain of Hell?

Suppose he got across somehow and found the far shore of the river was only the far shore of the river, no worse and no better than the shore we was on?

Suppose not even there could Maeve make out so much as the print of God's shoe?

A tree branch floated by. Downstream a ways a bird stretched out a pair of black ragged wings to dry.

When I took hold of Crosan under the arms to help him sit up so he could breathe better, his flesh felt cold as fish. He couldn't speak without bringing on a fit of coughing. He made his fist into a small face again. He tried to make words come from its lips like it had a voice for speaking other than his own.

Brendan waded up to his chest in the river. The rush of water swirled about and almost tumbled him. For a moment I thought he meant to try swimming across. Then with a great thrashing of legs and arms he turned topsyturvy like

197

a duck after fry. He was under so long I feared he'd gone and drowned himself. Then he come up spewing water and gasping. His eyes was red. When he clambered back onto the bank again I saw in each hand he had a fistful of black muck. He took it to Crosan in his litter.

"It's for your healing," he said. He crouched down beside him.

He dabbed muck crosses over Crosan's chest and belly. He added one on his brow then and one on each of his two cheeks.

Crosan reached out to draw him closer.

"It should be blue," he said.

The muck was dry on him the next morning. Brendan was kneeling on one side of him. I was on the other. The river was fuller and greener. It was moving slower. Etain was sitting on a rock letting it tumble about her brown legs. Crosan give me a sign he wanted a word with me. I placed my ear close to his lips.

He told me to go fetch Christ.

I knew it was Malo he meant. I found him back under a tree mending one of his brogues.

"Come for the love of Christ," I said.

"There's none with less cause to love him," Malo said. He come though. He crouched by the litter.

"Tell me, my lord," Crosan whispered. "What good have I done to deserve you by me at the end?"

"You deserve far better, my dear," Malo said. He covered his dark face with his hands. I doubt Crosan heard him.

We made a rough raft for Crosan before we left. We washed him first. Etain wove him ferns for a coverlet. We folded his hands on his chest and slipped between them the wood cross Finnloag give Brendan years before. We heaped flowers and green leaves about him. I tied his hair in a topknot. Mahon and Brendan on one side, Malo and me on the other, we lifted the raft and laid it in the river. It turned slowly about a time or two before the current caught it.

The way the tale goes, when the Etain we named the king's daughter after was changed to a butterfly she was blown down the smoke hole of a house one day and fell into a woman's cup. The woman swallowed her without knowing it and a certain time afterwards bore her forth once more as a human.

It was the sea in the end swallowed Crosan. Maybe by now it's bore him forth once more as a man and he's back at thumping folk over the head with a new bladder.

[XXII]

NOT far from where Beothacht drowned the Shannon widens out to make Lough Derg. Thanks to the mischief of the Sea King's daughter the salmons there have no red spots on their bellies but the lough itself is spotted with yew-covered small islands. The world passes them by mostly. It eddies around their banks much as the river does. You'll find wild swans thumping their great wings here and there. You might see a heron standing still as a stick with the proud sweep of black from her eye to the tip of her crest and her cry like a man retching. Sometimes a fisherman rows out to drop his line where stones show dark under the froth. Nobody comes much otherwise. There's nothing to come for. The islands was there at the start of time. They'll be there still at the end of it. Brendan lived on one of them a year or two after we come home. By now I doubt there's a trace of him left.

Mahon was one of the three of us lived there with him. When Brendan wasn't there to lead him he got about by feeling. He held one arm crooked before his face and with his other hand touched his way from tree to tree or rock to rock. Sometimes he tapped the earth before him with a stick to tell rough from smooth. If he was looking to find where he'd laid something he'd walk at a crouch patting the air for it on all sides. He felt his way about the world like that. But it was far from being the only kind of feeling he was master of.

When Crosan put out to sea for the last time on his raft Mahon was the only one of us couldn't see for himself the withered small face as the current turned him or watch the green water wind him slowly out of sight. Yet none of us surely felt it more than him. You could see by the look of his blind eyes that he was himself the river Crosan was winding away on. You could see from the way he held his hands how his fingers was the ones Crosan was slipping through like sand. It was the same thing when we told Tara goodbye. The old man said he'd taught Para a new stunt he wanted us to see. It turned out it was only the same old stunt he'd showed us already. He got the beast up on his mangy haunches again. He had him bow his head and fold his paws and snarl his nasty prayer again. Brendan stood by like a man in torment. I twisted my shirt into a knot. But Mahon felt the old man's delight like it was his own delight and laughed till the tears rolled down.

"I am his eyes. He is my heart, Finn," Brendan said once.

Malo was his stag beetle then, gnawing at him under his shirt like Ita's. Malo lived with us on the island as well. He slept away from the rest of us. He mostly ate apart. Mahon was the only one he spoke to much. Yet he gnawed at Brendan just by being near him. I don't suppose Brendan ever so much as glanced at him without remembering how he'd sent Beothacht to drown in his stead, but that was the least of it. There was no sinful thing Brendan ever did or thought he did his whole life long, I think, but what he saw it peering out at him through the dark of Malo's eyes.

Crosan's death was one of them. Brendan believed Crosan would never have died at all if he hadn't hauled him off to sea. He believed even that mightn't have been the end of him if on top of it he hadn't taken him a week's worth of jostling through the forest and then slimed his chest with muck in the bargain.

Dismas's death had its fangs in him as well. Often he spoke of it nights when we'd perch on a spit of the island that jutted into Shannon like a ship's prow. He could never forget the look of that befuddled fat face bobbing in the waves off Hell with his hair on fire.

"He'd be safe in his cell this very day if I hadn't sailed off with him on a fool's errand," he said. "And Gestas worse yet!" he moaned. "Gestas, Gestas . . ."

He buried his face in his hands.

"Gestas cursed God to his face because of me," he said all muffled. "He cursed God's eyes, Finn."

The water chuckled about our rock.

"Better they should hang a millstone about my neck and pitch me in the sea myself than I should turn a man's faith to hate by the drowning of his friend."

Brendan believed he'd killed Maeve's faith for her just as surely. Thinking she was a man changed to a woman by heathen wizardry the monks all stood in deep awe of her till she put them straight on the voyage home. She told them the truth of who she was then. She told them as well of her war school at Cashel. To her way of thinking, she said, they'd serve God better learning to take sling and spear to cattle raiders than mumbling their monkish prayers at mass day in day out. So it wasn't just that she'd lost her own faith because of him, the way Brendan saw it. She was out to wean others as well from cowls to cudgels. Indeed more than a few of the younger ones left holy orders to follow her counsels when we got home.

"Ah but it wasn't because of you at all she lost her faith," I said to him. "She said from a child she was never sure of God."

"She would have been sure, Finn," he said. He stared at me so hard it was like he was reading his words in my eyes. "If I'd found what I was after she would have been sure."

"All the same you got closer than any ever did before you," I said.

Did I believe he had truly? Do I believe it now? My believing is as muddled as my hearing what with only one good ear to do it through. If I had to wager what's left of my life on whether or not Hy Brasail lay across the river, which way would I wager? Which way would the monks wager? To hear them tell their tales today you'd think they hadn't a doubt in the world but who knows the tales they whisper in their hearts? Who knows what they thought when we limped out of the forest with nothing to show for our pains but Crosan's empty litter and our flesh all ragged from thorns and brambles?

Maeve set off for Cashel soon as we landed home anyhow taking a few of the younger monks with her as I said. Had Brendan showed her the King of Heaven himself swinging from a tree by his tail I doubt she'd have done any different.

As for me I went off by myself a week or two. I went to Jarlath's, Lugh's I should say. I was black still from the sun with a beard on me where before I was smooth. Nobody'd ever know me got up like that it seemed. They probably thought I'd drowned long since if they thought of me at all. Even so I took the back way around the hill and across by Erc's and Jarlath's graves once I got there.

There was a row of monks filing into church. They had their hands folded over their bellies. Their cloaks was blowing. One of them chanced to spot me crouched among the stones. He crossed himself. He thought me a ghost more than likely. So I was. If I'd walked on the sand I'd have left no footprints. I'd have cast no shadow if I'd stood in the sun.

I found my wife in the kitchen yard. It was where I was cutting up pig parts the time Ita picked me for going to Cashel with Brendan. I hid behind the wall. My wife didn't see me. She was lopping the heads and tails off herring and gutting them. When her hair got in her eyes she would

brush it aside with the back of her wrist. She had the same
shawl over her shoulders as the last time I saw her. Her
face wasn't the same though. There wasn't so much as a
glimmer left of what lit it sometimes when our small Brendan was about still. The back of her neck looked stringy
and lonesome. I felt my lips take the shape of her name only
I didn't speak it.

She had stitched together a life for herself out of the
snippets left her. She had the chores she did for the monks
still. Lugh was a kindly man. More than likely he was good
to her. She had her health by the looks of her. Suppose I was
to step out from behind the wall and wrap my arms about
her. How long would it be before Brendan beckoned me
again? What would it do to her to have me leave a second
time? What would it do to me? What would it do to Brendan even if the day ever come when he saw that too as one
of his sins? I turned and crept down the hill again with the
wind in my eyes. I could have been a ghost indeed for all
she ever knew I'd been there close enough to touch her
nearly.

Brendan went straight to Clonfert with his monks. It's
where I found him when I got back. Clonfert was teeming.
Word he was home again carried the length and breadth
of the land it seemed. Folk come from every corner to feast
their eyes on him. There was far more of them than Clonfert had shelter for so they had to make do for themselves
the best they could. They curled up under hedges or in
ditches to sleep though it was the fall of the year and the
nights chill. Some huddled in the lee of walls or crept into
stalls with the beasts. Word was we'd found the Land of
the Blessed indeed.

The copying and coloring of parchments, the learning of
the ancient tongues, the study of Scripture and the Fathers,
the hours for prayer and mass even—all was shirked whenever it was known any of the fifty was telling their tales.
Sowing and herding and choring stopped as well. People
gathered about them in the meadows or shinnied trees some

of them to get a better look at their burnt faces and bleached beards. Scribes took down their words with quill and ink. Bards threaded them into their songs. Walls was daubed with pictures of them.

They told how the King was twice the height of a man. He had feathers growing on him like a bird and was hung with gems. They told how the wizard was born in Abraham's time and could change a man to a woman or himself to a toad or any shape at all if the notion took him. They told there was an ancient monk of the blood of the high kings of Tara that taught the birds and beasts the art of human speech. The women was fairer than the fairest of the gentry, they said. They went about bare, but their shining dark hair grew so long it covered them chaste as a nun's cloak. For every bathe you took in the warm sea, they said you shed five years off your age. From the look of them I almost believed that part myself.

It was Brendan they all of them wanted to see most of course but he was seldom to be found. Gone was the time he used to gather any would listen together in the church or out in the fields and talk and talk till the stars come. Hours he would stand there in the old days going at it with his eyes closed and his chin drizzled. After we got back with Bishop's Joy though he stayed in his cell mostly. He got Con and Niall to bar the way should any come looking for him. They'd say he was at prayers and penance though they'd as well to have saved their breath for all any could understand a word they said. He went to mass only when it was foul weather. There was less about to pester him then. He left his part at the altar to others and tried to lose himself in the crowd though it was easy enough to spot him by the tallness of him and the point of his head.

Once he was coming back at a run when a flock of them cornered him. It was raining but they paid it no mind. They trapped him up against the wall of the bake house so he couldn't flee. There was herders and scholars and nuns among them and some small king from nearby as well. This

king had a fur hat on his head and some dozen or so of his
bullies. They was all of them calling to Brendan at once
and knocking each other about to get close enough to touch
him for luck. He was flattened against the wall wild-eyed
as a stag set on by hounds. It was all he could do to keep
them from tearing the clothes off his back for scraps to
ward off the evil eye or heal warts. Some of the monks tried
to drag them away but it was plain they'd never leave till
Brendan spoke of his voyages to them. It was the shortest
I ever heard him do it.

"I'll tell you about my voyages then," he said. "They
never did anybody a bit of good least of all Christ." The
wet was pelting in his face.

"There's only one true port," he said. "That's Heaven.
God grant we never shipwreck on our voyage thither. God
grant we never put our souls in danger of sin, for sin is the
only death in the world worth fearing."

The jaws of the herders hung agape. The king's fur hat
was sodden and his bullies dripping. They listened like he
was telling them the secret truth of life itself.

"Pray for yourselves and your kindred," he said. "If
you've any breath left in you pray for me then for there's no
worse sinner in the land nor a greater fool."

They parted then without a murmur to let him pass
through them. In silence they watched as he went splashing
off. It was that very day he fixed on going to dwell on
the island in the Shannon.

Near the center of the island was an old yew with one
side sheared off by lightning. It was still hanging by the
bark though so there was room enough beneath for a man
to shelter. Brendan made it his cell. Month after month
he spent before it. I've seen him there with snow on his head
and his breath coming out in puffs. I've seen him there so
still when the sod was green a linnet might have built her
a nest in his beard and never known. I've come on him

stretched out with his bare back flat to the earth and his arms flung to either side staring at Heaven through the dark branches. Sometimes his eyes was clamped as if to shut the sight of Heaven out.

He was sailing the seas inside himself. His prayers was his craft. Rue and shame was the winds that drove him. His back was bloody when he rose. You could see the mark of roots and stones in it.

Malo was the one he picked for confessing to. He told the one that hated him most the hatefullest things he knew of himself. Mahon said it was yet another way he scourged himself. He did it to make Malo hate him all the more.

"It won't come out that way though. You'll see," Mahon said. "Malo will end by pitying him instead. He'll pity Brendan for being Brendan the same way Brendan pities him for being Malo."

The way he fixed his eyes on me I couldn't believe they was sightless.

"Mark my word," he said. "They'll fall on each other's necks like brothers some fine day and weep."

Brendan would kneel by the yew with his face in a knot confessing. Malo would sit on a rock with his chin in his hand listening. I can't believe the pardon Malo granted him in the name of mercy was something he wished for him in his heart. But maybe his listening alone had a pinch of pardon in it. Maybe there was a grain or two of mercy just in sitting on the rock.

We had a bit of a boat for rowing back and forth to the mainland in. We had little need of it. There was plenty to feed us right where we was. Roots and berries was plentiful. There was fish to catch. Briga come visiting a few times. She'd stand on the bank with her mouth cupped and we'd row over to fetch her. You could tell it pained her to see her brother all skin and bones from fasting. He was sunken about the eyes. His voice was croakish. He used it rarely save for telling his sins. Not even Briga could cheer him. She'd chatter on about her nuns. She'd tell how the round roof we built on her church was in want of patching. Maybe somebody had stolen one of her cows. Brendan would nod now and then but that was the most of it. He was far off sailing the dark seas within himself.

Monks as well would come from Clonfert once in a while if there was squabbling among them perhaps or questions about the rule they couldn't answer. More often than not Brendan wouldn't see them even. He'd send them word by us they should take their troubles to the council of six he'd put in charge when he left. So back we'd row them in a pout. A time or two I spotted Brendan peeking out at them gaunt and haggard from the trees. He would like to have welcomed them but told them no as penance. He viewed his whole life now as penance. Apart from a visit now and again our days on the island was like as oysters. Until one special summer's day.

I was on the rocks scouring a pot with sand. There was swarms of midges over the water and a great tumble of white clouds in the blue overhead. All at once I heard a whinnying and nickering from the shore. A meadow lay there with dandelions in it thick as stars. A roan mare was skittering back and forth so close to the river's edge you could hear the suck of her hooves. She was flashing the whites of her eyes and tossing her head and bridle. Her ears was pricked forward and her tail high. Something in the water was driving her mad.

I've seen monks skid on ice the way it went. Their feet slip out from under them and they arch first this way then that way to keep from falling. They flap their arms to the sides for balance and hoot like lunatics half at the peril of the thing and half at the sport. Out on the river a brown-clad figure was carrying on in just such a fashion. Glittering great fans of water shot out from its feet as it lurched and scrambled forward. It listed in every direction at once filling the air with whoops and cackles. How it stayed afloat I'll never know. No wonder the mare was in a frenzy. The eyes was starting out of my own head. Closer and closer it come teetering fast as a man could race though nothing solider under its feet than the Shannon. When it run up onto the island at last the force was such it had to grab hold of a yew to keep from slamming into it. It was a leathery small woman in a brown cloak. Soon as she turned her face I saw it was Brigit.

"Praise be to Christ, Mother!" I cried. "However in the world did you do it?"

I've seen wonders in my time. I saw Maeve spit the stone in two. I saw the wizard pop every bone in his body. I was with Brendan when he healed the man with the spear in his nipple and told Bauheen his and Fiona's names though he'd had no way of knowing them. I have looked into the eye of Jasconius. Most wondrous of all I was there at the birth of my boy and at his death as well. I could not say which was more wondrous either, the way he popped into the world who'd never been there before or the way he popped out of it so soon he left no more trace than a pebble cast in the sea. But they was none of them wonders to match how Brigit crossed the water that day.

The bottom of her cloak was soaked and she was splashed some, but from the sight of her you'd have thought she'd only got caught in a shower of rain.

"Never look down if you can help it," she said huffing and puffing. "Never look back." She bared her white shanks plucking up her cloak to wring out the hem. "Never stop calling on the Queen of Heaven till you're safe ashore."

She had a shawl about her shoulders worked with a gold shaggy sun. She used it for drying her hair with and peered out at me through the tousle bright-eyed as a weasel.

"Here, and my blessing with it," she said when she was done. She made the shawl into a ball and tossed it to me. "Remember me in your prayers then."

I took her to Brendan straight off. We found him on his knees by his yew. Before he could clamber to his feet, she started having at him.

"Briga told me I'd find you dumpish and starved half to

death, my dear," she said, "but I never expected the likes of this!"

The place under the sheared branch where he slept looked like a beast was kenneled there. It was filthy with rotted leaves and twigs and no more than a ragged piece of sacking spread over them to keep out the damp. His bowl was fuzzy with mold. When she called his name he come crawling out on all fours. He fluttered his lids like Mahon in the bright sun. His matted hair was in his eyes.

Across the river there was reapers. You could hear the sound of them whetting and calling to each other. Bit by bit the stubble was widening and there was less corn left standing for the breeze off the water to riffle through. Brigit stood with her back to them looking at the wretched creature before her. She had her hands on her hips and her head cocked sidewise. You could see where her cloak was scorched from the holy fire.

"You're no Jarlath, Brendan," she said. "You were never cut out for this sort of monkishness. It's a grand way for those with a gift for it. I've got more than a few of them at Kildare, the Virgin be praised. You can see Heaven itself in their faces and catch the blessed whiff of it like loaves fresh from the baking when they pass. But you're a nimble-tongued footloose man. They say there's none since Patrick with a knack like yours for winning heathens. You should be out there with the reapers." She waved her hand at them. "You should be harvesting souls for Christ, Brendan. There's the truth of it."

"It's no longer Christ they want from me, Mother," he said. He stood there so helpless and feeble it hurt to look at him.

"What else do they want then?" Brigit said. "Not your great beauty surely. You weren't much to look at the first time I saw you what with more teeth in your mouth than you've room for and a queer shape to your head. But now they could use you for scaring off crows if you don't mind my saying."

She was trying to jolly him along you could see but it was no use. She could as well have been jollying one of the heads at Cashel. His jaw hung open. His eyes was lifeless.

"All they want from me now is my voyages," he said. "It's God curse upon me."

"They tell you've seen the Blessed Land if I'm not mistaken," she said. She said it with a hushed little rise at the end like it was his voyages she wanted from him herself.

"Whatever I saw," he said, "it wasn't worth the price of seeing it."

His eyes filled with tears. Was he remembering Crosan afloat on his raft? Was he thinking on his own wretchedness? Maybe they was tears of joy at just talking to another human soul again.

Brigit held out both her hands and drew him to her. She took a kerchief out of her sleeve and wet a corner of it with her spittle. She dabbed at his face with it till she had it part clean at least. Then she tucked the kerchief down the front of his shirt and give it a pat for a way of telling him he was to keep it.

"Go to a place where nobody knows you then," she said. "Find a place where there's folk who've never heard of your voyaging and all that. Bring Christ to them, Brendan, and in God's good time perhaps they'll bring him again to you."

He was white as a corpse there in the sun. His beard was filthy. His rags was scarce enough to hide his nakedness. As to Brigit, where she wasn't scorched she was damp yet from the river and her hair every whichway from touseling. They both in their own ways looked as much clowns for King Christ as ever Crosan was clown for the yellow-haired kings of Cashel. To see the way they stood there staring at each other it was almost like they was thinking the same thing. They could have been a pair of children playing at who could keep a straight face longest. The next thing I knew they was in each other's arms.

That brown small woman shriveled as a nut. That shipwreck of a man. Whether they was cackling or sobbing I couldn't tell. Maybe it was some of both. But this I do know. Brigit called Brendan out of the grave that day sure as ever Christ called Lazarus out of it. Perhaps it was the greatest wonder she ever worked.

I rowed her ashore again when the time come round though I don't doubt she'd have managed boatless otherwise. Maybe she'd have let herself be wafted through the air like a cobweb. She didn't weigh much more than that when I give her a leg up on her mare anyhow.

She was so old she'd known Saint Patrick when she was a girl. It was her that wove his winding sheet for him with her own two hands. Yet she could have been a girl still the way she went cantering off past the reapers. I stood in the stubble watching her with the shawl she'd given me tied round my middle. I've no doubt she'd have given me her mare as well if she'd happened to think of it.

Brendan was standing at the edge of the island to see her go. Before she vanished over the first ridge she turned and tossed him a wave of her hand. Her tangle of hair was bright as fire.

[XXIII]

IT was to the land of the Welsh Brendan went at Brigit's bidding. He was so set on nobody knowing his fame I had to swear I wouldn't breathe a word of it to a living soul even if they put red coals to my feet. I think he'd have left me behind altogether except he needed someone he trusted to ferry him across to the Welsh rocks and a stout arm to lean on once he got there. He was weak from his fasting still and stiff-legged from all the months he'd spent on his knees. Blind Mahon he left behind at Clonfert knowing Malo would look out for him there. He might have sent him back to Ita instead but she died soon after the day she suckled him in her old age. It was the last bit of life she had left in her, it seems, and she give it to Brendan for his voyage.

We lived in Wales with a monk name of Gildas. He was a friend of Brigit's and she sent us to him. They've come to call him Gildas the Wise since. Gildas the Sour fitted him better back then. He was half Brendan's age but you'd never have known it to look at him. He must have tickled his mother with his long grey whiskers coming out of her. He was stoop-shouldered with parchment skin and a way of drawing in air through the corners of his mouth like he was stepping on a thorn. I've never seen a greener lovely hillside than the one he lived on with his monks yet it could have been the bottom of a pit for all he noticed. He spent his days in his hut with a quill in his hand scratching out on his parchments the nastiness of his times.

A hundred years and more had passed since the last Romans picked up and sailed from Britain for home. They stained their skin and their clothes both the same green as the waves so none would mark them on the journey. The day they left was a dark day though there was many rejoiced in it at the time. The heathens that come in their wake have been working their deviltries ever since. Pictish and Saxon and who knows what-all else they sailed across in their curraghs and long-boats. Naked as beasts they was with hairy dog faces. They carried short one-hand swords and hooks for pulling down the stones of Roman walls. They spoke the harsh tongue of swine rooting. Their parts was stout as swans' necks, it's said, and no woman was safe from them. Slaughter and pillage was the work they was best at. Those they didn't slay or ravish they starved to death with robbing them of their herds and crops and putting to the torch anything left over.

The Welsh was the lucky ones. They had their high hills for a wall to keep the devils out. They had bullies manning their borders the Romans taught war to before they left. So for a time anyhow they was safe. You might have thought Gildas would at least have had Welsh luck to crow over then but he was too busy bewailing Welsh sins instead. Cynan and Cyneglas and Maelgwyn was the kings he come down on hardest. They had known Christ from their grandfathers and great grandfathers before them yet even Maelgwyn that was himself a monk for a time, Gildas said, was little better than a heathen. He feasted and whored and flouted the law as bad as the worst of them.

The only king Gildas had a good word for was one name of Artor. He said he was a true follower of Christ in his heart. The year Gildas was born, it seems, this Artor won a mighty battle over the Saxon bullies at Badon Mount. Nine hundred and sixty men fell there in a single day their corpses strewed about so thick you'd have thought the mount itself was torn and bleeding flesh. But cruel though the cost was, the Welsh was free from heathens from that day forth till past the time me and Brendan first set foot on their shore. Save for that though, Gildas was so steeped in the badness of things he was as blind to goodness as he was blind to the sunlit meadows he hobbled to mass on with his quill over his ear or to the tangle of honeysuckle decking the posts of his low door.

"You've come to win souls for Christ, is it?" he said to Brendan when we first met him. He sat at a table in his hut. His lips was black where he'd been sucking on the point of his quill.

"Some say only Christ wins souls for Christ," he went on. "They hold once Christ has cocked his holy eye on you, you're as helpless to flee him as a bird in a net. There be others as well howsomever—like your countryman Pelagius the heresiarch here not so many years back—that hold the High King of Heaven himself can't tinker with men's freedom to flee him to the uttermost parts of the sea even if that's their fancy."

At the mention of the uttermost parts of the sea, Brendan went pale as curds. He thought the man must know of his voyages. He thought this was Gildas's way of telling him he'd spent all those years at sea not seeking God at all but fleeing him. "Maybe he's right, Finn," he said that night. "Maybe he's hit the mark square." It kept him awake hours tossing and moaning. Out of one eye I watched him at it in the moonlight.

Gildas was too caught up in his own words to see how he'd rattled Brendan though.

"Rome planted her eagles in our coombs and hills," he went on saying, "and many a long year before Patrick sailed holy faith across to you she planted that here as well. You'd never guess it to look at our kings though. I've got it all set down here to their everlasting shame." His eyes glittered under their heavy lids.

"*Peccatores. Hypocritae. Ebriosi.* That's our kings for you," he said. The names he called them was all the more fearsome for the hushed way he spoke them. "*Adulteri. Fornicarii. Sepulchra dealbata. Progenies viperarum.*" The Roman words was as bitter in his mouth as the smell of the honeysuckle was sweet.

"Cynan with his gold-nippled bawds. Cyneglas with his wizards. That dragon Maelgwyn that's giddy in the head from the bards braying his praises day and night. What do they care in their coastland keeps for the faith of Christ? Ah well, they're great for feeding on his precious blood and flesh you can be sure. Kennels of lapdog bishops and priests they keep to that end thinking it's a way to buy their way to Heaven. But they give no more thought to the plight of their poor Welsh folk than to the earth they tread on."

"There's work for us then," Brendan said.

Gildas looked sharp at him.

"This is my work," he said.

There was a heap of parchments at his elbow. He pressed them flat with his hand till they crackled.

"When the Day of Judging comes, there'll be so many sinners running about some may escape the flames altogether. My work is to set their names down here with all their sins written after them so the angels don't let a solitary one slip through their fingers."

"It was work for the poor Welsh folk I was thinking of rather," Brendan said. The roof was so low he had to stand with his neck crooked.

"You won't be winning many of them to the faith if that's your meaning," Gildas said. "After a fashion they've been won long since, you see. They've had little good from it either they'd most of them say if you asked them."

"Perhaps it's from us the good must come," Brendan said.

"We must pray for their souls surely," Gildas said. "My monks are at it day and night."

"That's our monkish way, Father," Brendan said, "but the King of Heaven asks more of us than that, I think."

"He asks from each of us what we have in us to give," Gildas said. "I've given so many years at these parchments my eyes have gone asquint. Doubtless you've done as much yourself from the looks of you."

"Perhaps we've given all but what he truly wants," Brendan said.

"And what is that, Father, if I may be so bold?" Gildas said. You could see he was starting to rue the day Brigit sent us to him and itched to pick up his quill again.

"I only wish I knew for sure," Brendan said.

Filling the walls of his cell with a mark for each soul he'd won? Sailing the grim deserts of the sea? Starving himself into his grave nearly? Scattering monkeries and nun houses over the green earth like corn at spring planting? Was all that what Heaven wanted of him truly? Was any of that what Heaven wanted of him truly? The question he was asking himself was plain as the furrow between his brows.

"He wants us each one to have a loving heart," Brendan said. The words come slowly. "When all's said and done, perhaps that's the length and the breadth of it."

"You'll forgive me. I've much to do here," Gildas said. "Wickedness is multiplied and the times of tribulation draw near just as Scripture foretells it. I've no time to lose before the end is upon us." He jabbed his quill in the ink dish like he saw the end gathering in the sky at that very moment like a storm.

"How beautiful upon the mountain are the feet of him that bringeth good tidings," Brendan said. It was his jesting way of saying all Gildas's tidings was bad.

Gildas stopped his quill in mid air. "You'd best not look to me for feet," he said.

Pushing down hard with his fists on the table-top he heaved himself up to where he was standing. For the first time we saw he wanted one leg. It was gone from the knee joint down. He was hopping sideways to reach for his stick in the corner when he lost his balance. He would have fallen in a heap if Brendan hadn't leapt forward and caught him.

"I'm as crippled as the dark world," Gildas said.

"If it comes to that, which one of us isn't, my dear?" Brendan said.

Gildas with but one leg. Brendan sure he'd misspent his whole life entirely. Me that had left my wife to follow him and buried our only boy. The truth of what Brendan said stopped all our mouths. We was cripples all of us. For a moment or two there was no sound but the bees.

"To lend each other a hand when we're falling," Brendan said. "Perhaps that's the only work that matters in the end."

There was an old woman name of Olwen lived in the woods some half a morning's walk from Gildas. Her hut had been gutted once and the walls was charred black. You could see the sky through the roof. She was skinny and humped with a rattle in her chest when she breathed. She was forever hacking and spitting up. She'd had a flock of husbands in her time, she said. Now that she'd outlived them all she had nothing but a flock of children to remember them by. She dwelled by herself. All the years we was in Wales Brendan never missed more than a time or two of seeing her. There was days he set off to her moaning and groaning there was a hundred other things he'd better be doing or liefer be doing but he always went. After a while Olwen come to think he was dead if he didn't.

She had a wood cup and a pair of dice one of her husbands had whittled her out of horn. Every time Brendan went the two of them would play at them together. They'd sit with their heads bowed over the board they rolled on. The board was on their knees. There was no sound between them save the a..e. They grew so rapt you'd have thought it was their immortal souls they was rolling for. Olwen was happiest when Brendan won. She'd count up wrong or miscall throws or anything else she could think of so it would go his way. When they was new at it Brendan would stop her. Later when he saw how she had her heart set on him winning he'd let on he didn't notice. It was as queer a game as ever was. Each of them played it wrong for the other's sake and each knew that's what the other was doing but never owned it.

Brendan needn't have worried over keeping his fame a secret from her. It didn't matter a whit to Olwen who he'd been before she clapped eyes on him whether a sinner like the rest of us or an unblemished saint. She didn't care what he did when he wasn't with her either. She never thought to ask him about such matters any more than she ever took it into her head to tell him the parts of her own life he didn't know about. She never went on to him about the husbands she'd lost or her children that was scattered here and there over the green earth and it would have meant nothing to her if he'd told her he was abbot of Clonfert and a famed voyager. The only Brendan she cared to know was the Brendan before her. The only part of his life that mattered was the part they passed together under her wrecked roof. She spoke of nothing farther back than his last visit or farther off than his next one. She spoke of nothing weightier than the dice or the weather or such little news of the world as she might have heard if she'd heard any at all. It made no difference to her if they filled their time with any talk at all. It was the time itself she treasured beyond all else.

Always when their game was done and the cup and dice stowed away against his next visit she'd ask him to pray for her soul. They'd get down on their knees together. They'd bow their heads and screw their eyes shut. She'd ask him to take hold of her two hands in his. She could feel the good of the prayer better that way she said. It was against both his rule and his nature as well but he did it anyhow. Then he'd set in to praying like it was the church at Clonfert with a thousand tonsured monks packed in tight to amen him instead of one old lone woman that wheezed like a leaky bellows.

"You'll never know the good you do me," she'd tell him every time he left. She never once in my hearing called him by name. It wasn't his name that mattered but only himself. She'd tip her head sideways and study his face. She'd keep hold of his hands till finally he was the one to unloose them. More often than not she'd press some small gift on him then. It might be pigeon eggs or an apple. Sometimes it was a bit of stuff she'd worked with some holy sign. But you might say her chief gift was how she took him to her heart just as he was. If you'd told her he was the great abbot of Clonfert it would have added nothing. If you'd told her he was a braggart and a hot-head it would have taken away nothing. After that fashion she fed him at her shriveled teat as much as ever Ita did though to her way of thinking it was Brendan was the one that fed her.

There was many besides Olwen he went to. It was the new work he believed Heaven set him the day he kept Gildas from tumbling. He believed it was penance as well for all the time he'd spent chasing after Tir-na-n-Og on the waves when he'd better have been caring after the naked and hungry and sick at home. In winter when the snows was over his knees and his beard froze he went at it. He went at it as well in summers when the meadows was yellow with broom and the white hawthorn flowers glittering delicate after a rain. Every day and every weather he'd go tramping off in search of them he thought needed succor most. He brought mass and shriving to any too old or too feeble to seek it. He touched the hands and the feet of the dying with holy oil. He touched the lips of the new-born with salt. If there was a man died leaving his wife and babes with none to care for them he'd see they had bread enough not to starve. Many's the hour I've helped him gather faggots or dig turf for a widow's fire.

You'd never have guessed it was the same Brendan folk trudged to Clonfert from miles around to gawk at. Miles he went with green dung on his brogues to settle some herdsman's quarrel or pray for the opening of a barren woman's womb or lay his hands on a child with fits. Some of them he brought no more to than a pair of ears for pouring their woes in. Then the same Brendan that once was wont to blather for hours on end of the wonders he'd seen would for a wonder sit silent as a stick while some poor soul spun out his own drab story. It was duty drove him more than a loving heart maybe but no matter. Many a one drew comfort from the sight of his pointed head bobbing up over the rim of a hill or the sound he made slogging through the muck of a spring pasture. What he brought them of Heaven I'm not one to say but he brought them himself. They none of them seemed the worse for it anyhow.

Gildas couldn't have thought him queerer if he'd taken to sticking straws up his nose. To him a monk's business was either down on his knees or with a quill in his hand like himself. If folk come looking for shelter or food he'd see they got a bit of it but the notion of seeking them out to succor never entered his shaved head. Having but one leg for seeking them on was part of it maybe. Another part was he spent so long each day peering into the wretchedness of the times he stopped noticing the wretchedness at his own door. He got used to Brendan's ways though little by little and as time went by they got to be friends after a fashion though there was never a pair more ill-sorted.

There was a shallow cave up the hillside from Gildas's cell. They'd go there together every now and then, Gildas wobbling along on his stick and Brendan shortening his sailor's stride so as not to shame him. They'd sit in under the high stone ledge of it if there was a wind blowing or out in the sun if it was fine. There was a great boulder there they'd rest with their backs against like a pair of lizards. Gildas would talk of the Romans like as not. He'd tell of the mighty wall they laid up with castles and turrets against the murderous northmen. It reached from the waters of the Solway clear to the Tyne. He'd tell of the princely houses they left behind them with heated water for bathing in and floors of gay colored tiles and pictures true as life itself painted on the walls. These was most of them all gone to ruin long since for there was icy-fingered Roman ghosts haunted them still, they said, and none but owls and foxes ventured near them though Gildas had spoke to some as still remembered the years of their glory.

For Gildas Romans was the darlings of the age. They kept the peace. They maintained the law. They held fast against the ghoulish forces of evil and misrule that's always roaring at the gates of the world to swallow it whole. To him the darkest of all dark days was the day they sailed off at last and the Saxon and Pictish bullies come ravening the land they'd left helpless. Save for Artor the king and his blessed victory at Badon Mount, he said, him and his monks would have long since been strung up like pigs with their gullets slit and their parts hung shriveled and black as smoked herrings from the belts of their slaughterers.

"Artor is King at Caerlon to this day, saints be praised," Gildas said, "though full of griefs now as years from what I've heard of him. Gwenhwyfar his queen was taken in the act with one Llenlleawg, it seems. He was the one friend the King had he trusted past all others. Could there be a crueler pair of blows than that? At a single stroke he got both his two legs lopped out from under him at once instead of just one from the knee down which is cruel enough for any man I'll tell you. To make matters worse yet there's a bastard they say he got of his own sister, may Christ forgive him, that's a thorn in his flesh as well. I've heard he takes comfort from neither God nor man. It's a bitter end surely for one that saved the Welsh land from pillage and rape."

Brendan heard the words from Gildas's inky lips like it was the old king himself crying to him for help. He thought there was nothing for it but he should go seek him out and bear him whatever of Christ's peace he could. He told Gildas as much right there. Gildas was sitting against the boulder with the sun glowing rose-color through his ears. His eyes could have swelled no wider if Brendan had told him the world was to end that very day.

It was no small journey to Caerlon on the river Wysg where Artor lay. Brendan had put some flesh on him by then but was stiff in the legs still and I was grown paunchy and short-winded with no work to keep me trim. We stopped for breath at the top of every hill we come to and was so weary by dusk each day not even our sore joints could keep our eyes open much past it. Better than a week it took us to make our way through the dark hills and forests and over the red crumbled Welsh rocks till we reached Caerlon at last.

It was crowded with Artor's bullies and the small kings from roundabouts that looked to him. There was plenty of priests afoot as well for Artor had crowded the place with churches. There was a church for himself and another for the Queen when he still had her about. He built still others for women and strangers and so on, some of them no bigger hardly than for the two or three Christ said was enough gathered together for him to be with them though it's a puzzlement where they'd have squeezed him if he'd ever come. The King kept to his chamber we was told. None could remember the last time any had seen him out of it. They pointed to the proud castle the Romans had built on a hill over the river. Next to Cashel I never saw such heap of turrets and porches and iron gates and massy walls of tight-packed stones. There was banners hung from it that snapped in the breeze as bright as flowers. At the foot of the battlement ravens was pecking about for slops. I doubt they could have got into the air if you'd chased them they was that fat and slow-footed.

The Saxons and the rest of them was ever at their wolvish raiding and pillaging to the east and the King's bastard Medraut was stirring up trouble right there under their noses but they told us the King give orders none was to pester him about any of it. They told us his bullies and lords had to manage on their own the best they could. Nobody we talked to ever come straight out and spoke ill of him quite but they shook their heads at his name. They rolled their eyes about and looked wary. We cooled our heels a week and more before we found somebody who said he could get us in to the King's chamber though at grave risk to himself and us both. It was a whispery old priest with rheumy eyes that was the King's confessor. He knew who Brendan was straightaway from having heard him spin his tales once at Clonfert. He stood in great awe of him and vowed he'd never tell.

The chamber was dim and chill as winter though without all was merry with spring. The priest pushed the studded door just wide enough to let us through and then fled barefoot down the winding stair. There was skins and spears on the walls together with all manner of other arms. I saw a battle-axe half a yard across from ridge to edge that was keen enough by the looks of it to draw blood from the wind. Cloths painted with proud men and fierce gaping beasts hung there as well. A haze of blue smoke hovered in the air from a smudge of a fire. A brace of creamy-breasted wolfhounds dozed next it in silver collars.

A tinkly thumping bit of a tune reached our ears such as I've seen maids dance to among the willows at spring lambing. I thought there must be two or three players from the sound of it but as our eyes got used to the smoky air I found it come from one only and him no higher than a man's thigh. He had a head on him bigger than mine with a steep brow bulged out like a cabbage. His bandy little

stumps of legs would have done for a child of three. With
one hand he was beating on a drum he had strapped to his
knee. With his other he was playing on a whistle. Both his
feet had bells on them and he was jigging up and down on
them in a choppy way in time to his playing. Sweat was
running down from under his cap.

He might as well have spared his pains for all the king
give signs of minding him. Off at the far side of the chamber
Artor sat slumped sideways on a pile of green rushes. He
had a heap of cushions to prop his elbow. There was a pot
of wine in his hand. His eyes shone glassy through the
haze. A gold chaplet sat crooked on his brow. His mantle
was the color of fir needles. You could see where he'd
slopped wine on himself and his lips was blue as a dead
man's with it.

The dwarf stopped jigging and playing when he saw
us. One of the hounds raised her head and made a low
rumble. The King glanced up as well but from the look of
him you could tell he thought we was only part of whatever
the dream was he was dreaming. I thought if an old soaker
like him was all that stood between us and the Saxon
butchers it wouldn't be long before they was wearing
Brendan's and my parts at their belts along with the rest
of them. Or maybe the King would take it into his head to
wear them at his. I held my breath as Brendan's brogues
went slap-slapping to him across the stone flags.

He spoke so low when he got to him I couldn't make out
his words. He stood with his head bowed. There was a gash
of sun down one cheek from the slit window. When he
stopped speaking I heard no sound out of the King. I had
no sight of him either with Brendan in the way. Brendan
sunk down and knelt in the rushes. He spoke again soft as
the stirring of wind in the boughs. Slowly the King's head
turned. I caught a glimpse of his face for the first time. All
rutted and loose it hung, the lower part lost in the shadow
of the great nose. After a time they could have been at dice

together the way their heads was both lowered. Their brows touched nearly. At the first quaver of speech from the King, the dwarf come tiptoeing over to where I waited by the door. He had a ring in his nose that glittered as he whispered. He'd been dancing blisters on his feet for months just to keep the King from hanging himself, he said. He couldn't even remember the last time he'd heard him speak.

What the King said was it was his own bullies kept him shut up in his chamber. It wasn't his own wish at all whatever men said. He said they thought he'd gone soft in the head from age and drink and wouldn't let any in to see him. He said he was as much a man as ever he was. To prove it he sent the dwarf to fetch him his sword off the wall. It was longer than the dwarf was tall and he could scarce reach up to it with his little arms. It was all he could do to carry it back at the run. There was gems at its hilt and the upper part of the blade was worked with twisting vines. The King got to his feet to take it. His whole frame shook like a tree in a storm and his face turned black but he got it raised over his head at last. It set him coughing so hard I feared he'd let it fall and take Brendan's head with it.

When it was back on the wall again he took a long pull from his pot and made a fearsome face. He said they was out to poison him. He said Gwenhwyfar was a slut. He said Llenlleawg was a Judas. He wept a little. He give Brendan a ring off his thumb wrought like a serpent with its tail in its mouth. He offered him land and herds and a high place in his court if he'd stay and be his beadsman. He threw his arms about his neck and smothered him nearly with winy kisses.

With one hand on top of the dwarf he shuffled out on the battlements to tell us farewell in the end. He got me and Brendan mixed. He offered Brendan a woman for his use while we was at Caerlon and it was me he got down on his knees to, creaking and groaning. He said I'd brought peace to his soul and asked my blessing. I had no wish to shame him setting him straight so it was Finn in place of Brendan that raised a hand and signed with the cross of Christ him that routed Christ's foes at Badon Mount.

A row of gulls off the river was hunched on the wall with their backs to the wind. Artor's face was white as his beard. He'd had the dwarf buckle on his sword for him before we come out and from its scabbard the hilt of it flashed in the sun. He raised both his arms over his head to wave us off when he spotted us far below among the fat ravens. He looked like he was made of the same stuff as the castle the way he towered over us there still as stone. I pictured him standing there all the rest of the day and the night as well with his arms in the air and his beard blowing. If I went back in a thousand years it wouldn't surprise me to find him standing there yet if there's anything left standing by then in the world.

It wasn't many months after we got home to Gildas we heard he'd fallen in battle. Once Brendan got him back on his feet he took heart again, it seems, and laid about him with his sword like in the old days. They wrapped him in a mantle sewed with gems and laid him out in a high-prowed boat with his sword at his side and his gold chaplet on his brow and set him afloat in the river like we did Crosan. The news of Artor's death was almost the death of Gildas. He wouldn't set quill to parchment for weeks. He set his monks to praying day and night for the old King's soul. He said the ruin of the world was at hand.

As to Brendan, I think it was the first time he ever truly believed in his heart he'd lie in a grave himself some fine day. If Artor the King was no match for the bully Death— him that held ruin at bay long years after he was himself half ruined—what chance had any of us?

It was not wishing his bones to moulder among strangers in a strange land that led him to make the last of his voyages, which was his voyage home.

[XXIV]

"THERE'S heads yet on the walls of Cashel," Brendan said. "They've gone black and leathery most of them though. I'm happy to say I saw no fresh ones at all. King Hugh is no butcher like the yellow-haired kings before him. Mind he's no Artor either, but he's a god-fearing decent man all in all. It wasn't the worst thing I ever did setting the iron crown on his head that day."

We was by the carp pond at Clonfert, Briga and Malo and me. It was known the cowlords of Cashel was fixing to raid the herds of Connacht and the King of Connacht had asked Brendan to go see could he coax them out of it. Brendan was the man to do it if any could for he was held in great awe among them and King Hugh was beholden to him for the very throne he sat on as well. Brendan was freshly back and the three of us gathered to hear him tell of it one summer dusk toward vespers. You could see the shadows of the fish slow in the water.

"Hugh is no handsomer than he ever was," Brendan said, "but he's learned a kingly way of carrying himself over the years. Besides he's got whiskers now for hiding his face behind, praise God. I saw Hugh Black as well, Finn. He's grown so stout he can hardly raise himself off a stool. His lips are thick. He oils his hair and paints his face overmuch. So they've played turnabout, you see, the two Hughs. Kingship's turned the Handsome handsome nearly and the Black is puffed up like a green toad from overfeeding and lechery."

We'd all of us changed. Briga had lost so many teeth her nose come close to resting on her chin when her mouth was closed. Malo's black head was white as snow though his face still lean-jawed and young enough.

"Here's what I said to him," Brendan said. " 'King Hugh,' I said, 'the men of Connacht are lying in wait for you. They've honed their spears to sting like horse leeches.

They've patched and bound their shields. They've gathered sling stones enough to fill Lough Derg. Come pilfering their herds like they fear and many a poor woman of Cashel and Connacht both will sleep a widow that night. Many a mother will rise the next morning without a son to comfort her old age. All the wolf packs and wild women of the glen howling together will be nothing to the din of the slaughter you'll bring on their heads. The grating of sword against sword. The axes hacking flesh. The slings whistling.' " He closed his eyes as he spoke like he could block out the terrible din of it better that way.

" 'King Hugh,' I said, 'you're a man of peace. You treasure the Gospel in your heart. It's why I gave you the blessing of Bishop Erc at your crowning, may the sod be sweet in his mouth. It's why I'm here this day to beg you to call off your raiders.' He sat there with his fingers to his lips hearing me out polite as you please, but all the time I could see he was at work on his answer."

He plucked a primrose and tossed it into the pond. In a trice the dark water was freckled with gold mouths nibbling it.

"His answer was no," Brendan said. He raised his voice a notch or two then and sent it out through his nose to sound like Hugh Handsome. " 'Father,' says King Hugh, 'I'm a man of peace as you say. I'm no more for warring and hacking and cow-thieving than yourself. Yet I've given the cowlords leave to raid and, saving your holiness, raid they shall. I'll even tell you why since you've come all this way. I've given them leave to war for the sake of peace.' Those were his words."

"He'll be daft then surely," Malo said. "That heavy crown has crushed his brains." His blue-shaved face glowered in the dusk like the old days.

"Say cunning rather," Brendan said.

Vespers was tolling by then. The clang of it over the fields was mournful as Brendan's tale of his failed errand.

"He said it's better they should slay a few score raiding

cows now and then than be braining each other by the hundred the whole year through as they'd do if he kept them on too tight a rein," Brendan said. "That's how he reckons it anyhow."

"A score of corpses better than a hundred is it?" Briga said shaking her head. "That's no way to reckon with human souls surely."

"It's the way of a dark world, my dear," Brendan said.

"And all the holy monks in Christendom helpless to stop it," Malo said.

There was a time he would have said it to jibe at Brendan mostly. But there in the blue dusk he said it more in the way of a sigh like he counted himself helpless as the rest of us. A bloody time was coming and there was nothing a one of us could do. There was nothing a one of us could say. The first stars glittered bright as carp in the deep sky.

"You must do something, Bren," Briga said.

All Connacht was in arms when the day come round. Cashel would strike at sun-up they thought. The cows had long since been harried into one great herd and led up lowing and skreeking to a high pasture. They had bullies aplenty to guard them and a spiked ditch as well. It was night still when the others took their places on a scrubby slope of moorland below where the herds was. There was moon enough to make out the gold of the broom and the dark purpling of the heather. Far off through dips in the hills to the south toward Cashel you could catch silvery glimpses of Shannon. A lovelier peaceful starlit sight there never was in all the world.

The men moved about like shadows. Only their whispers marked them. They muffled as best they could the clatter of their weapons and the leathery creak of their harness. Some had their faces daubed white and their hair limed into points stiff as antlers. Some was naked as heathens. Others wore leggings and was shirted in waxed skins and helmed. The King of Connacht was there with a crown on his head and a crimson shawl. He sat a frothing white-eyed gelding of better than sixteen hand that kept wheeling about and nickering. Far off across the river the High King Hugh was doubtless there as well hid like a coney in the thicket of his whiskers.

Pots and pot lids and hollow logs was only part of what the women come lugging. They brought stout sticks and rocks as well for pounding them with when the killing started. They'd howl and pound and carry on to make Cashel think the very specters of the air was after them. Yet they could have been women of stone for all the sound they made getting ready. The crouched men too was like stone once they took their places. By the time the first brightening begun at the far rim of the sky you'd have thought you was all by yourself there if you'd come by not knowing.

Brendan picked his way through the heather with a staff. Stiff-jointed as he was he took care not to stumble. He had a cloak wrapped about him and over his shoulders for luck what was left of the saffron wool shirt Cara give him when he was a boy at Jarlath's. He moved slow as a cloud down through the stone women and stone men. Now and then he rested his finger-ends on somebody's head for a moment. I think it was less to steady himself then draw some bit of comfort from the touch perhaps or give some bit of comfort. He had no face to speak of in the shadows but Artor's gold serpent ring glinted on the hand he held his staff by.

When he got downhill of the rest of us a few paces he stopped. He sat down on a boulder and laid his staff on the sod beside him. There was a wallet hanging across his shoulders and he drew it around to where he could reach down into it. He took out two things. The first was a square of cloth. He unfolded it and laid it out over his knees. The other was three or four handfuls of white wool. Bit by bit he plucked the wool to pieces and then plucked the pieces to pieces till he had a feathery mound of it heaped up on the cloth on his lap. The air was gone grey by then and starting to swarm and seethe in your eyes like it does at the coming of dawn.

Brendan got to his feet and stood tall and pointed against the sky. All those silent waiting eyes was upon him. I thought of that other dawn when he'd taken his iron-studded club to Bauheen's lewd stone. I doubt he could have hoisted it again now but I doubt too if back then he could have done what he did there with the silver Shannon at his back and all of Connacht waiting on him. He held the square cloth with the wool in it as far out in front of him as his arms would reach. He held it stretched tight with the wool sagging it a little in the middle.

"I am the wind that blows over the sea. I am the tear in the eye of the moon," he said. "The honor of Christ be as the dew on the grass. The strength of God's peace be in my hands."

He let the cloth sag then pulled it tight again. Two or three times he did it and each time more of the fluff was wafted away. Light as thistledown it floated off. Pale as a starshower it swelled in the grey air. He let go of the cloth save by one corner then so all that was left of the wool drifted out of it. It begun settling soft as snow into the heather. Before my very eyes it turned into a mist.

The mist lay shallow on the ground at first. It licked around Brendan's brogues. It spread uphill till it lapped about the crouching warriors. When it started drifting downhill it was thin as the first flat riffles of the tide coming in. It deepened as it went. It curled and tumbled and spilled out to the side wider and farther. Brendan was up to his waist in it. The whole valley was flooded with it. There was no valley any more, only a great sea stretching off toward the far hills toward Cashel and the glimpses of the Shannon beyond.

"Dimness to their eyes," Brendan said. He called it so all might hear him. "Confusion to their feet. Christ's cooling to the blood in the bowels of the cowlords of Cashel."

I could no longer see him though I was scarce a mast length off. I could see none of the others either for the matter of that. Thick and clammy the mist swirled about us in clouds till there was nothing left of the whole world you could see.

The raiders got so far as fording Shannon it seems but little farther. They stumbled over each other and wandered in circles. They run into trees and sank to their knees in bogs. They give up at last and headed home. Hugh Handsome was doubtless just as glad to have them back again unbloodied.

Brendan never said much about it afterwards though as a younger man he'd have added it to his other tales surely. I believe he thought it among the grandest deeds of his life though. For one, it was the closest he ever come to working a wonder like Brigit's. For two, Erc would have been proud how well he did the druidry of it. There's no question either but what he saved many a mother's son from dying in mortal sin that day and hoped the King of Heaven would thereby forgive him some black sins of his own. Best of all, he heard Maeve was among the raiders. He said he hoped the mist he'd raised by the power of Christ had given her back again the holy faith he feared he'd lost for her not getting across the river to Tir-na-n-Og. Maybe it did.

Brendan did less and less of the running of Clonfert as he grew older. Much of the time he spent in prayer. He made visits often to see Briga and her nuns. He taught the monks holy Scripture and the blessed lives of the saints. Patrick was the one he taught most. There wasn't many left alive by then had talked to folk that had known him and he passed on much he'd heard of him from Erc like the whispery way he had of talking and his youthful looks and the small bells he give away such as the one Erc lay in his grave with. For a time he tramped about visiting the old and the sick and the grieving like in Wales but his bad legs put a stop to that in the end.

Often he wouldn't leave his cell for a week or more at a stretch. Sometimes he'd summon Mahon to play at chess with him. Once I come on him sobbing over the board like a child. He said it was because it put him in mind of Olwen and how they used to play at dice together. He said he never went to tell her goodbye when he left Wales just like he never told Finnloag and Cara goodbye either when he set sail the first time. He hadn't the heart for it.

"God counts the tears of all the ones I've brought misery on, Finn," he said. "Heavy as stone they'll weigh against me when I stand before his judgment seat at last."

One time I found him in his cell with the air so full of smoke I could hardly spot him. He was on his knees by a heap of ashes. His eyes was round and haggard.

"I've burned my parchments," he croaked like an old raven. "There was no good ever come of all that was in them."

"Don't forget the crystal hill rising out of the sea where you said mass," I said. I'd heard the tales so often I had them by heart. "Don't forget the merry small dog that whispered Fiona's name in your ear. Surely Jasconius was a blessing. You'll remember to the end of your days the way he was trying to fit his tail in his mouth to the glory of God."

"To the end of my days I'll remember Judas," he said. "He called to me to succor him, Finn. I did nothing. I hardly heard him even. My ears was ringing still from hearing a holy monk tell God to his face he pissed in his lovely eyes."

He spoke the words like they scalded his mouth coming out. A draft sent the ashes drifting across the floor.

"I've seen Hell, Finn," he said. "I saw poor Dismas drown in the sea of fire."

He sank back on his heels and covered his face with his hands.

"You've looked on the fair shores of Heaven as well," I said. "You've bathed in the white foaming waters of blessedness. You've seen brave lovely women and men walk about in their nakedness without shame."

I thought of Etain. I thought of her skittering through the giant ferns like a butterfly. I remember her waking me in the night cloaked only in shadows and brushing my eyes shut with her finger-ends.

Brendan uncovered his face.

"Would I could burn the parchments of my mind as well," he said.

Sometimes in fair weather he'd wander about among the buildings of Clonfert with his stick to lean on. By then it was crowded as Cashel nearly. Monks and scholars and priests come to it from all over. There was Romans among them and Franks and many other hairy queer sorts from over the water. Brendan had shrunk some with the years but he was taller than most even so and it was enough to spot his white head bobbing along. His gait had something of a sailor's roll to it still. He'd pass among the monks' huts and the chapels. Sometimes he'd look in on them at their copying from their great books or their studying. He'd stop by at the bake house maybe or the wash house where they scrubbed their hands and necks for mass at the long stone trough and cleaned their teeth with their fingers to sweeten their breath. Now and then he took a meal with them at their tables.

Mostly he moved in silence among them. It was rare anybody ever made bold to talk to him unless he talked first. Gone was the days they flocked about and badgered him for tales. They'd sooner have dared badger Saint Patrick if he'd come back among them with his stained hair and the wrinkles of his face drawn smooth with the white of duck eggs.

More and more of his time he spent with the fosterlings. Malo was the one had charge over them. Malo had softened toward him by then from hearing him confess the dark times of his life all those years. It was just like blind Mahon foretold on the island in Lough Derg. Pitying a man is little more than a skip and a hop from taking him into your heart.

The fosterlings dwelled upstream of the wash house. Hazels grew about dropping their blossoms in the water. The willows was bent with weeping in it. Brendan might sit there a whole morning through hearing Malo put them through their lessons. I've seen him myself take one of their hands in his and guide it through the shaping of a letter or lend an ear as they spelled out the words of a psalm.

Most of them knew the old man with the crooked teeth was holy Brendan himself. It didn't rattle them like it did their elders though. They grew as easy with him in time as they was with Malo. They'd sit on his knee. They'd chatter at him. If they did something to make him speak sharp or strike out at them with his stick even, they'd run off only to run back again the next time he come by. The small girls showed him their dizzies. Cut out of cloth and stuffed with straw they was with gay faces painted on them. It was an old dumb man made them, Malo said. Dizzy was the only word he ever spoke so that was what they called them. One day Brendan and me went to see him.

He'd made himself a hut in the branches of an oak with sticks lashed across and a roof of leaves and wattle. There wasn't a trace of him when we got there but after Brendan called out a time or two he come leaping down to us on all fours. Bald as an egg he was and brown as a berry. His face was so full of creases you had to look sharp to find which crease his eyes was in. Malo said he was more than half daft. If so we'd all do well to drink at the same spring. I never saw a merrier man.

All nods and grins and winks he was when he dropped to our feet. He wrapped his arms about us each in turn and hugged us to his fuzzy chest. Save for a breech cloth he was naked though it was the fall of the year and the sun with little warmth in it. When Brendan raised his hand to give him a blessing, the dumb man clapped his hand to Brendan's and started making pat-a-cake. He bent nearly double cackling. Brendan himself couldn't forebear to smile.

"God's peace to you then," Brendan said.

You'd have thought God's peace was the grand joke of the world. The dumb man threw himself down in the leaves. He rolled about holding his sides like they'd crack.

Brendan waited till he was through before he showed him why we'd come. He drew from his cloak a dizzy he'd brought. It belonged to a red-haired bit of a bow-legged girl. One of the arms was long since pulled off and lost. The other hung by a shred or two only. The face was faded away altogether. He asked the dumb man could he patch it. The way the man listened you could tell he understood the words well enough though he spoke none himself. He took the dizzy out of Brendan's hands and held it like it was alive.

"Dizzy," he said. "Dizzy."

He softly raised the loose arm a time or two. He pushed back the wisps of straw that was poking through where the other arm was pulled off. He run the flat of his thumb where the face belonged. He cuddled it in his arms. He pressed his cheek to it. He hummed to it some daft little air.

Brendan knew who he was then. Perhaps he knew from the start. Many's the time he'd seen him crouched in Cara's bilges humming like that to his first dizzy, the one he made of Dismas's kerchief and stuffed with dulce.

If Gestas knew it was Brendan, he give no sign. Brendan called him by name, but it seemed no more to him than if another dry leaf had dropped out of the branches to the ones already thick on the ground. He didn't so much as raise his eyes from the poppet.

When Brendan reached out his hand to him though, Gestas took it in his own whether he knew whose hand it was or not. Deep in their creases his eyes glittered with mirth. Brendan's eyes was shadowy and crooked like he couldn't bear to look at him head-on. Gestas's cheeks was ruddy from living at the heavens' mercy like a squirrel. Brendan's was ashy white.

Seeing them there with their hands clasped I thought how queer a thing it was. The one that had cursed God to his face looked a man at peace. The one that had spent his whole life long serving God the best he knew looked a man in torment. Maybe it was God's jest. Maybe it was the very jest set Gestas to rolling about again in the dead leaves. I doubt he even marked when Brendan raised his hand to bless him as we left.

Brendan told Malo the whole story of Gestas when we got back.

"I cursed God like him myself," Malo said when he'd heard it through. "I cursed Christ for how they used my wife and babes."

The fosterlings was down by the stream floating sticks. They could have been birds from the chirp of their voices. You could see them fluttering bright through the hazels.

"There's part of me that curses him still perhaps," Malo said, "though with most of me I've forgiven him."

"A sinner forgiving him that was sinless!" Brendan said. His voice was hushed with the blasphemy of it.

"Crosan thought I was myself Christ," Malo said. "That's what led to it. I couldn't tell him he was mad. I couldn't tell him I wasn't the one he thought I was but only Malo, bitter and hateful as ever. I even saw why I couldn't too. It was because he'd touched my heart with his daftness and his dying. It was because I knew I'd be dying myself one day and that made us brothers. It was because I couldn't bear to think what telling him the truth of who I was would do to the poor soul with his withery clown's face you'd dabbed with muck and that fist of his he could make into a little head that talked. I'd taken him to my heart, you see. Yet I could no more keep him from dying by that river there than Christ could keep my babes from dying. I could no more keep him from dying than Christ could keep himself from dying when the time came."

The muscles worked in his blue jaw.

"All at once I saw in myself the helplessness of Christ.

237

That's when I forgave him," Malo said. "He's so helpless he's got no hands to help with save our own."

"Christ have mercy of us then," Brendan said.

"Amen to that," Malo said.

I said amen myself even.

It wasn't so long after that Brendan let it be known he wanted Malo to be next abbot of Clonfert after him. Malo never said he would but he never said he wouldn't either. I think Brendan knew in his heart he'd do what he asked when the time come round. And so he did. The monks stood in awe of him because he was Brendan's confessor. He was one of the voyagers as well and as time went by and there was less and less of them about, the few there was was held in special reverence, nor any of them more than Malo because of his grave dark air.

Brendan took to passing months each year with Briga and her nuns. All his life he fancied the company of women though he spent most of his time with them with his eyes to the ground. The last years he started looking at them more. He'd sometimes come and sit in the chamber where they weaved altar cloths. When the weather was fine they would set a stool for him in the doorway where he could feel the sun on his shoulders. He rarely spoke or seemed to listen to them chattering but I've found him there gazing at them sometimes the way a man might gaze at birds flocking in a green meadow or waves washing up on the shore. He come to where he liked to listen to the sound of them singing even. Around his neck he still wore the two balls of wax for working into his ears because earthly music was like cats screeching next to the heavenly music he heard once in the cave, but he rarely used them any longer. Maybe by then he believed the nuns' singing was itself from Heaven.

Once I come on him all by himself in that same chamber after the nuns had left their looms and gone off. From the way his shoulders shook I thought he was weeping.

"Ah, Finn," he said. "Will you ever forget how Saint

Patrick picked up that bit of fruit with his tail?"

His cheeks was wet with tears of mirth.

"Covered all over with red hair he was. And his feet like hands!"

It was like the jest had grown riper and sweeter from waiting all those years for him to cackle at it.

One winter sabbath he said mass for the nuns in the same church we built for them with a roof like the Cara's hull. You'd have thought he was aboard her indeed the way he wobbled about like he was walking a stormy deck. It took a nun under each arm to get him up again each time he kneeled. We was coming out the door afterwards when he told Briga he had to sit and rest. The snow was falling thick and we turned to help him back inside the church again. Before we could manage it he sunk down on the stone steps.

The nuns had filed out ahead of us hurrying along with their heads bent. They was most of them already dim as shadows in the flakes. A few of the last ones saw what had happened though. I remember them standing about at the foot of the stairs with their cloaks pulled close.

Briga was down on her knees by Brendan fussing over him. She took off her shawl and wrapped it about him. She pulled his cowl up over his head. He took his hands in hers and breathed on them. The snow itself was no whiter than his face. Already his beard was white.

"Pray for me, Brig," he said the best he could. "The tide's at the flow. I'm not half ready."

"You've nothing to fear, my dear," she said, "at all, at all." She was trying to keep the snow from his face with her hands spread.

"I fear going alone," he said. "The way is dark."

It was hard to catch his words over the wind. We was both of us bending close to hear.

"I fear the unknown of it," he said.

A pair of the nuns come up. They knelt on the step below us. They clasped their blue slender hands at their lips.

"I fear the presence of the King, Finn," he said. There was flakes in his lashes. "I fear the sentence of the judge."

Of all the words he'd spoken his whole life through those was the last. They was like the last hazels to fall from a laden branch or the last pitter-patter of a rain. His jaw didn't close after them till my hand closed it. It was Briga closed his eyes.

Briga and me and the two nuns carried him the rest of the way down the steps into the winter.

We buried him at Clonfert like he wanted, far from the sea.

Hugh, High King of Cashel, come to do him honor. The King of Connacht come as well and many small kings and cowlords, brehon lawmakers and druids.

Great and small alike, the whole land mourned him. Sailors call on his name in high winds to this day.

As to the sentence of the judge, I'm not one to know nor even if there be a judge at all. If I, Finn, was judge I'd know well enough though.

I'd sentence him to have mercy on himself. I'd sentence him less to strive for the glory of God than just to let it swell his sails if it can.

He said he feared going alone. If he has an ear to hear with yet, I'd tell him maybe he won't be alone at all. There's many in the Country of the Young will welcome him among them surely should there be such a country and the true Saint Patrick to ring him ashore with his bell.

Lest he ever think back on his old friend Finn and how I come to be so tangled in his life I never got round to living my own, I'd tell him maybe it was worth it even. I'd tell him he has my pardon anyhow.

Brendan, navigator, friend Bren, pray for us all then. Now and at the hour we're sentenced ourselves. Amen.

HISTORICAL NOTE

BRENDAN, son of Finnloag, was born in 484 near the sea at what is now Tralee, Ireland, and died some ninety-four years later at the convent he built for his sister Briga at Anaghdown. His day in the calendar of saints is the 16th of May. At the age of one, he was placed by his kinsman Bishop Erc in the care of Saint Ita of Kileedy, County Limerick, with whom he began his education. He continued his studies under Saint Jarlath of Tuam and upon their completion was ordained by Bishop Erc. During the course of his long life he founded many monasteries including the great one at Clonfert. When a dispute arose between two claimants to the throne of Cashel, he helped bring about the succession of Hugh the Handsome over his cousin Hugh the Black as Cashel's first Christian king. At this same time Brendan converted the bard Mac-Lennin, whom he renamed Colman and who later became a saint himself.

Brendan is chiefly famous for his voyages in search of the terrestrial Paradise or Tir-na-n-Og, during the course of which he may have sailed as far as Florida. The fanciful 10th century account of his adventures, the *Navigatio Sancti Brendani*, became one of the most popular of all medieval legends and was translated into many languages. Tradition has it that on one of his voyages his crew included one Crosan, a king's jester, and Saint Malo. It is also said that, obeying a command of Saint Ita to spread the Gospel, he visited the historian Gildas the Wise in Wales and King Arthur.

Of the many sources I have drawn upon in writing these pages, I would like to acknowledge my particular indebtedness to Katherine Scherman's *The Flowering of Ireland*, Robert T. Reilly's *Irish Saints*, and of course the *Navigatio* itself in various versions. I am greatly indebted as well to *The Brendan Voyage*, Tim Severin's fascinating and splendidly written account of the 4500 mile journey he made in a leather-covered curragh across the North Atlantic following Brendan's route as far as Newfoundland. For a sense of what those ancient Celts endured in their seafaring and for many a detail along the way I found it invaluable.

FREDERICK BUECHNER was born in New York City. He was educated at Lawrenceville School, Princeton University, and Union Theological Seminary. In 1958 he was ordained to the Presbyterian ministry. He has written eleven novels and a number of works of non-fiction including two volumes of meditations (*The Magnificent Defeat* and *The Hungering Dark*), *The Alphabet of Grace* (delivered as the Noble Lectures at Harvard), *Wishful Thinking: A Theological ABC, Telling the Truth: The Gospel as Tragedy, Comedy and Fairy Tale* (delivered as the Lyman Beecher lectures at Yale) and *Peculiar Treasures: A Biblical Who's Who,* illustrated by his daughter, Katherine A. Buechner, and two autobiographical volumes, *The Sacred Journey* and *Now and Then*. He lives in Vermont with his wife and family.